Robert Villier is a retired naval officer, having spent forty-four years in the Royal Navy. He is an active eighty-year-old and is happily married to Sandra. They recently celebrated their golden wedding anniversary.

Throughout his career at sea, Robert was a keen runner and cyclist, peddling and running his way around most parts of the world, until a hip replacement put an end to these much-loved pursuits. In the last ten years he has turned his attention to writing and has written a number of novels; *Acres of Diamonds* is the latest.

I have changed my mind with regards to this dedication. Originally, my immediate thoughts went (perhaps not unnaturally) to my loving family, dear friends and hopefully not too many foes. However, on reflection and having had ample time to ponder – the benefit of a happy retirement – I have decided with a clear and generous conscience to dedicate it to YOU!

Robert Villier

ACRES OF DIAMONDS

AUSTIN MACAULEY PUBLISHERS™

LONDON * CAMBRIDGE * NEW YORK * SHARJAH

A CIP catalogue record for this title is available from the British Library.

ISBN 9781398407930 (Paperback)
ISBN 9781398407947 (ePub e-book)

www.austinmacauley.com

First Published (2021)
Austin Macauley Publishers Ltd
25 Canada Square
Canary Wharf
London
E14 5LQ

I am respectfully reminded of one of Sir Winston Churchill's many sage remarks: *Writing a book is an adventure: it begins as an amusement, then it becomes a mistress, then a master, and finally a tyrant.*

For my own humble effort, I would agree entirely, especially with 'tyrant' and the desire to be correct concise convincing and coherent throughout. In these aims, I need to say a few very sincere Thank You.

Firstly, my enduring love goes to my darling wife Sandra, for her ceaseless support and encouragement. She retains that uncanny knack and intuitive ability of knowing when to enquire and when to stay silent. It's a skill honed and refined over 50 years of happy marriage – most spent not attempting to write.

Secondly, to Charlotte, who again proved ruthless but invaluable with a discerning ability of knowing what chunks to ditch whilst being ever constructive, and her attention to detail? She has this innate and incisive ability to make me feel good and bad at the same time!

My thanks also go to Rupert Horner, a distant relative and ex-Cambridge man himself (Gonville & Caius College), who kindly provided valuable practical knowledge of the actual graduation ceremony in the Senate House (his reward for such enthusiasm, or penance, is a copy – as requested).

I also need to thank another good friend and an old naval colleague, Les Maddock, known to all as Les, but as Brian by his wife, Belinda. He remains a member of my very small fan club and repeatedly says, "I don't know how you think them up," then politely points out any number of grammatical and punctuation errors.

It would also be remiss if I did not say a word of appreciation for my friendly printers ADP of Waterlooville. They are a small, professional outfit who provide the most excellent and friendly service. I bribe them occasionally with packets of biscuits and they respond like Pavlov's salivating dogs and produce the required finished product.

I also have to acknowledge the part played by Google and Wikipedia. The amount of information provided is truly staggering and it was the source engine of many hundreds of hours reading and research. If nothing else, I have gained a great deal of knowledge in reading on subjects and places of which I had not the foggiest. I'm sure my old schoolteacher would be impressed to know how many times I say and write – knowledge is never wasted, but how true it is.

Lastly, I thank the Royal Navy for teaching me to touch-type, making this book my own complete work, save that of the small matter of collating, printing and turning it into a book! OK, I admit it, I've had some help along the way, but I'd like to have it acknowledged that it was my own creative numerous neurons that did it!

It would also be remiss if I did not say a huge word of appreciation to the publishers, Austin Macauley, for their excellent support and advice in producing *Acres of Diamonds*. This was particularly laudable having had to work through such difficult times of COVID. Thank you greatly for making an old man happy!

Author's Note

A friend (who kindly said that she enjoyed reading my two previous novels) asked me how I thought up such strange ideas, and worried about my evil mind. I have since reassured her that I'm really just an eccentric old fuddy duddy of a fart that is trying valiantly to keep both brain and bones working for as long as humanly possible. I am, after all, 80, and should know better at my age.

The truth is that I find writing to be therapeutic and balancing, as it forces and offsets my lifetime problem of being unable to sit still and relax. My brother's the same – we have this inane desire and ability to stay out in the garden working until barely unable to straighten up, let alone talk. However, it's too late for either of us now to change the habit of a lifetime, and to be perfectly honest, I prefer it this way. Therefore, the opportunity to create and compose a readable storyline provides a satisfying equilibrium. In this, I am ably supported and encouraged by a wonderful wife who says all the necessary things at the right time, and when not to say anything.

I also depend upon my darling daughter Charlotte to act as my unpaid assassin of a proofreader and critic (have you ever seen a grown man cry?). Fortunately, and to my own modest credit, I am now able to accept criticism in a far more manly and grown-up way. It is, after all, me that has asked for constructive comments, and oh boy do I get them! But I have to admit that it's provided on the clear understanding that they are only trying to help, but it still hurts, I can assure you.

As for where I get my ideas from, well, that's easy, normally in bed and during the middle of the night, and not what any lewd-minded reader might be thinking – remember my age! I will routinely wake up thinking of a particular character and his or her part in the plot, and presumably whilst subconsciously play around with possible scenarios. I then get up early (normally around six o'clock) and put the remembered flashes of inspiration down on paper before the brain reverts to its normal dormant state. That's not strictly true, as I type it directly onto my computer file (the benefits of being a competent touch-typist). Or an idea might come whilst mowing or walking down a fairway trying to find my ball, probably why my golf is so dreadful (but still enjoyable). The amazing thing is how amazing our brains are, and its ability to think up and remember people and events of years gone by, with instant recall.

Seriously, what my writing does, it keeps the brain active, which supplements my usual busy and active day – if you want something done, then ask a busy person. I have seen other naval colleagues (no names, no pack drill), who seem to me at least, to lead sedentary lives and everything seems to be too much of an effort. The result is a definite decline and a slowing down, with the ultimate and unavoidable ending. Of course, there are some with health, mental and mobility problems, but I'm sure old age can be enjoyed to the full if you can remain active and have a reason for getting out of bed every morning. That, by the way, is not meant to sound like a lecture, just good advice from someone who has been very fortunate to have been blessed with a reasonable body and three pounds of functioning cerebral matter.

But, before I end, I have one more important thing to add. Friends have said, "I don't know how you do it, there's no earthly way that I could sit down and write a book." Our kind and friendly milkman Colin, is just one such person. I disagree. I bet you, if your life depended on it, and you were given a number of blank sheets of paper, you'd write! If your would-be executioner was really kind, he'd also give you some writing implements!

So, whether you have or you haven't enjoyed reading *Acres of Diamonds,* please, I beseech you; have a go at putting pen to paper. May I help by suggesting a subject matter that should be familiar – yourself? Write two full pages of A4 foolscap on your life to date and what you hope to achieve or aspire to. Then give it to your partner, friend or enemy, and see if they recognise who the author is and was it readable. You have nothing to lose, nothing whatsoever, and if nothing else, you may then remember the old codger that suggested it in the first place. I promise you; it is easier than you think. It's like being a dustman; you just pick it up as you go along. Remember what Mark Twain famously said: *Today is the tomorrow you worried about yesterday* – so best you make the most of it.

Robert Villier

Acres of Diamonds

Three Cambridge undergraduates embark on an illegal escapade (serious crime) to add sparkle to their final year at university by deciding to commit a diamond robbery.

Why do it and risk so much and so near to receiving their hard-earned degrees?

Find out for yourself in this enjoyable easy fast moving and entertaining novel.

Enjoy…

Prologue

Let us not be too particular; it is better to have old second-hand diamonds than none at all.

Mark Twain

A farmer in Africa heard of others who had become rich by discovering diamond mines. Filled with excitement and visions of finding such precious stones, he hurriedly sold his farm and set out to become a diamond prospector himself. For many years, he then wandered far and wide, crisscrossing the huge country with the ambition of striking it rich. Hope and change, however, proved to be a lame strategy. Alas and alack, the years took their toll, and finally, having grown old, tired and despondent over his failures, he ended his life.

Meanwhile, the man who bought his farm, settled in, and one bright day, while fording a stream on the land he now owned, was attracted to a gleam of coloured rock at the bottom of the shallow water. Out of curiosity, he picked it up and with pleasure displayed it on his mantel shelf as a decoration. One day, a visitor noticed the rock and almost fainted. He asked the farmer what he thought it was, the farmer innocently thinking it to be an attractive crystal. The visitor told him that it was probably one of the biggest diamonds he had ever seen. It turned out that the stream had many more such diamonds at its bottom.

The first farmer never knew he was standing on his own acres of diamonds. He already owned the land free and clear, which he had sold practically for a song. If he'd only taken stock of what he already had, by exploring and surveying his surroundings and working his own acres, his story might have had a different and happier ending.

This story is a staple used by noted motivational speakers and writers to make a point, and for good reason. 'Acres of Diamonds' is a powerful metaphor to inspire people to explore and harness their own potential as human beings striving to reach their goal of achieving the riches they seek, whether tangible or intangible, or a hybrid of both.

In the most of obvious of terms, riches could mean financial wealth, a successful career and a comfortable retirement, respected status and its associated perks. However, there are also those parameters that are harder to achieve and cannot be bought outright by money alone, like inner peace, contentment, a healthy mind in a healthy body filled with good spirit and wellbeing, or a long, happy, meaningful life. The wisest perhaps are those that opt for a mix of the concrete and the unperceived; they get to choose their very own definition.

Often staying the course and having the wisdom, patience and resolve is in using the resources we already have and were blessed with, far outweigh the enemy of envy. Our own innate personal gems would seem to offer better odds than seeking out those in greener pastures − whom for some it is ever thus. Surely, staying the course applies to us all, be it in marriage, family, education, profession, health and illness, or anything else you care to mention. The other field may well appear to be more verdant, but seldom is. Also, is it not a fact that we mine our own acres of diamonds in everything we do − every day of our life?

A Chinese proverb states that it is better to possess a diamond with a flaw than a smooth pebble. There is also a trite but true saying that money isn't everything. Whatever, diamonds − the product of millions and millions of years spent under extreme heat and pressure − still have much to answer for. Their pedigree, value and lustre are undeniable, but is undoubtedly depreciated and tarnished for those now staying the course − in prison!

Chapter 1

The three Cambridge undergraduates sat relaxing in Oscar's room, Raffer and Horatio having been unable to resist the intriguingly couched invitation to join him for afternoon tea. Oscar was now playing 'mother', pouring the Earl Grey, the selection of expensive-looking cakes now revealed from under a white linen napkin. The two curious visitors were close but not bosom pals of Oscar but had been unwittingly selected from a long list of initial possible candidates as the most likely partners to share in an undertaking that could change their three lives.

"Thank you for coming, gentlemen. I rightly calculated you would find my missive impossible to ignore or indeed refuse. However, I intend that you remain ignorant and in suspense, at least for the time being, whilst we enjoy this splendid selection of fare that 'Mrs B' has arranged."

Mrs Bates was the indispensable housekeeper that cleaned for Oscar, as well as the two adjoining rooms. In addition to doing his washing and ironing, Mrs B willingly ran errands and carried out his weekly shopping, it kept her young – being around 'her' undergraduates.

Having enjoyed and hungrily devoured the complete silver cake stand's contents, and drunk their replenished cups of Earl Grey, Oscar suggested a walk along the Cam. The two guests needed no second bidding, eager to find out the real reason for the short note which had arrived through their letterbox almost a fortnight since.

Having given the matter of my proposed undertaking considerable thought and due diligence, I have come to the conclusion that you have the right credentials, posture and attitude to share in the venture. However, whether you wish to become involved has yet to be discussed and agreed. Therefore, if your interest and innate curiosity has been sufficiently whetted, then please join me, and one other, in my room on Wednesday 24 February 2017 at 3 o'clock.

Irrespective of your attendance or absence, please burn this letter without a word to any other living soul. I look forward to seeing you.

Yours
Oscar Ormsby-Waite

Suitably replete, the three men now sauntered along the River Cam, which meandered its way through the Backs of their college grounds. A husband and wife swan silently neared the bank, perhaps in the hope of a thrown and welcoming tidbit. None was forthcoming as they changed direction gliding back out into the centre reaches of the faster moving body of water. It was a crisply cold but dry day, with all three sporting ski-jackets, gloves and scarves.

Even in winter garb, one could tell that these were confident men and comfortable with wearing expensive attire, as if it were the norm. The wealthy and well-off have a confident knack and assured way of showing it without seeming to do so.

"Come on Oscar, you irritating bastard, you can't keep us in suspense forever," Horatio being the first to break.

"Gentlemen, what I am about to audaciously propose could well alter the course of our lives and must not be shared or heard by another living person." The other two nodded from behind wrapped faces.

"The first thing to say is that you were both selected for your honour, integrity, build and sense of daring-do. I also know that should you decide not to join me in my adventure, then I can trust and rely upon you as gentlemen for your eternal silence. I therefore fully understand that it is not axiomatic you will elect to join me in what you may consider to be a sheer act of folly, or a patently stupid undertaking given our privileged positions."

"Oscar, you know bloody well we're just bursting to know what this is all about, so please stop all this theatrical preamble and spit it out, as I'm not sure I can bear all this cloak and dagger nonsense," Raffer interrupted.

To which Horatio backed him up with a, "hear hear, old man."

Oscar smiled. He knew he had a captive audience, and with no other person within earshot, he opened the bidding.

"I think you would both agree that we are three extremely fortunate blighters, with every chance of the likelihood of successful careers ahead of us, and not wishing to sound too immodest, we're all three likely to leave King's with a First with honours. Is that not too proud a boast to make?" The other two nodded, not wishing to stop Oscar's divulging flow of information.

"What then, say you both, if we were to pull off a modest but successfully audacious diamond robbery that would remain unsolved for years to come?"

"Are you serious?" Horatio exclaimed, in shock at what he had just heard, if not completely frightened off.

"This is a joke, Oscar? Please tell me it's a joke," Raffer countered, but inwardly interested.

"Yes, Horatio, I'm deadly serious, and no Raffer, it's far from being a joke; those cakes cost me a tidy penny, I'll have you know."

They all three laughed, the ice had been broken. The initial shock had been received, if still being inwardly digested, whilst waiting to hear more. Oscar was not upset or surprised by their predictable reaction – it was what he had logically and rightly expected.

"When we leave King's, we will all go our separate and hopefully successful ways. Yet, wouldn't it be wonderful – the icing on our academic cake – to plan and execute a small but worthwhile diamond robbery and not be caught? Gentlemen, be in no doubt, I would not be contemplating or suggesting such a venture if I thought for one moment that we were not clever enough to pull it off. Surely, we have the intellect, resources, time and guile to achieve such a crime, whilst fully appreciating the magnitude of what I am suggesting? Therefore, we all need a period of deep reflection and heart-searching before we make any firm commitment, one way or the other. I propose, therefore, that we meet again in a month's time to give our decision. I promise that there will be no loss of face or stigma attached if either or both of you feel that it is not what you wish to be involved in." Neither said a word, their faces hidden by scarves as they both nodded, understanding the gravity and rationale behind Oscar's measured words.

A month later saw the three men punting on the Cam. Horatio had been the cox of the victorious light blue eight from the previous year, punting to him was considered boringly pedestrian – but it was extremely private. No one had as yet ventured a single word on the subject which had occupied many hours of the three minds, all waiting for the opening card to be laid.

"I'm in!" declared Raffer, deliberately looking away from the other two, as if merely discussing the weather.

"Me too," the man with the long pole echoed, "but against my better judgement, I might add."

"Splendid," replied Oscar. "However, let us make haste slowly. Your final commitment and decision will again be required once I've explained exactly how we intend to successfully deprive a certain fat cat London jeweller of his stock of raw and unpolished diamonds. Before then there is a lot to plan, as I have no intention that any of us should ever be caught."

Chapter 2

It was a life-changing roll call. As the admissions tutor read out the names, the men and women gathered around the table replying confidently to each one: "yep…yep…yep." Each yep was actually a no. It was in fact a rejection of a candidate who had applied for a place at the University of Cambridge. The weakest of the field had already been sifted out, with up to a fifth of the applicants having been declined before reaching the interview stage.

With the wind vigorously shaking the bare branches in the grounds of King's College, the tutors gathered round a long rectangular table in a light-filled room to consider the results of those interviewed. There were five women and seven men – a jury of 12. They were there to discuss admissions to study Law. On the table were white china cups of tea and coffee with two barely touched water jugs and plates of cellophane wrapped biscuits untouched, well, no visible sign of any empty packets. Perhaps all were waiting for someone to be first?

The easy ones went first. Those were the candidates whose academic track record were – by Cambridge standards – marginal, and whose performance at interview had been disappointing. As a candidate's name was read out, one of the academics noted that he'd got an interview score of two, out of a possible ten.

"Oh dear," said Malcolm Althorpe, the senior admissions tutor, who presided at the head of the table. Next to him was a steel trolley, not unlike a supermarket version, containing all of the applicants' files.

Then, they got down to business. After the straightforward rejections, and those they had already decided to offer places to, there was a band of candidates who fell somewhere in the middle. They might have been teenagers who had done well at interview, but whose academic performance seemed patchy. There were some with impeccable credentials on paper – but, in a phrase repeatedly used, 'failed to shine' at interview. Suffice to say, that great care, thought and deliberation went into the assessment of each and every candidate.

Both Oxford and Cambridge had been regularly accused of bias against state school applicants. The tutors now gathered at the table were all too aware that Cambridge was committed to admitting between 61% and 63% of its UK students from state-sector schools and colleges. At present, the proportion stood at 59.3% (which displayed a certain measure of pedantic accuracy). The university had also agreed with the 'Office of Fair Access' – an official watchdog set up when the Blair government brought in top-up fees – to increase the share of students from neighbourhoods where few, if any, people had gone to university.

Competition to gain admission to any of the Cambridge universities (around some 30 colleges), and presumably Oxford for that matter, remained intense. There were around 16,000 candidates chasing just under 3,400 undergraduate places. At the close of play after five or so hours of painstaking deliberations, the academics made a number of offers; the letters arriving on a successful candidate's doormat, in most cases likely to be their parents' doormat.

First up was a girl from a leading private school, who was strong on paper but stumbled at the interview.

"She seemed surprised by quite a lot of the things we asked and were talking about. She would all too often say, 'Oh right,' as if she hadn't seen it or heard of it before," one of the academics offered in explanation.

"Had she revised?" Althorpe enquired.

"We asked what work she had done recently, and based our questions around that, so it was starting with something that should have been familiar, but seeing it in a different context," one academic continued.

Althorpe suggested, "One possibility is that she's someone who's learned in a compartmentalised way."

Another tutor said, "The comment I've put down is: 'needs help with the next steps'."

Althorpe looked up to the heavens and noticed a large undisturbed cobweb, as he wondered aloud if tutors could lead a student through an entire degree?

"We could," one of the seven just men responded dryly.

Althorpe went on, "If we gave her a chance. she would do what everybody else would do and think: 'I'll probably be all right' and she would in all probability be wrong."

There was a despairing consensus around the table that the university could not repair or fill the gaps in this candidate's knowledge. A damning line from the school's reference – which laid bare its inability to teach the candidate – was read aloud by a tutor who raised his outstretched hands in exasperation, as if seeking divine help. The candidate's file went back into the Tesco or Sainsbury's style trolley – with a resounding clang.

A few of the academics paused for a cup of now-cold tea or coffee, whilst leafing through multicoloured spreadsheets with the candidate's names, their exam performance to date, predicted grades, interview scores, contextual flags and ranking – based on exam results – compared with all of the university's applicants this year.

Suitably refreshed and with the wind continuing to shake the trees, the jury of academics moved on to discuss the next interviewee who hailed from a well-known Birmingham sixth form college. It was a candidate by the name of Oscar Thurstan Ormsby-Waite.

One tutor noted, "He considered him to be thoughtful, articulate and extremely careful with everything he said, even if not appearing to be entirely or fully engaging in the topic under discussion. However, on balance, I think he would do well, even if he didn't exactly shine."

"I liked him, let's take him," the eldest tutor at the table called out. It was Professor Dunstan Dodderington. The oldest academic present who was affectionately known simply as 'DD' by all tutors and staff alike and as Doddy by the students. Both titles seemed to sit perfectly well with the man who had made this command decision.

Althorpe immediately agreed, "Everyone content?"

And so, Oscar duly received his letter of acceptance, which he'd assumed he would, and this was not a matter of being big headed or overconfident. He'd carried out his own post interview assessment, privately conceding that it could have gone better. He had rightly come to the pragmatic but accurate conclusion that most of the 12 fair-minded jurors nodded and looked satisfied rather than questioningly anti. This was very much in line with Oscar's outlook, attitude and approach to life: don't under or oversell oneself, be honest and concise and trust in what you truly believe – wherever possible.

Such was Oscar's mental modus operandi that he had immediately contacted King's College, enquiring as to the accommodation and rent, something the average undergraduate failed to do until the very last moment. Oscar Ormsby-Waite had got off to a good start. He was going to King's College Cambridge to read Law.

Chapter 3

As soon as Oscar had received his letter of acceptance, he wasted no time in contacting the Graduate Admissions Office, who in turn put him through to the College Accommodation Officer – a Mr Reginald Turnbull, who was extremely helpful.

"Yes, young sir, I can either send you all the relevant information through the post. Or if you have five minutes to spare, I can explain it to you now over the phone."

"Thank you kindly, Mr Turnbull. I'd very much like to hear what is available now, if you don't mind. I can then discuss it with my parents. Is that all right by you?"

"It's certainly all right by me, young sir. So, if you've got a pencil and paper handy, I'll give you my standard spiel. Accommodation here at King's College for all you undergraduates is fit for a king, well I would say that, wouldn't I?" Oscar twigged this was not the first time he'd made this quip. "The first reassuring news is that accommodation is provided for the full three years of your course. It will be either here onsite at the college or in nearby hostels, which have their own student rooms, and only a few minutes' walk from the college. Between you and me, it's better to be onsite, that is if you're lucky enough to be pulled out of the hat.

"Your rooms cover a wide range in terms of size, shape, age and, of course, rent. All have a bed, desk, chest of drawers, wardrobe, bookshelves and a reading lamp. They also have an easy chair and a coffee table." It was becoming clear to Oscar that Mr Turnbull was simply reading from a prepared and much used script. He obviously enjoyed imparting such valuable information to any enquiring undergraduate.

"Some of the rooms are cosier than others and have interesting shapes and features associated with such old buildings. Inevitably, they look Spartan when empty, but are soon made to look homely once your own things have been placed or rather strewn about. Most of the buildings have a shared kitchen or 'gyp' room, where snacks can be prepared. They are deliberately simple, but all are fitted with fridges and microwaves, some are lucky enough to share a cooker and an oven, which are rarely used. One additional luxury, but not uncommon, is that most bedrooms have their own small fridge.

"As I've said, some of the rooms are very old with interesting architectural features, such as mullioned windows (a vertical member between the casements of panes of windows) and uneven floors. You will soon get used to the several flights of stairs to the nearest loo and bathroom, although most of the rooms have their own wash basin. Some of these are 'sets', that is, two rooms, one a bedroom, the other a sitting-room-come-study. There are, of course, many beautiful views to admire.

"In the case of the hostels, they have an additional common room area, where students can socialise or study including laundry facilities. Here on the college there are also music practice rooms, a large bicycle storage shed and a small gymnasium, which is heavily used and overbooked. Students tend to be either very energetic or the entire opposite, I'll say no more."

"What can I reasonably expect to get in my first year as a Fresher, Mr Turnbull?"

"Young sir, please call me Fred or 'FT'. Everyone does. When you start as a first year, you are allocated accommodation by me – the Accommodation Officer and it's all done in an impeccably fair way. You will be given a choice over two things: your preferred building and the length of lease. You can also specify if you wish to be guaranteed a room at the lower end of the rental scale. I also take account of the small number of students with special needs, such as a disability and access.

"The next first years will be allocated to either Keynes building, which is onsite with en suite rooms, or in the Spalding hostel. This may change from time to time according to circumstances, which will not concern you."

"Fred, are we all grouped together by subjects?"

"No, young sir, you will be living with other students, both men and women, studying a wide range of subjects."

"Are there any rules or no-go areas regarding the fairer sex, if you get my meaning, FT?"

"Now, come on, young sir. You are all highly intelligent people, or you wouldn't be at Cambridge. So, there is little point in trying to create artificial barriers to which you are all clever by far to circumnavigate. You are treated as adults and expected to act like adults. Need I say more?

"It's worth mentioning the ballot system we employ. As your first year comes to an end, you will be placed on a list according to a King's ballot. This is in the order in which you choose your room for the following year. The list is then reversed for year three, so if you get a low ballot position for choosing your second-year room, you will have a high position for your third year. The third years always choose before second years, and groups of friends can enter the ballot together so that they choose rooms at the same time, which helps to find rooms near one another. It's all very fair and sensible as you would expect – we've been at it for long enough and we seem to know how to get the most equitable results."

"What about the terms and the rents?"

"Good point, young Sir. I was just coming on to that. All undergraduate rooms are available on either a 28- or 29-week lease, covering term times and a bit either side, or a 35-week lease running from October to June, minus two to three weeks over Christmas. Some rooms are available only on a 29-week lease, because they are used for interviewing candidates at Christmas, school visits and conferences which are held over the Easter recess.

"Rents for rooms are set according to the facilities they have; size, amenities, desirability, etc, and are arranged into six bands. The highest rent is £1741 per term, which is the most expensive band covering a 35-week lease. The cheapest is £962 per term, for the least expensive rent band on a 28- or 29-week lease. Also and in total fairness, we guarantee that students can choose a room at the lower rent band in the ballot, which remains private information and not declared at any time, to save any embarrassment, you understand?

"We have many treasures here, young Sir, and as you might or might not already know, the college library here at King's has been in continuous existence since the foundation of the college in 1441. As well as preserving many rare books and manuscript treasures, the library serves the current needs of all you undergraduates, and other graduates and senior members of the college.

"That, young sir (all were called young sir or young lady by the affable Mr Turnbull, Fred or FT, who had served King's since leaving school some 52 years ago) is about it. If you will now give me your full postal address, I will send you a fuller version of what I have just briefly explained. At least you are ahead of the field, which is always a good sign and to your advantage, as I already have your name lodged in my memory box. I look forward to hearing from you in due course as well as welcoming you to King's. You've made a wise choice, young sir. I'm sure that both the college and Cambridge will not disappoint."

Chapter 4

Dear Ormsby-Waite,

By now you should have received your letter of acceptance to read and study Law here at King's College, Cambridge. May I be the first member of the staff to both congratulate and welcome you on what is undoubtedly no small measure of achievement.

I will be both your prime mentor and tutor, along with a further cadre of eight chosen few. Therefore, I do not wish you to waste the remaining precious time you have left before joining King's on any unnecessary swotting or background reading. Be assured, there will be time enough for us both to stretch your mind and intellectual bandwidth after you have arrived.

For my sins, I remain an ageing but contented bachelor, thus afforded the privilege of permanent accommodation within the college (Bodley's Court, top floor, room number four). Please come and present yourself, as and when, at a time convenient to you.

Yours in anticipation…
Dunstan Falcon Dodderington
King's College

3 March 2017

FT was absolutely right, neither King's nor Cambridge disappointed. Oscar fell in love with the college of his choice the moment he walked through the large and impressive entrance. His first impressions were more than favourable, he felt a physical excitement in his loins and an immediate sense of belonging, which would have been difficult to describe or explain to a stranger.

The transition, having attained a string of outstanding A Levels, from sixth form to university had seemed seamless and made in remarkably short order. Oscar already had warm and favourable vibes, having spoken to Fred or FT. He thought on reflection he preferred the handle of Fred, which he spontaneously decided to use. He was further impressed and reassured to receive an unexpected personal letter from his tutor. This made him feel far more than just a statistic or a number, in the way of being yet another new undergraduate.

The letter of acceptance from King's had not only thrilled Oscar but had been welcomed by his parents with evident pride. They were proud beyond belief and far beyond the boundaries of their wildest of dreams. They had always known that Oscar was bright and displayed an incisive and quick mind, but they had never thought for one moment that he was that bright or that clever. After all, they were both comparative duffers with not a single O, let alone an A Level, to show between the two of them.

Yet this lack of academic qualifications had not prevented Oscar's father from becoming a wealthy and successful jeweller in his own right. In this, he had been ably supported by a loving and devoted wife. The success of his business now paled against the knowledge and pride of telling friends that their son was going up to Cambridge to read Law, with the aspiration of a further year at Harvard in America. This rightful proud boast counted for more than the 'glass rocks' he had locked in reinforced steel vaults on his business premises.

The Ormsby-Waites, for all their apparent success, were not an extravagant family or overt in their wealth. True, they lived in a large and secluded gated property abutting Sutton Coldfield Park, with the only visible sign of opulence being the luxury of a Roller and full-time chauffeur. They were, therefore, more than happy to fund the tuition fee of £9,250 per year without batting an eyelid, with a more than reasonable day-to-day allowance. For his part, Oscar was appreciative and never extravagant, as he derived most pleasure and satisfaction from cerebral challenges rather than expensive gismos.

Mr Ormsby-Waite senior now employed over 50 men and women in his company located in the jewellery quarter of Hockley in the heartland of inner

Birmingham. He had left school at the age of 15 with no educational qualifications whatsoever and had been grateful to be accepted for a jewellery apprenticeship. He then, at the tender age of 25, had the balls and confidence to branch out on his own: small and steady had been his byword and his business had gone from strength to strength, building a reputation for excellence and fairness. Now and by far the zenith of his considerable achievements, was for both him and his dear wife to see their only son being accepted by King's College, Cambridge, to read Law. How good was that!

Oscar had found Cambridge a breath of fresh air after the outskirts of the industrial hub called Birmingham. The beauty and serenity of the many college grounds, set against the backdrop of old and fine buildings, was a far cry from the hustle, bustle and grime of the country's second largest city. He could well understand why his tutor lived in and seldom left the College.

His father had insisted they drive him to Cambridge and help him settle in. Having had his first year's rent and tuition fees taken care of and a not ungenerous monthly allowance, Oscar was hardly in a position to refuse. At least a flying visit enabled Ma and Pa to see at first hand, where he would be residing and the wonderful facilities on offer; if only to confirm what a privileged position and opportunity he had been given. He had also acquiesced to their request for a further weekend visit when the weather improved, and he had his feet firmly under the table.

Fred, or the ballot, had done him proud and he was allocated second floor rooms, a bedroom and a separate sitting room with en suite facilities in Keynes building.

Secretly, he had not relished the thought of being assigned to the hostel; he was a private person by nature and the idea of sharing and having to use a common room did not sit comfortably. Had his good luck been influenced in anyway by his prompt action in contacting Fred; impossible to know?

He had first reconnoitred the college, its magnificent library, the grounds, the Backs and the riverside walks. He had spent time marvelling at the College Chapel, a fine example of late gothic architecture built over a period of a hundred years (1446-1531), which featured the world's largest fan vault ceiling and 26 large stained-glass windows – most dating from the 16th century. It was all too splendid and too much for Oscar to take in. He wondered how much he would remember, such as taking lunch in the splendid King's College dining hall.

Suitably prepared, Oscar presented himself at the door of his tutor. At least he wanted to give the first impression of someone who had taken the trouble to stake out the lie of the land before entering the lion's den. What had his sixth form master told him; "Always remember the seven Ps: prior preparation and planning prevents a piss-poor performance!" Perhaps the most important person in his life, at least for the next three years, may not be a lion and more akin to a pussycat? The truth turned out to be somewhere between the two.

Chapter 5

The door to room number four at Bodley's Court – King's College of Our Lady and Saint Nicholas in Cambridge – to give it its full and rightful title, was finally opened by Professor Dunstan Dodderington.

"Welcome 'Ormsby', please, do come in." The professor had already and unilaterally decided that he could not be doing with hyphenated names and certainly not for the next three years.

"I'm afraid you're going to have to get used to Ormsby as your new moniker, if only for the sake of convenience and expediency." Oscar nodded. "By the same token you might as well know that I'm known throughout the College as 'DD' by colleagues and staff alike, and as 'Doddy' by all you rebellious and disrespectful undergraduates," he said, smiling broadly, extending an outstretched arm and a large plate of a hand.

"This, as you can see, is my humble abode, which you will be seeing a great deal more of over the next three years," the professor continued. He handed Oscar a cream sealed envelope bearing his name written in a beautiful manuscript hand, at the same time inviting Oscar to sign the visitors' book. The leather-bound tome lay open at the day's date, its contents of many pages almost full. "Would you prefer tea or coffee? By the way, I rarely drink alcohol, so don't expect to be offered anything stronger. In the meantime, you might care to wander around my den or lair whilst I make the brew. Have a look to see if you can learn anything, and perhaps offer any pointers for either the prosecution or the defence."

"Tea…milk with no sugar, thank you, sir." Oscar had been in the room barely but a minute and already he'd been asked to make a decision and been given two separate directives. *It was certainly not going to be a dull or pedestrian three years*, he smilingly thought, musing to himself. Oscar, alias Ormsby, now had time to study his tutor, who seemed to be busying himself in what looked to be an improvised kitchen-come-recess area.

He appeared to be something akin to a large green canopy, topped with a wild but sparse head of wispy white hair. The professor was a big man, over six feet with a spreading stomach which seemed to indicate he enjoyed his food, if not physical exercise. He was wearing a dark green corduroy suit, the green interrupted by a purple velvet waistcoat with matching bowtie. The waistcoat boasted a gold chain and presumably a fob watch, securely hidden in one of the small side pockets – more a slit than a pocket. A large yellow silk handkerchief flopped from his jacket pocket, as if on the verge of falling out. He fittingly wore large brown but eminently sensible brogues, which had never seen a lick of polish in all their many years of use, and heels badly in desperate need of repair. His long and thinning calico-coloured hair, which remained bushy at the back, gave the impression he'd just received an electric shock, as it shot out in all directions of the compass.

His long and angular face was adorned with bushy pinnacle eyebrows that had never been plucked nor trimmed during his entire life. Under which sat pince-nez glasses, perched precariously at the end of a long and narrow beak of a nose. To complete his distinctive facial features, he sported thick and generously greying sideburns and a goatee beard. Here was a man who could not easily have hidden in a crowd. His appearance certainly made a statement, if it was not exactly one of sartorial elegance – he somehow looked right.

Professor Dunstan Falcon Dodderington had himself received a First with glowing honours at King's many moons past. Following a short sabbatical of a month's walking holiday spent alone in the Lake District, he had promptly returned to the college to take up a position offered on the teaching staff. It was to be a career spent entirely in the safe and cossetted world of academia, which suited perfectly. Here at King's, he had thus remained quite happily for the ensuing 35 years, fiercely resisting any overtures to be promoted to any higher exalted position. He was utterly and entirely content and would not brook any suggestion or offer to do anything else. He was happy with his lot, and didn't his 'lot' do well by him each successive year? How many can profess or claim a career of sheer contentment?

Professor Dodderington was a bachelor, with no distractions other than his academic devotion. There was little surprise then, when his students seemed to achieve an inordinately high number of First-class degrees – with honours. Was this due to his availability and ever open-door policy, by virtue of living within the college in a small and pokey one-roomed apartment? A man who rarely left the college, apart from his walking breaks.

This was Doddy' résumé, together with the experience and time offered in the way of encouragement and advice to his students. Here was a man who had spent his entire adult life secure and protected in the world of academia, and shortly to celebrate his 60th birthday. Dunstan would not have known a tin of paint or a hammer if they were opened or fell on him, let alone be used in anger. But his skill was immeasurable in mentoring each of his students. Each was treated as if they were the most single most important person ever to tread the streets of Cambridge, let alone the quadrangle of King's College or his tutor's study-come-home.

The room was an Aladdin's Cave, with two walls a mass of crammed bookshelves, with further piles of hefty looking tomes scattered or abandoned around the floor, appearing to encircle the two comfortable and obviously well-used leather armchairs. In a small, recessed corner now stood the professor brewing the tea. In another recess was a door housing a toilet and washbasin. *Self-contained?* he thought. His eyes then settled on what was clearly an expensive and top-of-the-range music and audio suite of equipment, under which was housed rack upon rack of vinyl records, CDs and tapes. The professor was a lover of classical music and chess, looking at the number of books on the game. Along the remaining wall were many photographs of past students, a few wearing wig and gown, but mostly alone or now with a wife and family.

Oscar peered out onto the college grounds with the River Cam clearly visible beyond the paved path that followed the curve of water. There were people out punting; it looked a picturesque sight and surely one that he or the professor would never tire of seeing. Having been invited to take the other green leather armchair, he was handed a large hot mug of tea. The professor clearly didn't cater for any unnecessary saucers!

"Well, Ormsby, you've now had time to have a quick look round. So, what are your initial observations – if any, and do you find for the defence or the plaintiff? Remember that every word you utter is being heard and assessed by members of the jury and the judge."

"Your Honour (Oscar had already decided to play his tutor at his own game), as counsel for the defence, I have much to say on behalf of my innocent client." The professor smiled as he filled his large briar pipe, warming and pleased with the newcomer's response and ability to think on his feet.

"My client claims he is a bachelor; that he is, but only in the strictest definition of the word. He is in fact happily wed to a lady called King's College, with his large family here on display in this very courtroom." Oscar dramatically and expansively waved his arm, deliberately pointing to the many photographs one by one, as if to emphasise the size of his supporting siblings.

"It may also interest the jury to learn that he has two mistresses, namely, classical music and the cerebral game called chess. He is, therefore, far from being a bachelor and is rarely alone as he is regularly visited by unescorted people seeking his advice and company. In conclusion, My Lord and members of the jury, my client's only crime is that of having spent his academic life in the pursuit of helping many alumni down their chosen road of law. Therefore, I am confident that you will have no hesitation in finding my somewhat eccentric but likeable client innocent on all counts wrongly arraigned." The professor smiled and slowly clapped his hands.

"Well done, Ormsby, that was a fine effort and I am impressed and encouraged by three qualities shown; your ability in responding to my demand, thinking on your feet, and your evident sense of humour."

"Thank you, sir, I hope I didn't overstep the mark by alluding to the possibility of any eccentricity?"

"Not at all, Ormsby, I admit I have my odd ways, but anyone can be normal, and if that were to be the case, wouldn't it be a dull and boring old life?

"You were, however, quite discerning in your scout around my boudoir. I do indeed have a passion for music, in particular that of Wagner. That is why I was so long in answering the door I was waiting until the end of the London's Philharmonic Orchestra's beautiful rendition of Wagner's *Tristan und Isolde*. As for my love of chess at which I consider myself to be a reasonable exponent of what is a truly fascinating game. Do you play?"

"Yes, sir, I played at sixth form but sadly not very good. I tend to be too aggressive instead of being more patient and biding my time, as my last schoolmaster advised – not a chess master, if you get my meaning."

"Well, we might get round to having a game at some stage, but for the foreseeable future, I'm going to be loading you with more than enough to occupy your every awakening and even sleeping moments. You have a busy three years ahead of you, very busy indeed. But remember, you have already jumped the biggest hurdle, you are here! That in itself is a tremendous achievement, and you should be rightly proud. I have only a few words of advice, as too much advice and information, no matter how well intentioned, merely serves to overload the system and achieve little. You will find the atmosphere here at King's is generally considered to be a little easier than that of other colleges to integrate into, if you come from a working class or minority background. Having said this, a survey conducted by the Varsity newspaper in January 2009 revealed that the parental income of students who participated in the survey here at King's were slightly higher than the university average.

"The college, of course, has its own student unions, both for undergraduates and graduates, who use both organisations to assist in the decision-making in the college itself and the university. The college students have a reputation for radical political activity going back to the 1960s, and the college has not infrequently been the centre of demonstrations, rent strikes and so forth, sparked by political events. Therefore, I would advise if I may be so forward, that you stay well clear of any active involvement. You will be up to your ears with legal work and studies and any added distraction would not help or serve you well. That is, of course, only my own personal advice and I will not punish or demean you if you wish ultimately to get involved.

"The best advice I can give you, is that you enjoy your time here both in the college and Cambridge. There is a lot to see, admire and appreciate, so remember all work and no play makes Jack a dull boy. If the going gets tough, and it will at times, stand back and take a breather. We have beautiful grounds, and we could always mix business with pleasure, by talking as we enjoy a walk along the Cam. There is also our magnificent chapel, should you feel in need of any divine help or intervention. However, if there is none forthcoming from on high, then you can always use me as a fall back to depend upon. We work and live in a very privileged environment and we should all do well to remember it, so please never take the college and its people for granted. And please let your parents share in your success by inviting them up to spend time in Cambridge, if only so that they can see and appreciate what a fortunate person their son is.

"Here endeth the introductory sermon, according to the eccentric Doddy. I think, Ormsby, that is more than enough to take in on our first and enjoyable meeting. Now, take your envelope, study the contents and its advice and I'll see you next together with the other eight cohorts in our group. Welcome to King's, now clear off, as Wagner is waiting to soothe and satisfy."

Oscar walked out of Bodley's Court and found an empty bench to sit and read his tutors first instructions. He stared at the expensive looking envelope for at least five minutes before carefully opening it. The one inner sheet was also a textured cream and almost akin to vellum in appearance. Was this deliberate? A message of evident excellence he was meant to keep for years to come? Whatever, he certainly intended to keep and treasure it, as it clearly indicated both thoughtfulness and class. He slowly read, taking care to absorb each and every word, slowly and carefully, not to miss any possible nuance. The first thing that struck him was the thought that the professor had probably gone to the same effort in writing a similar handwritten letter to all of his new students. Oscar was suitably impressed.

Collegium Regale beate Marie et Sancti Nicholai Cantebrigie
Welcome to King's College Law Faculty

The first thing you should be aware of is that once someone has been admitted to the College, he or she automatically becomes a member for life. You should also be aware that you are walking in the steps of Robert Walpole, John Maynard Keynes, Rupert Brooke, Alan Turing and Stephen Poliakof, to name but a few.

There is no specific set of subjects that need to have been studied prior to studying Law here at King's (and taking Law at school provides or gives no particular advantage). What you do need, however, is a clear logical mind, a willingness to think through and argue a case, and the ability to assimilate, condense and use large quantities of information. The most important criteria are enthusiasm, dedication and potential and we will consider each case on an individual basis. Please, be under no illusion: the course requires a considerable commitment in terms of time and energy. Law is quintessentially a language-based subject, so the ability to speak and write coherently and precisely is vital.

...

Things to consider:

What is Law, Law at Cambridge, Law at King's, Student perspectives, King's Fellows in Law, What are we looking for and what careers follow a Law degree.

...

Recommended reading:

Allan Hutchinson, 'Is Eating People Wrong?'

'Great Legal cases and How They Shaped the World' (Cambridge University Press, 2010). All chapters are useful, but see particularly Chapters 1,2,6,8 and 10.

'What about Law: Studying Law at University' (2nd revised edition, 2011) by Catherine Barnard, Janet O'Sullivan and Graham Virgo − editors.

...

Finally, congratulation on your wise decision in choosing to come to King's. I now look forward to the many hours of personal one-to-one cut and thrust of our intellectual legal chess encounters. My door is always open should you wish to avail yourself of my willingness to help at any time − good luck.

Doddy

Oscar thought it a good letter which he read three times. He paused to watch two pairs of swans glide past, the first time he'd ever seen a black cob and pen. Was this an omen or a sign of good luck, impossible to say? Whichever it was, it was worth capturing as he used his mobile phone to photograph and record the sighting. He liked the professor's use of Doddy; it showed he had a sense of humour, together with a somewhat distinctive if slightly eccentric dress sense!

He'd recalled what his father had told him: 'Oscar, it's not the wrapping that counts, it's what's inside that matters.'

He sat and recalled his earlier interview, which had lasted but barely 25 minutes. He had been asked to read a text in the half hour immediately prior. When inside much of the interview was a discussion centred on what he had read. This is where his memory and ability to recall and retain facts and figures seemed to help, plus his skill and quickness to sort out the wheat from the chaff. He could have said more and perhaps should, instead of being too economic with his answers. The one thing that had apparently shone through was his articulation.

He rose and made his way to the library to get copies of Doddy's recommended reading list. Later that day, he phoned his parents to explain what had taken place on his first day, being both encouraged and happy to be at King's, and thanked them for helping him to settle in.

Chapter 6

Oscar was bright, exceptionally so, and had immediately elected to read Law, as a career at the Bar was all that he ever wanted to do. He was fully aware that the three years at King's would be a demanding and relentless slog from day one, having pledged himself to be assiduous in all that he did. Indeed, he relished the thought and challenge of testing his cerebral knowledge and ability to the limit amongst other like-minded intellectuals. Hadn't Doddy already intimated as much?

He'd been greatly heartened by his meeting with Professor Dodderington, and could live with being called Ormsby, as his peers would still call him Oscar. Even before arriving at King's, he had decided that his future lie in the field of Law − Criminal Law. The others laws: chancery, commercial, family and the suchlike did not appeal. He desired the cut and thrust required when pitted against the finest brains in the country. He knew, however, that attaining a Law degree was not a given or a mere tick in the box. Only the exceptional and very best eventually went on to qualify and practise as barristers.

He wanted it with a passion, after watching many, if dated, television courtroom dramas − it has to be said, with predictable decisions and happy endings. Perhaps in real life, the baddies didn't always get caught and the crimes remained unsolved, he conceded. Apart from watching *The Idiot's Lantern*, there appeared no other compelling reason why he'd chosen a career in law. There didn't seem to any other motive or legal family connection − his father, after all, was a jeweller.

Oscar was joining King's with no prior knowledge or preconceived ideas. He was starting with a clean sheet of paper − if not exactly vellum, on which he hoped to make his own distinctive imprints. To this end, his aim was to attain his degree in law (a first with honours was his private ambition), then to spend a further year in Harvard, Massachusetts, the supposed fount of American Law. He was confident that his father would not be too reluctant in finding the additional required fees. Yet the guilt steadfastly remained, that of feeling he was the only one to benefit and perhaps unfairly so?

Oscar had had for the first ten years of his life an older sister called Jessica whom he'd loved dearly. Tragically, she had died at the young age of 13 from an inoperable brain tumour. The shock, the timing and the realisation of its invasive presence, to her dying had been a mere and inappropriate six months. In the precious short space of time left for Jessica, the family did all that they possibly could, but the knowledge and spectre of imminent death cast a long shadow over the family.

It was a shadow which still clouded the Ormsby-Waites with an unavoidable feeling of guilt whenever they smiled, laughed or enjoyed something. Oscar felt it perhaps even more so, as he was now the sole beneficiary of his parents' love, attention and financial help. His father's mantra had been: 'Money isn't everything, Oscar, as we all well know, and as you will undoubtedly come to appreciate as you grow older – God bless Jessica'.

It may well have been this perpetual shadow, this invisible pervasive cloak that consumed the family home, the catalyst that turned Oscar into something of a 'geek' or an 'anorak'. Not that they blamed him or dared to mention Jessica, or allude to his size, well at least not to his face. Perhaps somethings don't need to be said with everyone aware of the status quo? For these or any other unknown reasons, he could invariably be found in his room, his head hidden in some book or surfing the net, instead of being outside playing with the other boys; which, in fairness, his parents actively encouraged.

Was it his small and rather puny frame that deterred him from mixing and taking part? He never actually said as much, but he was definitely self-conscious of his concave chest. At one time, he had secretly considered applying for a body-building course, if only to put at least some muscle on his slight frame, but his intellectual reasoning had won the day. *Both of my parents are on the slim side, as was dear Jessica, so this is how I was meant to look and be.* This was Oscar's own mantra, although never entirely convinced by his own argument – *Better to have brains than brawn,* he would try to reassure himself.

His mother took the death of Jessica far worse than Oscar or his father, if that were humanly possible. She virtually lost the will to live, becoming lethargic, vacant and uninterested in their lovely home and family. After a full year with no visible sign of any appreciable improvement in his wife's forlornness, Mr Ormsby-Waite recruited the services of a Mrs Featherstone to come in and help. The arrival of another woman neither upset nor annoyed his wife, as grief remained her constant and unforgiving companion. But as Mr Ormsby-Waite had rightly opined, "Life has to go on," as both he and Oscar also needed staple and sympathy. If the truth be told, the new woman was a blessing in disguise for all.

Mrs Featherstone, 'Feathers', as she was affectionately known by, had lost her husband for reasons never declared or indeed enquired after. They were never sure whether Mr Featherstone had cleared off or had died. She never offered an explanation and so it was deemed prudent not to ask, but for whatever reason, it was certainly to the betterment of the Ormsby-Waites. She soon became the pivotal point around which the family operated, astutely without undermining anyone. They all came to depend upon her more and more, and invited her to move in. The offer Feathers wisely declined, stating that she wished to keep some semblance of independence, her own house and bolthole, should it be necessary or opportune to leave at any time.

Feathers had a heart of gold and a turbo-charged engine; there wasn't anything she couldn't do or solve; and all this with only a secondary modern education. What she did have, however, was energy and pragmatism by the bucketful, and an A Level in common sense. She had no children of her own, and so Oscar became her surrogate son, aided and abetted by Mrs Ormsby-Waite, who slowly shed the shackles of grief with her now friend and daily companion. Feathers had been wise and wary enough not to try and replace 'Mrs O's' position.

The only apparent failing that Feathers had was her weakness for cakes and sweets, which accounted for a high body mass index, and the only 'family' member with a weight problem! Her obesity resulted in all manner of dietary regimes, but as sure as day follows night, the diet of the day would lapse, and solace would be found on a plate or in a packet of sweets. It became something of a household joke and Feathers took it all in the right spirit. After all, she wasn't looking to impress any other fella – and was totally content looking after Alfred,

Winifred and Oscar. Needless to say, she too was immensely proud when the letter of acceptance arrived from King's, now feeling one of the family.

Chapter 7

Horatio and Raffer left with serious misgivings. Yes, it was true that out on the Cam they had declared their commitment, but certainly not a declaration of faith. It was like saying, 'Yes I'll buy the car even though I haven't seen or driven it.' Not unreasonably, they both still needed to know what they were getting into before buying a pig in a poke, namely their lives and their future! Admittedly, Oscar had promised to explain the basic outline of the plan, if not the complete circuitry. Was this sop good enough to satisfy the curiosity and reasoning of two barely committed and confused undergraduates?

There also remained the undeniable and most vexing question of all: why attempt it in the first place? They were in an extremely privileged position, enjoying an environment and opportunities afforded to only a fraction of the country's population. Why then, for heaven's sake, go and abuse it by possibly throwing away the prospects of a successful life and career in blowing it on some egotistical exploit, which even if successful they could never boast or talk about. How daft was that?

Both men still needed convincing on what they had half-heartedly signed up to.

Rupert Alexander Fordham, known to all as 'Raffer', even to his sister and parents, was without doubt the most confident and flamboyant of the three would be robbers. This extrovert, outward-going persona was suitably illustrated in his choice of degree – electing to read Drama. It was his known and broadcasted wish to leave Cambridge with a degree and be accepted into RADA, there to pursue a career on the stage in some form or another as a thespian. Was this the main reason why Oscar had picked Raffer from a cast of many?

Raffer was not unlike Oscar, being slight of build and openly effeminate, which most attributed to his theatrical bent. The truth was more bizarre. Raffer was bisexual and had had regular relationships with both genders. In most walks of life, this sexual promiscuity may well have been frowned upon by the average man in the street. Here at Cambridge, it was accepted as an educated personal choice, and prudes, cynics and Freudians could think and say what they liked. Whilst keeping his peccadillo-type activities to himself, Raffer didn't impose or intrude upon others − so best let sleeping dogs lie?

That said, this grown-up and ambivalent attitude might have been all well and good within King's and Cambridge, but it would hardly have gone down well in his hometown of Truro in Cornwall. It was thought that the locals were not quite ready for Raffer's diverse and varied sexual orientation. That was why he wisely left his deviant side of his personality in Cambridge and adopted a conventional and accepted heterosexual stance when at home. His sister, Rosemary, was the only one to suspect there was another 'side' to her brother, but that was probably due to a woman's uncanny intuition. Had he slipped up or said or acted untoward? Impossible to say.

Raffer's parents had done well, owning a large and successful garden centre which they had built up from scratch. Now, like many garden centres, plants were only a side line. It was more akin to entering a glass-encased emporium offering furniture, china and bedding. You name it, they sold it − to say nothing of the cafeteria-come-restaurant. They employed a staff of 30 and it kept them all busy but comfortably happy with their lot; and extremely proud of their son being up at Cambridge.

Raffer had had to work hard at his A Levels, not being a natural academic. In fact, he had been one of those Mr Althorpe and a separate jury had procrastinated over before giving him the benefit of the doubt, with his file saved from going into the trolley. His acceptance was due largely in his performance of 'shining at the interview'. He was the most handsome of young men, with a mop of fair to blonde hair and delicate features that most women would have envied. Despite his diminutive size, he possessed an air of self-confidence and assuredness without appearing to be cocky or too overbearing. It was not difficult to see why he could be both enchanting and beguiling to men as well as women!

He, possible more than his colleague Horatio, had been more than just interested by what Oscar had proposed. He rightly put this down to his theatrical inclination and the opportunity to play out a role, a role that Oscar had suggested would be right up his street − requiring him to dress and play the part of a woman! The offer had aroused his desire, but not the possibility of being caught and going to prison, though even that had its own attractions!

No. He wanted the opportunity to live a life amongst people with the same love of the stage and its inevitable accompanying life's drama that it entailed. It was in an artistic environment where he could express himself professionally and physically, without others casting asides and aspersions − except when required from the wings. Yet, he still needed convincing that they would not be caught.

Horatio Benedict Charteris was an identical twin, but apart from their spitting − can't tell them apart image − he and his other half, Tristram William, were alike as chalk and cheese. Horatio was the academic and clever one, whilst Tristram was sporty and a fine cricketer at that, but who would have had trouble keeping the scorecard, and not given to anything remotely academic.

Their parents had at first been amazed that their two sons, who had shared the same embryonic seed and pod, could be so entirely different in character. They were later informed this was not unusual and was often the case, with identical appearances belying two entirely different personalities and skills. Even though they both possessed this fascinating inner sixth sense which twins seemed to have. Therefore, both parents and boys were happy and relieved when Horatio was accepted for Cambridge and Tristram to the ground staff of Kent County Cricket Club, with the potential of becoming a player. Horatio excelled and shone in the classroom whilst Tristram had aspirations to enjoy lengthy innings at the crease.

Horatio was also like Oscar and Raffer. Indeed, the common denominator in all three had been their small, slight and rather delicate build. Horatio hailed from Ramsgate in Kent, his parents owning a string of boarding houses, which had made them wealthy over the years. He was an outstanding scholar and had excelled in all of his many 'A Levels' with a flair for languages, speaking fluent French, which had been enhanced by regular family holidays to most regions of France.

Horatio Charteris was reading Anthropology but didn't know what he wanted out of life. His only firm resolve was to obtain a First and then clear off round the world for a couple of years, and then see what fell out of his travelling sabbatical. He'd only seen Oscar's Doddy from a distance, but the idea of becoming an academic had certain attractions. He didn't like the hard work involved in becoming a barrister, no matter how attractive it may be from a financial standpoint. Neither did the worlds of drama or medicine attract. The continual furore over the NHS did not appeal, and certainly not being a GP – allotting ten minutes to examine old and horrible pensioners, no thank you. The more he thought, the more he warmed to the world of academia, the privileges and the sinecure that a university way of life provided.

Whatever, he had no intention of languishing behind bars, merely to satisfy a colleague's wish to do something daring and all in the name of mental masturbation! Oscar had mentioned the plan involved masquerading as women and having to speak French. The latter excited and interested him, but was it enough? Like Raffer, he needed more information before committing himself. There was also the not inconsequential hurdle of attaining a degree; wasn't that enough to occupy both body and brain, as it certainly seemed to be the case for the many other hundreds of undergraduates? If it was all a matter of priorities, then he remained to be convinced – it was no more than Oscar expected.

It was a number of unrelated events, which were probably nothing more than sheer coincidence that first got Oscar pondering the thought of entering the world of criminality. The first trigger had been his initial interview with Doddy when he'd first arrived at King's. It had been the montage of photographs proudly displayed on his study wall of previous students, now famous, that had attracted. He'd later asked himself, *What will I be remembered for?* It had turned out to be more than just a fleeting and rhetorical thought, but a subject that had continued to niggle and occupy his mind during the next two years of studying. It had been the first conscious seed to fall to the ground in his desire to break the law.

The second had been his total fascination in studying the Antwerp Diamond heist of 2003, where diamonds worth over a hundred million dollars had been stolen and never recovered. The Belgium and Italian police always thought it to be Mafia inspired, with the ringleader caught and serving a lengthy prison term. It would seem there was more to it, even though the gang leader had not 'grassed' – there was still honour amongst thieves.

The third and last embryonic plant had been the most recent, namely the Hatton Garden diamond robbery. It was here where a gang spent the weekend drilling through 18 thick, reinforced walls, then breaking open hundreds of safe deposit boxes. Again, it was a very cleverly executed robbery, but carried out by old and hardened criminals known to the underworld at large, who were well past their sell by date! It didn't take long for the whole gang (well, not all) to be caught within a matter of months, with much of the safe contents recovered (but not all). The gang, however, were not as clever as the actual deed, and lacked the intelligence and nous to get away with it.

From that moment on, he had been captivated, with many subsequent hours spent reading about the whys and wherefores of committing a crime, and more importantly – not getting caught! In fact, this crime-committing pastime acted as a therapeutic release valve from the enormous amount of research reading involved in his final law year. At the moment, he was deep into the bowels and ramifications of a complicated perjury case which Doddy had required a thousand words on why the prosecutor's main premise was flawed.

The more Oscar read, the more he became convinced a robbery could be successful, if executed with a kiss – Keep It Simple, Stupid! The exquisite beauty lay in its simplicity and carried out by non-criminals, with no 'previous'. The weakness and downfall in most failed robberies was that they were the work of hardened villains who treated crime and being outside the rule of law as a way of life, and therefore almost accepted the inevitable consequence of being caught. Indeed, most spent more than half of their adult life in one prison or another. What Oscar was thinking and aiming to do was breaking with tradition – by getting away with it!

It would seem the seeds of his outrageous plan had not fallen to the ground accidentally but had been carefully planted. Oscar, Horatio and Raffer were law-abiding citizens who had never once stepped outside the boundaries of law and order – ideal 'recruits' perhaps? It was a proposition that had now germinated within his mind, the attraction growing with each passing month.

The idea more than titillated, spending spare hours (which were few) devising and refining a fool proof plan; whilst at the same time cramming in this his final year of studies. It was a mental game that became obsessive as he tweaked and adjusted each phase of the operation. The seedlings he had subconsciously planted now beginning to sprout! Repeatedly, he rebuked his silliness, trying always to dismiss the idea of committing such a crime, but try as he might, he couldn't get it out of his mind.

Meanwhile, he threw himself headlong into his studying, aided and abetted by Professor Dodderington – Doddy, who was expecting great things from his latest star pupil. Little did his tutor, the likeable music and poetry-loving bachelor, know that he was harbouring a student – a possible would-be criminal – by stimulating and encouraging his ability to think laterally and outside of the legal box! Oscar had now decided to put his money where his mouth or his misplaced ambitions lie.

He also intended to feed off and learn from the mistakes made in Belgium and London. His was a far less grand and simpler heist that he had in mind, which involved fewer risks but elements of excitement. Moreover, it could be aborted if things didn't go according to plan and it went tits up, whilst also accepting that the other two might decide not to play. His aim was to convince them to join him in their King's swan song.

Chapter 8

All three arrived at the punt station a good ten minutes before the appointed hour, which augured well. King's had its own four punts which were available for hire by students, fellows, staff and even some conference participants. Oscar, with his attention to detail, had some weeks prior, reserved one of the punts for a two-hour session. They were not cheap; the normal standard charge was £27 per hour. He knew he had a lot to say with much to consider, and they should not be rushed.

"Gentlemen, a month has now passed, and we meet again to give our decision as to whether we wish to undertake the venture I have in mind. However, before I invite you both to cast your vote, please bear with me whilst I describe the background research I have carried out. I'm reasonably confident it will prompt questions that you will no doubt wish to raise," Oscar opened.

"That's good to hear and I'm all for that, as we still haven't a real clue as to what we've actually being invited to get involved in," Horatio said.

"Ditto, and not only that, I'm now in my final year and this is my first time in a punt," Raffer declared, as Horatio held the pole, moving the craft away from the jetty.

"Well, if that's the case, then perhaps Horatio will enlighten us all with his punting prowess and knowledge," Oscar replied.

"Delighted," returned Horatio, who was skilfully manoeuvring the punt out into the centre of the river.

"You probably already knew these were originally used for ferrying cargo and for fishing and fowling in the Fens. As you can see, their flat-bottomed design makes it an excellent choice for use in small rivers or shallow water. And as I will shortly demonstrate, it can be punted just as easily in either direction, which is handy in narrow waterways where turning around may be difficult, or when faced with congestion along the Backs," he exclaimed, whilst adeptly avoiding an oncoming punt.

"The basic technique is to propel the boat along by pushing a pole directly against the bed of the river or lake, like so," as the punt obliged. "The traditional punting position is to stand in front of the flat deck which is called the 'till' facing towards the stern, and to punt from the side. But of course, clever sods at Oxford and Cambridge tossed this tradition aside. Now here in Cambridge, as you can see, I'm standing on the till and punt with the bow or 'open end' forward. It goes without saying that in Oxford they do it differently. They stand inside the boat and punt with the till forward. Devotees − such as yours truly − believe that ours is the only true style, and the till end is often known as the 'Cambridge end', and the other as the 'Oxford end'. I hope you will agree my standing on the till looks much finer." Both Oscar and Raffer nodded and gave their self-appointed 'punter-in-chief' a gentle, if sarcastic, round of applause.

"Before we get down to the real nitty gritty of what I shockingly suggested four weeks past, may I beg your indulgence whilst I describe two diamond robberies, followed by a self-analysis. By which time you will hopefully have digested all or most, and no doubt suitably primed to voice your own opinions and suggestions, one way or the other." Both Horatio and Raffer nodded.

"First, I'd like to make you aware of the Antwerp Diamond Heist of 2003; then to describe a more recent robbery nearer to home, that of the Hatton Garden safe deposit case. Finally, I need to wear my heart on my sleeve in trying to justify my motivation and thinking. It will then be for you two to decide if I'm raving bonkers, or you are still willing and have been persuaded."

"Good. Let's first hear what you have to say, as I for one still remain to be convinced. The last time we met I said I was in, well I'm now dithering," said Horatio.

"That goes for me too," echoed Raffer, who was quite relieved that he was not the only one who was having second and third thoughts. "After all, we've now got two years of hard work under our belt, with less than a year away from a well-earned degree. Why jeopardise it now?"

"Fair enough, but please first hear me out," Oscar continued, neither perturbed nor unhappy by the warning shots that had crossed his bow by his cautious colleagues. "Just pin your ears back and listen to what I have to say; then we'll stop for a break to enjoy a special treat of Mrs B's egg sandwiches."

With that, Oscar produced a thick wad of rolled-up written notes on A4 paper, more akin to a scroll, as if about to make a proclamation.

"I have here the salient points taken from an article in the *Diamond Dealers'* magazine. It was written by an American journalist who had interviewed a celebrated prisoner. I'm sure you will find it most interesting.

"In February 2007, Leonardo Notarbartolo was arrested for heading a ring of Italian thieves. They were accused of breaking into a vault two floors beneath the Antwerp Diamond Centre and making off with at least $100 million worth of loose diamonds, gold, jewellery and other spoils. The vault was thought to be impenetrable, protected by layers of security, including infrared heat detectors, Doppler radar, a magnetic field, a seismic sensor, and a lock with 100 million combinations. The robbery was called the heist of the century and even now the police cannot explain fully how it was done.

'The haul was never found but based on circumstantial evidence Notarbartolo was sentenced to ten years. He had always denied having anything to do with the crime, refusing to discuss the case, preferring to remain silent for the next six years, when he told all to an American reporter. What the inducement was, I don't know.

'Notarbartolo said he intended to set the record straight, after all, he'd had long enough to think about what he was about to say.'

"'I may be a thief and a liar," he says, "but I am going to tell you a true story:

"'We had executed the plan perfectly, no alarms, no police, no problems. The heist wouldn't be discovered until the guards checked the vault the next morning. The rest of the team were already on their way back to Italy with the gems. We planned to rendezvous in Milan to divvy it all up. There was no reason to worry, all Speedy (my accomplice) and I had to do was burn the incriminating evidence sitting on the backseat in three extra-strong plastic bags.

"'I pulled off the highway and onto a dirt track that led into a dense thicket. The area seemed abandoned and so I decided to burn the rubbish beside a small pond. When I returned to the car Speedy had really lost it. The contents of the bags were strewn amongst the trees and the underbrush; I spotted a half-eaten salami sandwich. The ground around the car was flecked with dozens of tiny, glittering diamonds, it would have taken hours to gather everything up and burn it, and I left with misgivings."

'The police arrived at the Diamond Centre the next morning; they had received a frantic call: the vault had been compromised. The subterranean chamber was supposed to be one of the most secure safes in the world. Now the foot-thick steel door was ajar, and more than 100 of the 189 safe deposit boxes broken open. The floor was strewn with wads of cash and velvet-lined boxes.

'"What is the status of the alarm?" the detective asked. "Fully functional," the operator said, checking the signals coming in. "The vault is secure."

'"Then how is it that the door is wide open and I'm standing inside the vault?" the police officer demanded, glancing at the devastation. He hung up and looked at his colleague; they were up against a rare breed of criminal.'

'A few years earlier in 2000, I'd rented a small office in the Diamond Centre, presenting myself as a gem importer based in Turin, Italy, and scheduled meetings with dealers. It's easy when you've got my contacts to get hold of the necessary paperwork to convince anyone doing background checks, if you catch my drift. They never knew they had just welcomed one of the world's best jewel thieves into their inner circle. Then one day, a Jewish 'dealer' came in and sat down for a chat.'

'"Actually, I want to talk to you about something a little unusual," the dealer had said casually. "Maybe we could walk a little?"

'We headed out, and once we were clear of the district, the dealer picked up the conversation. His tone had changed however, the casualness gone.'

'Leonardo then made some checks to ensure the Jewish 'dealer' was not an undercover cop. "I'd like to hire you for a robbery," he said, "a big one."

'For an initial payment of 100,000 euros, I had to answer one simple question: could the vault in the Antwerp Diamond Centre be robbed? I was pretty sure the answer was no, but I was a tenant in the building and rented a safe deposit box in the vault to secure my own small stash; it was the safest place in Antwerp. But for 100,000 euros, I was more than happy to photograph the place and show the dealer how daunting or impossible it really was.

'I managed to get into the vault and with a miniaturised digital camera in my pen poking out of my breast pocket, carried out my reconnaissance. A three-ton steel vault door dominated the far wall; it alone had six layers of security. There was a combination wheel numbering up to 99, with 100 million possible combinations. Power tools wouldn't do the trick; the door was rated to withstand twelve hours of nonstop drilling. Of course, the first vibrations of a drill would set off the embedded seismic alarm anyway. The door was monitored by a pair of abutting metal plates, one on the door itself and one on the wall just to the right. When armed, the plates formed a magnetic field. If the door were opened, the field would break, triggering an alarm. To disarm the field, a code had to be typed into a nearby keypad. Finally, the lock required an almost impossible-to-duplicate foot-long key. The vault was one of the hardest targets I'd ever seen.'

'It took five months for the dealer to call me back, after I'd told him the heist was impossible. I thought that was the end of it, but now he wanted to meet outside of Antwerp. When I arrived, the dealer was waiting for me in front of an abandoned warehouse.'

"'I want to introduce you to some people," he said. Inside was a massive structure covered with black plastic tarpaulin. The dealer pulled back a corner and we ducked underneath. At first, I was confused, I seemed to be standing in the vault antechamber. To my left, I saw the vault door. I was inside an exact replica of the Diamond Centre's vault level. Everything was the same. As far as I could tell, the dealer had reconstructed it based on the photographs I had provided.

"Inside the fake vault, were three Italians. The dealer made the introductions (Notarbartolo refused to reveal their names), referring to them only by nickname. They were the criminal world's best disabler of alarms, lock-picker-come-locksmith, and mechanic-come-electrician."

In the February of 2003 the heist was successfully carried out, with the three 'specialists' spending the night prising open over 100 safe deposit boxes, in complete darkness. By five the next morning, they had made their getaway in the hired lookout car driven by Notarbartolo. He then drove them to the railway station, where they departed to Italy with the haul of diamonds and other valuables.

After the fiasco in discarding the bags of incriminating evidence, Notarbartolo drove home to his family in Turin. Later, he again met up in Milan with the rest of the gang, to await the agreed arrival of the Jew boy who had set up the whole thing. Surprise, surprise, he never turned up, and the haul was nowhere near as large as first thought or predicted. When they opened the traditional blue and red velvet purses, many were empty.

The Jew boy had worked a flanker on them. Before the robbery, he'd emptied his own safe contents and advised his friends to do likewise. In the event, once the crime was officially registered, he and his cronies were in a position to claim exorbitant amounts in losses from their insurers. Whereas, in truth, they still had their diamonds! The only losers would be the insurers, Notarbartolo and gang, who were in no position to do anything about it. The Jewish dealer was never seen or heard of again.

However, Notarbartolo was still confident they had indeed got away with it and he soon returned to Antwerp with his wife, needing to clear his office, empty his safe deposit box and return the hire car. The authorities had reasonably assumed that the gang could by now be in any other part of the world. Instead, he walked straight back into the waiting and lucky arms of the Belgian police.

The gangs undoing was all down to a man called August Van Camp who owned weasels. The 59-year-old retired Belgian grocer had two and he enjoyed sending them down holes in the forest. In 1998, he bought a narrow strip of forest alongside the E19 motorway. It was an attractive 12 acres of trees with a gurgling stream, with plenty of holes and rabbits. But because it adjoined the highway, Van Camp found a lot of rubbish. When he found rubbish, he would phone the police, who'd got used to his calls.

"The kids have made a mess on my land again."

"I'm sorry to hear that, Mr Van Camp."

"I demand that you send someone to investigate."

"We will pass along your request." Van Camp rarely heard back.

While hunting one morning – Monday 17th February, to be exact – Van Camp was incensed to find yet another pile of junk in the underbrush. He knelt down and glared at the refuse. He wanted to be able to describe to the cops what he had to put up with. There was videotape strewn all over the place and a wine bottle rested near a half-eaten salami sandwich. There were also some white envelopes printed with the words Diamond Centre, Antwerp. Van Camp's irritation increased. At home, he called the police asking to lodge a complaint. The officer listened as Van Camp tallied the mess.

When Van Camp mentioned Diamond Centre envelopes, the officer broke in, "What was that?" he said.

"Antwerp Diamond Centre envelopes," Van Camp angrily replied. This time, the police did come running.

By mid-afternoon, half a dozen detectives swarmed the forest, painstakingly gathering the rubbish and collecting stray gems, as Van Camp watched with satisfaction. The police were finally treating his litter situation with proper respect. Within hours, the rubbish began to fill the evidence room at the Diamond Squad headquarters in Antwerp. A member of the squad bent over the clear plastic bags, looking for immediate clues. It didn't take them long to reassemble a pile of torn paper. It was an invoice for a low-light video surveillance system purchased by a Mr Leonardo Notarbartolo.

Back at Van Camp's property, another detective knelt amongst the thorny brambles and peered at a small, jagged piece of paper poking out of the mud. It was a business card that bore the address and phone number of Elio D'Onorio, an Italian electronics expert tied to a series of robberies. Notarbartolo had consistently refused to identify his accomplices, but all evidence indicates that D'Onorio was the Genius.

The laboratory technicians also examined the half-eaten salami sandwich. They found Antipasto Italiano salami packaging nearby and sent it along to the Diamond Squad headquarters. Four days later, the detectives executed a search warrant on Notarbartolo's rented apartment in Antwerp. In a cupboard, they found a receipt from a local grocery store for Antipasto Italiano salami. The receipt had a timestamp. A detective drove to the grocery store and asked the manager to rewind his closed-circuit television to 12:56 pm on Thursday 13th February, it showed Ferdinando Finotoo − likely to be the other member. The police had a lead, but were they too late?

As Notarbartolo drove back to Belgium, the police wondered whether they'd ever catch the thieves. They could be anywhere by now, Brazil, Thailand, Russia. It never occurred to the detectives that one of the robbers would walk right back into the district. But that's exactly what Notarbartolo did. While one of his friends waited on the street outside the Diamond Centre, Notarbartolo waved at the security guard and dropped in to collect his mail. The guard knew that the police were investigating Notarbartolo and phoned the building manager, who immediately called the detectives.

When the police arrived, they found Notarbartolo with the building manager and began questioning him. The other man left as Notarbartolo stalled for time, pretending to have trouble understanding French and claiming that he couldn't remember the exact address of his own apartment. He just knew how to walk there.

"Let's go then," the detective said and pushed the Italian into a car.

Eventually, Notarbartolo pointed out the apartment. As the police car arrived, Notarbartolo's wife and the friends, who'd come for dinner, stepped out of the building. They were loaded down with bags and one carried a rolled-up carpet. Another minute and they would have been gone. The police took everyone into custody. The bags contained critical evidence. The police dug out a series of prepaid SIM cards that were linked to cell phones used almost exclusively to call three Italians: Elio D'Onorio, aka the Genius; Ferdinando Finotto, alias the Monster, and the person most likely to be Speedy, an anxious, paranoid man named Pietro Tavano, a long-time associate of Notarbartolo.

On the night of the heist, a cell tower in the Diamond District logged the presence of all three, plus Notarbartolo. The day Notarbartolo was arrested, Italian police broke open the safe at his home in Turin. They found 17 polished diamonds attached to certificates that the Belgian diamond detectives traced back to the vault. More gems were vacuumed out of the rolled-up carpet from Notarbartolo's Antwerp apartment. The Belgian courts found Notarbartolo guilty of orchestrating the heist and sentenced him to ten years. With the mobile phone records and the peculiar salami sandwich evidence, the Belgian detectives persuaded French police to raid the home of Finotto's girlfriend on the French Riviera. They retrieved marked $100 bills that the detectives say belonged to one of the Diamond Centre victims.

Finotto was finally arrested in Italy in November 2007 and served a five-year sentence there. When questioned by police in Italy, D'Onorio admitted that he had installed security cameras in Notarbartolo's office but denied any involvement in the crime. Nonetheless, his DNA was found on some adhesive tape left in the vault. He was immediately extradited to Belgium where he completed his full time without any remission.

The highly-strung Pietro Tavano also served a five-year sentence in Italy for the crime. The King of Keys was never caught, and despite many false sightings, it seems he disappeared off the face of the earth.

'In January 2009, the reporter met Notarbartolo for the last time. There were still unanswered questions. Was $100 million stolen as the police estimated, or just $20 million as Notarbartolo insisted? Did it make sense that the heist was part of a larger insurance scam, or was Notarbartolo's elaborate story a decoy to throw suspicion on others? Whatever the truth, where is the loot now? The murky nature of the diamond trade makes it difficult to get clear answers. For instance, Detective De Bruycker reckons that three-quarters of the diamond business is under the table. Since there were roughly $25 million in legitimate claims at the time of the heist, he calculated that at least another $75 million in goods was stolen. That brings the total value of the heist to about $100 million.

'If Notarbartolo's insurance scam theory is correct, as he repeatedly claimed, it went like this: the dealers who were in on it removed their goods – both legal and illegal – from the vault before the heist, and then filed claims on the legitimate gems. The adjuster, who investigated the robbery for the insurers, calls this the 'double whammy' these dealers would have got the insurance pay outs and kept their stock. The $20 million found by the thieves belonged to traders who were not part of the scam.

'Or there was no insurance scam. The thieves actually found $100 million in the vault and Notarbartolo has spun a story to cloud the true origins of the heist. Regardless of which theory is correct, there is agreement that the thieves got away with millions that were never recovered. Notarbartolo refused throughout to talk about what happened to the goods, adding that it is something best discussed once he was out of prison. In the meantime, his share may very well be waiting for him, hidden somewhere in the foothills of the Italian Alps – perhaps 'acres of diamonds'?

"By the way, as you've probably twigged, I've skipped over how the three managed to access the vault, notwithstanding all the counter-measures I mentioned earlier. I've still got the magazine back in my rooms, if you'd care to read it, it's well worth a decko," Oscar concluded, as he prised open a silver, foil package.

Horatio had long since stopped propelling the punt; instead, he now rested or rather lightly balanced the 16-foot pole vertically on the till as the craft found its own silent way back to the riverbank. The two would-be recruits had been utterly enthralled listening to what had to be a true story, a story which Oscar had accurately and fairly graphically related. Indeed, he'd only needed the comprehensive wad of notes as an occasional aide-mémoire, such was his deep background knowledge and familiarity of the story he had told.

When Oscar had finished, it was akin to sitting in the cinema with the lights coming up but with the credits still rolling, by far too much information and too fast to read. Horatio still stood and Raffer still sat, both remained silent, both now aware of why their friend had regaled them with such a story. Still too soon to ask questions.

"Oscar, is that a true story?" Raffer eventually asked.

"Absolutely, as I've said, I still have the magazine in my room. So, gentlemen, what did you make of it all?"

"Bloody marvellous, rotten shame they got caught," Horatio added.

"That's my point exactly, and the reason why I related it to you both – chapter and verse."

"I think it's now time for an egg sandwich," Oscar announced, having finally managed to solve Mrs Bs customary double-wrapping system. It was time to break them out of their reverie and thinking and back to the River Cam, to get their reaction, having been given the full ramifications of the Antwerp Diamond Centre Heist.

A cob and pen instinctively glided across in the hope of being thrown a crumb or two. This couple were to be the lucky ones, with Raffer in a generous mood. For some reason, he'd suddenly lost his appetite – if only for food.

"I'd now like to explain a little of the Hatton Garden robbery," Oscar continued.

"I hope it's not going to take as long as that one," Raffer added, whilst accepting another egg sandwich being offered.

"No, I promise. I'll just briefly explain what happened and again why they got caught. Trust me, gentlemen; there is method in my madness."

"And what's all this cryptic nonsense of self-analysis, don't we all do that to ourselves all the time?" Raffer added.

"Not if you're in two minds as to whether you wish to be part of a diamond robbery, albeit not on anywhere near the scale of Antwerp or Hatton Garden, but still a sizeable number of white rocks to be had," said Oscar.

Horatio resumed his standing on the till and assumed his Cambridge end position, as the craft moved back out into the faster moving water. Just then a fellow colleague and his girlfriend, walking hand in hand along the riverbank, waved enthusiastically in recognition. Raffer waved back, instantly recognising both the boy and the girl. Well, he certainly should have, as he'd been to bed with both of them, although he doubted that either one knew the other's secret! Not that he was about to share these private goings on with his shipmates.

He smiled to himself, thinking what would they think and make of it, if they knew what the topic of conversation was that now focussed the minds of three men in a certain punt?

"Everyone gasped – the police and the public – at the sheer audacity of the great Hatton Garden heist of 2015. I'm sure you both must have remembered it, if only for seeing the pictures in all the tabloids of the drilled holes through the vault wall. The crime seemed to capture the imagination of everyone, and was reported as epic, with millions supposedly taken in both jewellery and diamonds valued up to £30 million. So much so, it had to be hauled out in giant containers not unlike wheelie bins. Reading between the newspapers' lines, there was almost a tacit hope that they would get away with it – which as we know, they didn't.

"It turned out to be the work of a ragtag of superannuated criminals masquerading as the last of the traditional British villains. In the words of the police commander in charge, Commander Peter Spindler, 'most were in their 60s and 70s, more a Lavender Hill Mob than James Bond. Run, they could hardly walk. One had cancer and he was 76. Another was 68, with a heart condition, and another at 75. There was a 60-year-old with two new hips and knees and one with Crohn's disease.' He said, he could have gone on, if not so funny or serious. Yet despite all this, they had defied age, physical infirmities, burglar alarms and even Scotland Yard to power their way through walls of concrete and solid steel and haul away a prize estimated at more than 20 million, of which 15 million is still missing."

"I promise not to make it another Notarbartolo length story, only to briefly describe the actual operation and how they got caught. It's worth listening to."

"We're listening," Raffer responded.

"The vault, belonging to the Hatton Garden Safe Deposit Company (HGSD) was located at 88-90 Hatton Garden, London. The building is seven stories tall and has around 60 tenants, most of them jewellers.

"The 20-inch-thick solid concrete wall would have been impenetrable to a drill in 1946, when the vault was constructed, but was child's play to the thieves Hilti DD350 diamond coring drill, a 77-pound £4,000 circular monster. Within two and a half hours, three overlapping circular holes had been cut through the concrete. It should have been cause to celebrate for the ageing thieves. Instead, they stared through the holes not into the vault but at the back of the cabinet housing safe deposit boxes – unmovable and bolted to the ceiling and floor.

"However, the thieves had come prepared for such an eventuality, having with them a Clarke pump and a ten-ton hydraulic ram, strong enough to force the doors off almost anything; but the pump broke and the steel cabinet stood firm, and so they temporarily left. Then, in a move that shocked the others, one of them left for good – the ringleader, Brian Reader. He was convinced that to return would mean certain capture and so he went home. Two of the others, not deterred, drove to a machinery-equipment store in Twickenham. There, they paid £140 for another Clarke pump ram and hose, cheap at half the price!

"Back in the vault, they used the metal joists they'd brought in earlier to anchor the new pump and hose to the wall opposite the vault, and the ten tons of pressure went to work. Eventually it gave, and they were looking through an opening ten by 18 inches across. Having slithered and struggled through, they opened the deposit boxes with sledgehammers, crowbars, and angle grinders.

"In the time they allotted themselves, they were able to ransack 73 of the 996 boxes, but it was enough: a vast array of loose diamonds and other stones, jewellery and cash. There was also gold and platinum bullion. With the job done and no incrimination evidence or DNA, the thieves must have thought they'd really got away with it. Moreover, the authorities never really knew how much had been stolen, because safety deposit boxes are used for a number of reasons, and one of them is undoubtedly – anonymity."

"Early in the subsequent police investigation, a member of the CCTV team made the Flying Squad's first break. It was a white Mercedes E200 with a black roof and alloy rims. It had passed through Hatton Garden a number of times prior to the Easter weekend. Whereas the other vehicle used, a white van, had been bought months beforehand and not tied to anybody. But the easily traceable Mercedes was a major mistake and tracked to one of the thief's home, and from there onto the store in Twickenham and the replacement hydraulic pump.

"Also, and quite foolhardy, the burglars had used walkie-talkies during the actual heist, but continued to use their own mobiles before and after the burglary. The police were then able to put them under surveillance, as they still needed to catch them with the goods. Interestingly, they used lip reading techniques whilst they monitored them in a local pub. They had also used a taxicab to carry the proceeds; who would suspect a London taxicab? The handover point was a public car park in Enfield, which was under CCTV surveillance, next to the workshop of a plumber who would later be charged and convicted as an accessory. How insane was that, using a car park with CCTV?

"Six weeks after the heist on the 19th May, 12 addresses were surrounded, front, back and sides, hitting them all simultaneously so no one could escape. Three of the robbers were at a dining room table, on which a smelter had been set up to melt down between three and four million pounds worth of precious metals that lay on the floor in holdalls. The officers burst through the front door, wearing riot helmets and flame-proof overalls, carrying what's called in the police parlance a 'commissioner's key' – a battering ram. They had no choice but to plead guilty and the seven were sentenced in the March. HGSD went into liquidation in the September, unable to recover from its damaged reputation.

"The thieves made one further mistake. There was a small camera fitted in the side alley outside the back of one of the jewellers, which was still working and recorded everything they did. As Commander Spindler said, 'they were analogue criminals operating in a digital world'."

"Right, gentlemen. I've now described two major diamond robberies, using skill, ingenuity and nerve. In the end, they were all caught and now serving long prison sentences. What we need to do is to ensure we prevent this from happening to us.

"Whilst you ponder this task, take as long as you like, in the meantime, please have another of these delicious egg sandwiches. I'll then explain why I contacted you in the first place and the rationale behind my desire to continue with this exciting undertaking, hopefully by all three of us in this boat – fingers crossed."

Chapter 9

"Come on Oscar, we've heard all about Antwerp and Hatton Garden, and by the way, you didn't mention the Brink's-Mat robbery," answered Horatio.

"Now, we need you to justify why you think we can all become successful criminals and more importantly – why for fuck's sake? Sorry for the expletive, I'm not normally given to using such coarse language, but it somehow seems necessary and appropriate," he continued, as Raffer tried his hand at punting. He had, however, had the nous to first look around to ensure they were out of earshot and not be overheard. Perhaps he was already subconsciously leaning towards the adventure without having yet decided or declared it. Horatio was by nature a quiet and measured person, who thought deep and long about everything, and not one to rush into anything – especially prison. He must have been the ideal undergraduate studying anthropology, with the world his oyster with everything and everyone in it.

Clearly, the choice and overture to both Raffer and Horatio had only been made by Oscar after he'd weighed all the pros and cons, as all three had quite different personalities and possessed different skill sets, which complemented one another, hence his selection.

"Gentlemen, I said earlier that I wanted to wear my heart on my sleeve. This is not strictly true, and I would not argue if you thought I was being somewhat disingenuous. What I'm really trying to say and indeed justify to both you and myself is our proposed illegal undertaking. I therefore need to try and explain what I mean from an honest and soul-searching standpoint.

"Horatio, I'm sure you with your studies will have far more eloquent and rational explanations as to why we human do what we do. Raffer, you with your artistic, sexual and dramatic slants on life, will no doubt have other thoughts as to why we behave so. Haven't you repeatedly said that life is just one big act, with all of us being but players and merely extras as part of the scenery? For my own part and thoughts, I've attempted to read Sigmund Freud, who seems to have an extremely complicated formula for what makes a criminal. He talks about a sense of guilt, overdeveloped superegos and relieving the guilt by being punished, with the guilt coming before the crime. According to Freud's view, crime is not the result of a criminal personality but of a poorly integrated psyche. All I can say is that I'm glad he wasn't trying to teach me law, as I neither understood nor accepted what he was trying to explain."

"What a complete load of old tosh," uttered Raffer, who appeared to be finding the art of punting far more difficult than Horatio had made it look. The other two smiled at their companion's succinct assessment of Freud. "Freud also identified the 'pleasure principle', that humans have basic unconscious biological urges and a desire for immediate gratification and satisfaction. This includes desires for food, sex and survival. He believed that if these could not be acquired legally, people would instinctively try to do so illegally. He also believed that people have the ability to learn in early childhood what is right and what is wrong, and though we may have an instinctive nature to acquire what we desire; such nature can be controlled by what is learned in our early years.

"Two other so-called authorities on the subject, Yochelson and Samenow, put forward the theory of free will to explain criminal behaviour. This has five points to it. One, the roots of criminality lies in the way people think and make their decisions. Two, criminals think and act differently than other people, even from a very young age. Three, criminals are by nature irresponsible, impulsive, self-centred and driven by fear and anger. Four, deterministic explanations of some crimes believe the criminal is seeking sympathy. Five, crime occurs because the criminal wills it or chooses it, and it is this choice they make that rehabilitates the need to be dealt with. Are you still with me, gentlemen?

"In truth, it is probably impossible to say what a typical criminal is – even if a 'typical criminal' exists. While there is a common perception that a criminal is from a broken home, has suffered a deprived childhood, lacks a good education etc, that would not include the likes of Dr Harold Shipman, Bernie Madorff or the recent cases of former Members of Parliament, both MPs and Lords, who were sent to prison for breaking the law. So where do I and possibly you two fit into this?

"There are many theories about why people commit crimes. Issues such as poverty, drug abuse and mental illness often play a role in driving an individual to commit a crime, as we all well know. Yet I suspect these are not the complete explanation of the phenomenon. Some theorists suggest that we humans are innately self-interested. Which category do you think we might well fall into? Others believe that people commit crimes because they are unable to achieve success in life through legal means. I shouldn't think we fit into that one.

"There are of course other reasons which include greed, anger, jealousy, revenge or pride. Some obviously consider a life of crime better than a regular job, believing crime brings in greater rewards, admiration and excitement – at least until they are caught. Others get an adrenaline rush when successfully carrying out a dangerous crime, some on impulse out of rage or fear. Then there are those that never commit a crime, no matter how desperate their circumstances.

"Gentlemen, I would suggest that what I am proposing has elements of credence in what I have just described, and you have both already, if unwittingly, cherry-picked the reasons you identify – both for and against. So, let me tell you what my honest and genuine reasons are.

"I'm 23-years-old and have been a boring swot since the age of 12, with the prospects of continuing to be a boring old fart of a swot into the foreseeable future – if I'm to make it as a barrister. I'm not saying in times ahead there won't be interludes of fun and relaxation, but nothing to mark me down as exciting and certainly not an adventurer. Look at me with my concave chest. I'm hardly likely to make it big on the sports field or make it with any desirable member of the opposite sex, apart from my chess potential not chest! Let's be honest, we're all built like rashers of wind!

"In my tutor's room, dear old Doddy has displayed many photographs of famous students that have passed through his hands here at King's. What will I be famous for, possibly winning some dubious case at the Old Bailey, perhaps? Is that really enough? No! So, I intend to have at least one daring episode in my life, even though I will never be able to brag or boast of it. That I don't mind. I can live with such a lifetime secret. At least content in the knowledge that I have accomplished something which the best detective brains in the country could not get anywhere near to solving, let alone catching anyone.

"The derived satisfaction and pleasure would be achieved by the meticulous planning and implementation, safe knowing that every *T* had been crossed and each *I* dotted, with no detail overlooked. Then to be efficiently executed without fear, favour or deviation once agreed upon. If you remember, the two robberies I have described, no matter how clever they thought they were, they made fundamental errors which should and could have been avoided. If we three agree to go ahead with my plan, I promise that we will all have unanimously agreed and triple-checked every single step with a fine toothcomb; utilising the considerable skills and talents that are present in this boat. That is, apart from the poor standard of Raffer's punting." All three laughed.

"Once it's all over and we have achieved our aim, we can then get on with the rest of our studies and lives. It will remain a secret that none of us will ever divulge to another living soul and we take to our graves. The icing on the cake is that we may also feel dishonestly better by making ourselves modern-day Robin Hoods. I would suggest that the entire money realised, after our dealings with the diamond black market, be donated to charities of our choosing. It will, of course, not excuse or exonerate us from the act of committing a crime, that we will have to accept, but it might make us feel slightly better when we go to bed. For me it is the thrill and challenge of beating the establishment, without anyone getting hurt, then to be able to put it to bed and forgotten. We are not known criminals and there will be nothing to relate us to the crime – it will be the perfect crime – I promise.

"I would also point out, that what I am daringly proposing has not suddenly just come to me. Over the past two years between my studies, I've found relaxation in reviewing various robberies, how they were done, what when wrong, and why they were caught. I've also read the book *The Diamond Underworld* and numerous magazines relating to the diamond industry. It may also surprise you both to know that I have more than just a scant knowledge of diamond testers, scales, gauges and other such paraphernalia. I have also been alarmed by the methods threatened by some thieves to achieve their aim. For example, in the Brink's-Mat case you mentioned, one of the gang threatened an employee by dousing him in petrol, then shaking a box of matches in his face. Needless to say, he did as he was asked. Another threatened to put him in a car crusher if he didn't comply!"

65

"Gentlemen, I think I've said quite enough. I hope you enjoyed listening to and learning about two famous − if not completely successful robberies? Now it's your turn."

"Crime doesn't pay, is that it?" Horatio declared. "You called us together to admit it was all a grand hoax and done just to get us all flummoxed. Am I right?"

"No, you're not right at all in fact you couldn't be further from the truth. What about you, Raffer?"

"It seems to me they were not that clever, with too many fundamental errors, proven by the fact that they are now behind bars. So, Horatio is right, crime doesn't pay. I assume you called us together to forget everything you said of venturing outside of the law. We are just to crack on with our studies as if nothing has happened, or indeed muted, and enjoy the river and Mrs B's egg sandwiches."

"I suspected that's what both of you would say – initially – but I'm here to persuade you otherwise. However, that was only part one of my two-part scenario. I've given you two good examples of robberies where they almost got away with it but were still caught. Why they were caught is more interesting and we need to explore the reasons in more detail. First, I suggest we need to take a long hard look at ourselves, get inside and ask what really makes us tick and what we truly are, and do we have what it takes to pull off a successful robbery.

"Horatio, I don't understand what part of anthropology you're in or at, it's such a vast subject. Where do you even start to begin? I know it's about where human life began, and how societies, languages and cultures evolved along quite diverse but often remarkably convergent pathways. Then as to how small bands and villages gave way to chiefdoms and chiefdoms to mighty states. Is that it?"

"It's along those lines, Oscar, but there's a little more to it than that. Remember, nothing human is alien to anthropology. Indeed, of all the myriad of disciplines that study our species, it is only us thinking anthropologists who seek to understand the whole panorama of space, time and evolution of human existence," Horatio answered, already thinking of becoming a criminal.

"Raffer, I think I understand you a little better, if not your sexual connotations. But just the thought of dressing up and playing the role model of a young French Parisian woman surely tempt you? You clearly have a love of the theatrical; it would be right up your street."

There followed a noticeable silence as all three went quiet, save that of the noise emulating from the other crafts that were approaching and passing. Raffer looked quizzically at Horatio, as if hoping to hear pearls of wisdom or the asking for more details and clarification of what was actually involved. It was undeniable that Horatio was the brightest and most deep thinking of the three and was not given to rash or flippant off-the-cuff answers. He considered all options and words as if they were valuable commodities and not to be given away lightly. He was infuriating at times with others impatiently hanging on his every word or response.

"Come on, you anthropological android, surely you've got more to say or ask," Raffer blurted out in exaggerated and dramatic exasperation.

"Just hang on a minute, you silly arse. This is not one of your so-called soppy stage productions where everyone can perform, take a bow and then piss off home. This is our lives we're talking about, not some fictitious farce."

Oscar interjected, "What do you want to know?"

"What do you have in mind?" replied Horatio.

"Tell us more, then I'll decide," Horatio responded.

"That goes for me too," echoed Raffer. The jury was still out, and there were still bridges to be crossed before everyone was totally convinced.

Chapter 10

Down on the river with spectacular ease, your boat glides on water whenever you please. But the tide gets stronger as the years go by and takes you off course when the river is high. Just be careful, my friend, or else you may drown. Choose the right line to go upriver, or down. Their fate is the worse, for those that try to go undecided, unsure, when the river is low.

– Lord Byron

The previous week, Doddy's nine law students occupied his room, eight of them sprawled on the floor, scattered between the permanent obstacles of mountainous piles of books. The only female present sat comfortably in the other green leather armchair, her obvious and overt boyfriend sitting propped up close by. The others were quite unaware of his need to be near her. If nothing else, undergraduates understood good manners and etiquette.

"As you are all aware, time is short, and I need to get you all in the right mind set for the forthcoming set of oral examinations in your next and final term. The first point to make is that the questioners are not trying to trip you up or catch you out. Their aim is to fairly assess and evaluate how much you have grasped and your understanding of the exactness of law. No one knows all the answers, not even me, nor the interrogators, but they will expect you to know the old chestnuts – cases which invariably crop up – time immemorial.

"From the longest case in English legal history to Lord Denning's rulings, judicial decisions are your – the law student's – bread and butter. Remember, law captures human stories, shapes public debate, and establishes new expectations of the state. Their wider effects can also reflect on society's consciousness often leading to new laws, most but not all of which are generally good. This can be well illustrated by the case of Roe V Wade; this being one from across the Atlantic and arguably no case better demonstrates the political and social impact of judicial decisions. Can anyone enlighten me?"

The attractive young lady showing ample leg in the green armchair raised her arm, volunteering an answer.

"I believe it was the landmark decision made in 1973 to uphold a woman's right to an abortion."

"Very good Marie-Jo, I had a suspicion that perhaps you would know the answer, especially having travelled here from across the pond. I can only but hope that our other students also knew the answer." Oscar didn't.

"Let me give you another favourite to ponder, the case of Jodie and Mary. In the year 2000, the plight of conjoined twins made front page news. The question was whether it was justified to separate and knowingly 'kill' the weaker Mary, in order to save her stronger sister Jodie, given both were destined for a premature death. In spite of the parents' favouring non-separation, doctors wanted a declaration that such an operation would be lawful. In a bewildering maze of ethical and legal conflicts, Lord Justice Ward rather hollowly declared that, 'this is a court of law, not a court of morals'. What was the outcome?" This time it was Oscar that answered most eloquently.

"After admitting to sleepless nights, the judges allowed the doctors to separate. Lord Justice Brooke – I'm not sure if the name is correct – declared the situation as one of necessity, allowing the option of a lesser evil. The stronger twin survived and made a full recovery."

"Well done, Ormsby, and it was indeed Lord Brooke. It was thankfully a rare case, which demonstrates the relationship between law and morality. I would suggest this will be one of the bankers amongst the written examination questions, but I haven't told you so," said Doddy, tapping his nose.

The professor threaded his way carefully over to the window, and whilst admiring the scenery, he again addressed his captive audience of budding alumni.

"Before we break for the day, let us consider Regina versus Casement in the July of 1916. Sir Roger Casement, it is sometimes said, was hanged by a comma.

This was a case about war, treason, syntax, punctuation, an ancient document and the noose. Casement was convicted during the First World War of conspiring with the Germans to further an Irish insurrection. Can anyone explain and perhaps elaborate?" Again, it was Oscar who answered.

"Are you trying to impress me even more, Mr Ormsby?" The professor smiled, inwardly pleased by the level of response he was receiving, which augured well.

"From what I can remember, the contentious punctuation mark appeared in some but not all versions of the law under which Casement was prosecuted – The Treason Act of 1351. Ultimately, the comma allowed the definition of a traitor to include someone whose treachery, such as Casement's, was committed outside the realm, in this case, Casement had made his plans, I understand, in Germany. But before the final decision was taken, two of the presiding judges went to the Public Record Office to check with a magnifying glass what was on the original state and parliamentary roll. Ergo, Casement's appeal was rejected, and on the 3rd of August 1916, he was hanged, but I can't remember where."

"It was at Pentonville Prison, but well done again on such an accurate account, most laudable," to which the other students gave him a generous round of applause. It was the first time for many years that Oscar had visibly blushed, but more in pleasure than embarrassment.

"I wanted to use the Casement case to make a point, although I didn't expect anyone to have heard of it let alone be so knowledgeable," Doddy continued, smiling in the direction of a still red-faced Oscar, alias Ormsby. "It illustrates how important the spoken and written word is in the revered and respected profession of law. By now, you will all have become accustomed to the precise, accurate and economy of words used by judges and barristers. It is a skill that I implore you all to be mindful of and practice. What was that Bernard Shaw once wrote, 'If I'd more time, this letter would have been shorter?'"

"Heed me well, when you leave King's and go your separate ways, you will be remembered and counted for by what you say. I will say no more. Thank you and enjoy your holidays. Ormsby, may I have a private word before you leave?"

Oscar wondered why he had been singled out. In the meantime, the others left, their minds immediately on other matters, mostly not law; with Marie-Jo linking her arm through that of a fellow student and lover.

"May I suggest a walk by the river I find the serenity and the sound of running water most soothing. Don't you find it so and almost therapeutic?" Doddy lightly offered. Oscar wore a worried and puzzled look on his face and was not at all sure why he'd been invited to this unexpected towpath talk.

"No need to look so worried or alarmed, Ormsby, you haven't done anything wrong. On the contrary, I'm somewhat impressed."

Not another word passed between tutor and student until they had reached the path which followed the contours of the River Cam. One was a large man clad all in green, the other a diminutive almost childlike figure in jeans and jumper alongside him. On the river most of the punts remained out in the middle, where the raised gravel bed was easier to propel against using their poles; some of the occupants happily talking, others with hands dangling in the moving waters.

"So many of you students spend your time here and take our lovely River Cam so much for granted. You must admit we are blessed with the most pleasant and well-situated river in the region. Are you like the others, or have you taken the trouble to learn about the waters that serve us so well? Go on, Ormsby, surprise me; it's a knack you repeatedly demonstrate, never failing to surprise me."

Oscar relaxed; Doddy was in one of his friendly, if somewhat philosophical and expansively laced moods, when he was prone to issuing forth on any number of subjects, most on which he was incredibly conversant. He then duly impressed his mentor by knowledgeably describing the background of the river, including Byron's Pool, where he used to swim and the naming of Cambridge. At which point Doddy uttered forth: "*Down on the river with spectacular ease...* I'll let you have the words, Ormsby, as I think you'll agree there are many hidden messages of advice therein."

Oscar smiled warmly, content to be interrupted and impressed by the professor's memory and passion for the love of music and poetry and the willingness to share them.

"Did you know, Ormsby, that the river is clear enough to support sufficient fish stocks for angling, as well as the obvious boating," as he waved to a heavily ladened boat of youngsters that he clearly recognised and they him.

"Birdwatching is also popular on the Cam, with over fifty varieties of birds to be seen, and so I often come armed with my trusty if dated binoculars. You probably already know that the area between Jesus Lock and Baits Bite Lock is the official training and race waters of the Cambridge rowers. I'm surprised you haven't been approached to be a cox."

"I was once, but rowing is not really my bag, I'm not really the sporty type."

"Well it takes all sorts," the professor countered.

"Is it true that people still swim in the Cam, because I've never seen any bathers during my time here? Not that I've ever gone looking."

"Yes, swimming is still popular further upstream at Granchester Meadows. There is even a tradition amongst the brave few who go for a dip there on New Year's Day. Now here's something I bet you or your friends didn't know. The stretch from Jesus Green to the Mill Pond that passes through the Backs of the university to the colleges has a towpath deliberately submerged under its surface. This was because, when the river was used for the transportation of goods to the old mill, the colleges would not permit the horses pulling the barges to walk within their boundaries. The horses walked through the water pulling their cargo, on the underwater towpath."

By now, Doddy was in full flow, as he and Oscar took their time walking slowly along the towpath. For the highly respected professor, it was the end of yet another term, with the feeling of imminent freedom in the air. Soon, he would be rid of his pesky students and would be off to the Lake District to stay with his long-time friends Wilfred and Eunice Pilkington. The latter was true but not the former. If the truth be told, he loved his position and the constant stimulant his youthful and knowledge hungry students both demanded and provided. They were his lifeblood, and he never tired of explaining and pointing out the importance of law – the written and the spoken word. The photographs and letters he received each year from past students was testament enough. The laudable fact was, many long-departed students still corresponded with him, and in a few cases – visited. These were tangible signs, genuine compliments, acts of kindness and gratitude which made his life so satisfying and fulfilling.

There was also the tacit and unspoken appreciation that hundreds of alumni felt. At least two couples had even tried some matchmaking for him, but this had ended in predictable disaster, but with no hard feelings, more one of all round amusement. Doddy was a loner by choice, who welcomed his solitude shared only with Wagner after a hard day of slogging over a hot stove of complicated aspects of law and general academia. Was he now thinking of making a change?

"Ormsby, we may be clever academics and barristers designate, but never forget the genius of the composers and the poets. What say you?" as he again acknowledged a waving trio in a fast-moving punt – someone undoubtedly trying hard to impress.

"I've never really given them much thought, Professor, not subjects that I've ever considered. Should I?"

"Yes, you should. There are other things in life outside of law, and we must always guard against being parochial. More to the point, I didn't invite you out here merely to impress you with my recitations. The real reason for this waterside chat was to point you in the right direction prior to the final term. We on the teaching staff shouldn't have favourites, but we do. You've done extremely well in your time here, but my fear is you will exhaust and fall before the finishing post is reached. Your work is excellent, and I have no doubt of your ability to leave here with a first possibly with honours. So, can I suggest you leave the books here at King's during your holiday and take a complete break? You will then return refreshed for the last lap. There is no need for any further midnight oil burning. Do you get my drift?"

Oscar left the professor, wondering how he would have reacted if he'd known that his erstwhile protégé was about to commit a diamond robbery before returning to King's. Some honour!

Chapter 11

"What I have in mind is that we deprive one fat cat jeweller of his stock of white rocks. For you uneducated, ignorant and ill-informed undergraduates, these are raw and unpolished diamonds. Our prize, however, should not come as any startling revelation, now that you've both been appraised of the Antwerp and Hatton Garden diamond robberies. The reason for my − sorry, our selected target − is a rather despicable character by the name of Abraham Birnbaum.

"It was in one of the many diamond trade magazines that I read of his outrageous behaviour. He openly, and quite unbelievably, boasted, that his daughter's engagement ring, which he had sold at an inflated cost price to his now son-in-law, was paste! So, what more a deserving target of a bastard could there possibly be?

"Of course, it goes without saying, that none of us three possess the skills of picking locks, drilling holes into secure vaults, or have a portfolio of suitable villains whom we could contact to advise us in our unlawful pursuit. So, what do we have? We have our rather puny bodies, which we can use to our distinct advantage, but more importantly, we have our sizeable and imaginative brains. I, therefore, propose that 'Mr Diddle-my-own-daughter' simply brings the diamonds to us, rather than the impossible task and risk of us trying to break into his shop, as we clearly couldn't even break into a sweat," Oscar declared. "So how do we go about it?"

"Yes, that's what we'd all like to know," said Raffer, in what sounded a rather truculent and almost demanding tone. Oscar held up both hands, as if in defence and acknowledgement. He knew he had a lot more to do if he were to convince his two friends to join him and become partners in crime. In horse-racing parlance, he'd jumped and cleared the first fence. There were still many hurdles to be surmounted before reaching the flat and the run to the finishing post. For Oscar and Co, there would never be the pleasurable ritual of a winner's enclosure, where they would receive the generous plaudits of the impressed gallery. Success for them would be measured in not being caught, returning to Cambridge and never to speak another word of their criminal adventure – ever!

"Last June when you were both starting a long, lazy summer recess, I was doing my homework. Not studying law, rather a way of breaking it! Instead of immediately going home, I made three detours by way of reconnaissance trips to Golders Green in London. I'd already researched and identified the jeweller and his shop in Hatton Garden, 21-23 St Cross Street to be exact, and more importantly, I'd also found out where he lives.

"It would not be unreasonable for you both to assume that a Saturday afternoon is the busiest time of the week on most high streets – not so in Golders Green. This affluent Northwest London suburb is home to a sizeable Orthodox Jewish community, and is therefore at its quietest at that time, in contrast to the nearby Hampstead and Brent Cross. Come the night, it bursts into life, with many food stores staying open well into the early hours.

"As you probably already know, the Jews strictly observe the Sabbath, which for them begins at nightfall on a Friday and lasts until nightfall of the Saturday. However, I discovered that Mr-Diddle-my-own-daughter works a modified 'Shabbat' or Sabbath routine. He goes off to work on a Friday morning, returning home at lunchtime, where he remains with his wife until precisely midday on the Saturday. He then contrives to bend the faith somewhat by going back to his shop until closing time at five pm. It would seem that receipts override religion, well at least for some part of his holy calendar.

"You can also well imagine that there are some very attractive and desirable properties around; the more upmarket ones I found bordered Golders Hill Park with its small zoo and tennis courts. It is here that our Mr Diddle-my-own-daughter lives, namely, 14 West Heath Avenue. So, whilst on a Saturday afternoon, when he's beavering away at his Hatton Garden goldmine, raking in yet more sheckles, his wife is left all alone in a very quiet but accessible large house.

"I found out – I won't bore you with the details or my methods – that their daughter now lives in Israel. She is married to an oil engineer…yes, the one her father had so unscrupulously cheated, working for a petroleum company in the Bay of Haifa. It would seem their hearts are in Jerusalem and not jewellery. This leaves Mrs Aalijah Birnham, an insulin-dependent Type 1 diabetic, in the house all alone. She also has a reaction to being in the proximity of animals and a dread of snakes, a fear apparently stemming from some childhood prank.

"It wasn't until my third recce that I was able to confirm she is a person of strict routine and habit. On a Saturday afternoon, she'll walk to Golders Green Road to do some light shopping, which always includes bagels. On the way back, she pops into the synagogue on North End Road before returning home. It was only then that I concluded that abduction was possible, practical and virtually painless. We could then demand that Mr Diddle-my-daughter return home post-haste, delivering to us a purse full of diamonds – Mohamed to the mountain."

"Bloody hell!" exclaimed Raffer. "You say abduction, old bean. Isn't that kidnapping by any other name? I think the authorities take a rather dim view of that sort of thing, and normally reflected in excruciatingly long prison sentences, where they tend to throw away the key."

"Yes, you're right and I confess it does sound all a little hairy and frightening. I cannot deny there is an element of risk, which surely adds to the thrill of it all? However, we have to accept that there can be no gain without some minimal short-term pain," Oscar was quick to reply.

Horatio and Raffer exchanged disapproving glances, the looks and faces pulled indicating that they were not at all happy or impressed by what they were now hearing.

"Go on," said Horatio, in a doubtful voice.

"Let me tell you what I have in mind. You can then come back at me with any comments and suggestions or pour water on the entire idea. As I said at the outset, what I am proposing is not yet set in stone, excuse the pun, and there is no commitment on anyone's behalf – I'm hoping two volunteers will be worth ten pressed men. I have a number of plans for you both to consider."

"One, we wait until Mrs Birnbaum has arrived home after her Saturday afternoon outing and whilst Mr Birnbaum is still at his shop. We drive up to the house in our Citroen, more on that later, dressed as three attractive French Parisian women. Access to the house will be easier than I imagined. Although it's a large property, it stands well back off the road behind a curtain of overgrown and neglected fir trees. The house and front door are virtually hidden from sight.

'When she opens the door, we'll force our way in with hopefully the minimum of resistance. Horatio will do all the talking in his best broken English with his heavily refined French accent, stating that we do not intend to hurt her in any way as long as she cooperates. Because of her aversion to snakes, I will be carrying one in a glass container as an added frightener. We will sit her in a chair and tie her wrists with an electric tie and tape her mouth with gaffer tape, but only if necessary. We will remove any rings and watch, at the same time demanding her insulin and needles. The photographs of these held in her bound hands will be sent to Mr Birnbaum with clear instructions on what he has to do. I believe the images and words will be sufficient for him to act. The only worry is he may have a direct panic button to the police. We therefore need to ensure that the words sent are cold, clear and convincing, with no ambiguity: SHOULD HE UNWISELY CONTACT THE POLICE, HE'D NEVER SEE HIS WIFE AGAIN."

"Blimey! You're not suggesting for one moment that we'd actually do away with the old gal?" Raffer interjected.

"Not at all, heaven forbid, but it has to come across in exactly that way, and we'll need to spend time agreeing the precise wording. Perhaps something along the lines that the safe location of his wife will only be given once we are in receipt of the diamonds and an assurance that we are not being monitored or followed? How best we achieve this we still need to agree.

"Alternatively, I could leave you two with Mrs Birnbaum and I take her ring, watch and insulin to his shop. There I would hand over the parcel and typed instructions stipulating where the diamonds are to be left.

"This is by far a riskier option, as it means additional exposure and contact, whereas the first plan minimises this. If for any reason, it goes pear shape, then we three attractive French women simply disappear forever. If all goes according to plan, and I believe it will, we can continue our holidays, return to King's and travel to Amsterdam at a later time and make the trade." There followed a long and deafening silence.

"To be perfectly candid, Oscar, old sport, I'm disappointed," declared Horatio. "I'm not impressed or convinced it'll work. From what you've outlined, this so-called diamond heist is nowhere near as good as that Italian chappies, or as perfect as you first intimated, and seems fraught with danger. There are far too many unknowns, maybes and what ifs."

"I agree," answered Oscar. "Let's be honest. To deprive someone of their hard-earned wealth at the drop of a hat, and a Jew boy at that, was never going to be a piece of cake. I admit the plan as it stands has weaknesses, but these I'm sure we can resolve that's why three heads are better than one. Up until now, I simply didn't want to count my chickens; at least not until I felt I had your lukewarm if less than half-hearted support. The only thing I'm sure of is that it cannot be done alone. I still believe with the correct disguises, the element of surprise, the health and fear factors, and the ability to disappear if it all goes haywire, still make it highly possible. Remember, we are not villains, merely three good-looking women who are not remotely like or connected to any undergraduates from a distant Cambridge university."

Oscar paused, looking questionably at his ship's company of two. One picture said a thousand words, two doubtful faces appearing to indicate their disinclination. He clearly hadn't sold the proposition well enough, or in anywhere near a favourable or attractive light. He was not beaten yet and decided on another approach, whilst endeavouring to keep the disappointment out of his voice. He could tell their vital support was slipping away, as were two majestic swans that silently passed by.

"You're both absolutely right," Oscar continued in a surprisingly confident or was it a possibly false upbeat tone? "I've been too close to it and for far too long and it's become rather obsessive. You two come along and see it with fresh minds, clearer eyes and valid concerns. So, can I suggest a completely new approach? We still aim to deprive Mr Diddle-his-own-daughter of his glass and white rocks but start again from scratch on a clean sheet of planning paper, as to how we go about achieving it. Don't forget, we can still use or modify any of my ideas as you think fit. How does that sound?"

"That's the first reasonable thing you've said in the last ten minutes," uttered Raffer. "Don't get us wrong Oscar, neither of us have said no, well not yet, but we do have serious reservations. I'm still persuaded that the whole escapade-come-crime will add an exciting new dimension to our lives, but not the prospect of going to prison old bean. I agree with Horatio, at the moment, your plan leaks like a sieve! Nonetheless, I'm still in if we can all be convinced that each and every phase is in our favour and under our control, and not endangered by the possibility of someone deciding not to play by our rules, by throwing a wobbly or a spanner in the works. As I've just made abundantly clear, I have no intention of going to prison. I remain mightily tempted by the excitement it offers and all it entails, but fearful of it going wrong and someone getting hurt. Also, my family and friends would never forgive me for doing such a stupid thing, and all in the name of some charity, come off it! A third-rate dungeon is a lot less desirable than a first-class degree."

"I totally agree and I'm of the same mind," declared Horatio. "The persuading factor for me would be if we can guarantee an escape route if it turns out to be a bag of worms. Like Raffer, I'm totally averse to the wife getting hurt or being deprived of her insulin and ending up in a coma due to our bungling. Using her as a threatening lever, I think will work and I believe it would be enough to stop old thingamabob from pressing any police connect panic button. The real sticking point seems to be the problem of the drop off and pick up of the diamonds without being spotted, identified or followed."

Raffer spoke again, whilst at the same time deftly pushing away a closing punt from what was on an imminent collision course, "I agree with Horatio, but I'm still to be convinced. You're right, Oscar. I'm sure we have the brains, balls and effrontery to pull it off, but only if we can remove the existing 'ifs and maybes'. By the way, I forgot to ask about this Mrs Birnbaum. How easy is it going to be to force her to do our bidding?"

"She's a poor waif of a thing, not much more than six stone soaking wet. For a wealthy woman who lives in a large and impressive house, she doesn't look to be the happiest of people. If that's what lots of money does for you, then I have no wish to be rich. I don't foresee any trouble or struggle in getting her to do our bidding, as long as we remember she's a diabetic. From what I saw of her, I got the distinct impression she'd much rather be back in Israel with her daughter and son-in-law."

"Where do we stand? Is it a complete non-starter or is one or both of you still attracted to the idea, if we can sort out a better plan? I'm still hoping you're not completely anti or averse to the idea, notwithstanding your valid concerns. I do, however, fully accept the plan postulated was far from being perfect let alone acceptable. Is that a fair comment?" Oscar asked. The punt had now reached a stretch of water with no other boats around, as all three sat attentive to what was being discussed.

"That's exactly so," Horatio answered. Raffer nodded. "Can I take it then, that to get your backing we need to sit down and start from scratch, eliminating the risk elements; where the leverage of abduction or kidnap is acceptable? This we feel is sufficiently threatening to the fat cat to ensure he delivers the diamonds to us, and not be tempted to inform the police. Thereby ensuring the safe return of his dear wife, whom we must assume he does love and would presumably not attempt to do a deal over."

"I must confess, it does sound tremendous fun, but what about the funding of such an operation? I'm afraid I haven't any spare dosh," said Horatio.

"Neither have I," added Raffer.

Oscar inwardly relaxed and breathed a sigh of relief − they were coming round. Their doubts were perfectly reasonable, and if the truth be known, he was still to be convinced himself. They definitely needed to have fresh brainstorming sessions to work out a strategy that minimised the risks and was acceptable to all.

"That's all taken care of. I've already purchased a left-hand drive Citroen with French plates. I also have sufficient funds to buy our female attire, train and ferry tickets, accommodation, PO Box, start a Swiss bank account and any other odds and sods. I might ask you both to stump up for the odd lipstick and mascara! Raffer might want to hang onto his!"

For the first time out there on the water, all three laughed. Oscar − the Bridge player, felt the cards had been shuffled, dealt and played well. The cautious openings had been made but had indicated poor hands with no responses and no deal − but the game was still on with more tricks yet to be played. It was time to reshuffle and perhaps deal from the bottom of the pack.

Chapter 12

It had taken five long evenings of brainstorming and wrangling for the three would-be criminals to settle on a revised plan (from start to finish) they were satisfied would work. A fresh approach had been required, which was desperately needed to resolve and expunge the earlier but valid doubts expressed by Horatio and Raffer out on the Cam. Their earlier scepticisms, once allayed, had now been replaced by genuine enthusiasm and an ardent desire to crack on and do the deed.

Similar to Oscar, Horatio and Raffer were not at all interested in any personal financial gain, they were in it for the adventure and the idea of stepping outside the bounds of respectability for one brief interlude in their life, that's what spurred and excited. Finally, with all of one accord, Oscar relaxed, content he'd made the right choice of accomplices. What now lie ahead were the preparation, rehearsal and execution. In the meantime, there remained the not inconsequential matter of continuing studies.

"So, what made you come up with the idea of the French car and female disguise?" asked Raffer.

"If you remember in the Antwerp and Hatton Garden robberies, silly clues were left as to their identities, which should and could have been avoided. I've studied the reports over and over and the mistakes made. In both cases, it was a lack of basic discipline and not being thorough, either by lack of concentration or not being bright enough. In the Hatton Garden case, it was definitely the latter, especially in using the same mobiles repeatedly.

"We therefore have to assume that every move and action we take is being monitored and watched from here on in. You must, therefore, be totally disciplined and take meticulous care when buying our props," looking at Raffer, "to ensure you are not recognised or remembered by drawing attention to yourself in any way.

"The reason for the disguise is a double insurance against being recognised or remembered during the minimum in-contact time. And if we are remembered, it will be for entirely the wrong reasons. If all goes according to plan, Mrs Birnbaum will be the only person in this country with whom we'll have the briefest of contact. Therefore, if we can present ourselves as French women in a French car, it's reasonable that's what she'll recall. The additional mobile phones and extra sim cards will ensure a brief once-only use. The spoken instruction inside the house will be uttered by Horatio in his well-rehearsed French-come-Pidgin-English accent. We will be suitably attired so as to deceive and fool even our friends.

"Raffer, your job is to dress us from top to bottom – wigs down to shoes. We also need to be wearing expensive French-made women's leather gloves for added effect, but more crucially we do not leave any fingerprints or DNA. Our clothes must look streamlined and nondescript with no loose fittings that can accidentally snag or catch."

"I think I'll get the shoes through one of the mail order firms, simple and anonymous," Raffer replied.

"Good idea," replied Oscar. "At least we've agreed the wording of the instructions to be sent with the photograph of Mrs Birnbaum, holding in her hands her watch, ring, insulin and syringe. We'll take a bottle of *Fairy Liquid* just in case the ring is difficult to get off. I'd rather we didn't have to amputate her ring finger," he jested.

"Jesus Christ," exclaimed Raffer grimacing. "That's not in the least bit funny, old bean. Remember, we're all agreed − no violence of any kind. I'm taking myself off to Peterborough tomorrow on my first shopping expedition to look for suitable clothes and wigs. I can now see why you chose Horatio and me. I reckon we're a size eight with Horatio a small ten. Gentlemen, by the time I've got us all togged up, you'll even doubt your own sexual orientation! We must of course remember to hide the old Adam's apple with either a scarf or a roll-neck jumper. Leave it with me and let's see what I come up with. Now, the awkward bit, I'm afraid I'll need some dosh." The 'old bean' immediately handed him an envelope already loaded with a thousand pound in crisp and unused twenties.

"Thanks, old bean, let's see how that goes."

The first dress rehearsal was an absolute hoot. It was difficult to imagine this was all part of some serious and dastardly crime. Raffer had enjoyed his task, acquiring virtually complete outfits for all three. The shoes were the first to be tried on. They were simple black canvas deck shoes-come-loafers, which could be seen any day in Rome, Ramsgate, Lisbon or London. They were light, cheap and beautifully nondescript and Raffer's artistic flair had done the trick. He'd also insisted they shave and oil their legs, as they would be wearing short to three-quarter length black slacks, revealing the lower leg and ankle. Now standing there in their knee-high 15-denier stockings, all convincingly passing the test of looking like women, indeed, many of the fairer sex would envy the size five and six loafers and shapely breasts.

Inside the size 34 and 36 black bras, Raffer had taped gel pads, similar to what women spent thousands of pounds on having implants. At first, he had mischievously considered frilly, lace bras, but reluctantly conceded they would only have served his own fetish, and also hidden under black roll-neck jumpers. With a last-minute flush of inspiration and an eye to detail, he'd purchased thongs, just in case their jumpers rose up. The accidental showing of a skimpy purple band would be far more convincing to Mrs Birnbaum than her spying men's M&S underpants!

The wigs were the most difficult to find and required Raffer to make a further errand into Newmarket, where he finally got what he wanted. Three good quality wigs, two brown and one black, were the most expensive of all the purchases. There was no point in spoiling the ship for a ha'porth of tar, and cheap wigs would have done exactly so, and ruined the desired effect of authenticity.

By the time Raffer had finished (painstakingly) applying a modest amount of makeup, the finished effect was remarkable. The *piéce de résistance* was the gold and black masquerade-type masks. They were not at all frightening, but subtly distracting. Later, the initial statement from a shocked and traumatised Mrs Birnbaum would affirm they were three masked French women but she wasn't sure of the regional accent. She could remember the car had a foreign number plate, and yes it was a left-hand drive. She also thought she recognised French cigarettes stuffed in one of the rear-door side pockets but couldn't swear to it. She did, however, remember that on the car floor was an almost new A to Z of London and a map of Calais. Her summary had been, 'to be perfectly honest I was in such a state and only thinking – those bloody French'.

Oscar had travelled to Calais a few weeks earlier. It had been a tiring weekend, starting with the train journey from Cambridge to Kings Cross, then from St Pancras down to Dover. He'd crossed the Channel and into France aboard a Britany car ferry as a foot passenger. Having looked around three second-hand car lots, he finally settled on a cheap high-mileage Citroen. He paid for the car in cash, all for the princely sum of 1500 Euros; no questions asked, and none given. Oscar's only fear was that it would break down on the homeward journey. It didn't.

In Newmarket, he'd already rented a lock-up garage for £50 per month; again no questions asked. Here was housed his five-year-old extremely low mileage Toyota Yaris (which his parents had bought his as a present for getting into Cambridge), which he swapped with the Citroen. He had finally returned to the college late on the Sunday night, relieved but exhausted. He did, however, remember to make the effort to appear as fresh as a daisy the following Monday at morning prayers in chapel.

Oscar had explained how diamonds can be easily traded, for a fraction of their true value, on the Amsterdam black market. It was very much a case of no one asked questions and everyone knew nothing! It was a place where diamonds and customers appeared and disappeared with a knowing silence that was almost reverential. The only difference being the deities were diamonds, white rocks that had been compressed below ground over millions of years. The raw and unpolished were paradoxically the more attractive and by far the most desirable. Here, diamonds pass through hands like ripples on a lake. Soon the ripples disappear, as if nothing had ever happened or any transaction taken place. Other items such as bracelets, necklaces and rings caused more ripples as they had to be dismantled and could later be identified and in some cases be recognised. As is often stated in the trade magazines: *Raw is unrefined − beautiful and untraceable.*

The task of setting up an unnumbered Swiss bank account had been simpler than imagined. The bank staff gave the tacit but polite impression that every client was a crook and should be treated like royalty and with strictest confidence. A direct debit to a charity was something common to them and easily arranged. Oscar had soon realised that he was not the first person to ask for such a transaction and arrangement to be set up.

"Of course, as is customary, we have well above the average bank charges, you understand? The arrangement will continue until you instruct otherwise, or until the funds are exhausted, you understand?" Oscar understood.

The three big unknowns lay within Mr Birnbaum's gift. One, they didn't know how many diamonds he had. Two, how he would react? Or would his professional or avaricious nature tempt him to keep some back. So be it. They could only hope the safety of his wife would work in their favour, but it was an unknown and there was no getting away from the fact. The third unknown was the stipulated drop off and pick-up location. This had to be as soon after the phone demand as possible, to avoid any short notice plans to be made in collusion with the police. This was the crucial time, whether to proceed or abort. To walk away empty-handed was preferable to wrists adorned in restraining handcuffs.

The punctured Citroen would be left abandoned in the Birnbaums driveway. Oscar in the Yaris (parked nearby), would drop Horatio and Raffer, having rapidly changed sex, at the nearest tube station, the start of their journeys home to Ramsgate and Truro. Oscar would later destroy the disguises at a suitable location, before driving home to Birmingham. Any celebration would have to wait until they all reconvened back at King's for the full Easter term before graduating in the June. In the meantime, they were three hardworking undergraduates and not three unscrupulous women from across the channel!

The next planning stage required a visit to London to carry out a detailed and timed dry run, to check out what Oscar had first described. It had to be concise and accurate, as you would expect from a prospective barrister.

The Birnbaums were indeed creatures of habit. A discreet surveillance shared by all three confirmed their comings and goings – almost to the minute, as Oscar had said. Mr Birnbaum epitomised the typical fat cat jeweller. He was short, tubby and sweated a lot. He wore an expensive suit, shirt and tie, badly. His small and podgy hands had an almost abhorrent look about them. Oscar could well believe he had diddled his own kith and kin. It was just one of those immediate, instinctively intuitive assessments that are so often amazingly accurate. It could only be hoped that he loved his wife almost as much as he loved money. One thing in everyone's favour was his punctuality. At least this augured well for their daring abduction; the word kidnap was too awful to say. How strange a simple spoken word can affect and upset a person's equilibrium? Was this the showstopper? The single word which could change the course of their lives?

Once more, they had to ask each other why they were going ahead with it. It was Oscar who seemed to falter, whose idea it was in the first place. Now so near, was he the one possibly getting cold feet, whereas Raffer and Horatio had become the dedicated disciples? It was as if once their doubts had been allayed, they had entered into the venture with an enthusiasm that was almost unhealthy and unexpected. It wasn't too late to abort, with no harm done apart from some financial expenditure.

"You're getting stage fright, old bean, I've had it many times, it's called first night nerves," offered Raffer, poking Oscar in the chest with his elbow (not breast). "Most people experience it at some time or another." Horatio reassured him that all would be well – the tables had turned. Raffer was right, Oscar was definitely nervous.

"It'll be all right on the night," Raffer affirmed. This proved to be the case, after yet a second visit to Golders Green. The stage was set. At least Oscar had had his panic attack before and not like Speedy with Notarbartolo.

Chapter 13

It was the final dress rehearsal before the big day. Oscar and Raffer had joined Horatio in his room. His room had been chosen for the sole reason that his whole floor had been vacated; everyone else had already cleared off on their Easter hols. They certainly didn't want anyone unexpectedly knocking on the door and seeing any of them wearing bras, tights, wigs, lipstick and blusher!

After countless rethinks and major amendments, they finally arrived at a plan they were all happy with and keen to execute. At last, they had one that would work. Not only would it work but it would also excite. After all, wasn't the thrill of it all the object of the exercise, to undertake this once-in-a-lifetime venture that would set the heart pumping and the adrenalin soaring? It seemed the successful catalyst-come-remedy to all their previous what ifs and maybes was their own specific studies, which had also occupied their minds, and the stimulus needed.

The day agreed dawned. They had shrewdly chosen the last day of spring term, with almost everyone off campus, except three otherwise preoccupied undergraduates, who remained in what was a virtually empty King's.

Friday, 17th March 2017

King's College looked and resembled a ghost town; it was Saint Patrick's Day, with not a shamrock in sight. It was the last official day of the Lent term, which had begun such a seemingly long time ago on Tuesday the 17th of January. The evident lack of people and activity (with not a single punt in sight) was to be expected. It was generally accepted that everyone – both students and staff – had packed up by the Thursday lunchtime, with most having departed well before the weekend had begun. That was, of course, apart from our three would-be diamond robbers, who intended to drive south to London during the silent hours of that night and the Saturday morning. Their Thursday had been spent having a quiet evening going over the plan, yet again – practise makes perfect. They had wisely agreed to keep a low profile.

Early on the Friday morning, Oscar had made a solitary visit to the empty chapel. Was this to pray that all would go well, or was he asking for some divine help or forgiveness in what he and his chums were about to do? He didn't tell the other two of his visit; his religion and beliefs were something he kept very much to himself, especially as they were a million miles from what they had planned. However, his visit was noticed. Doddy was already up and about, enjoying his pipe and morning constitutional brisk walk along the towpath. He just happened to be standing behind a convenient oak, hiding out of the wind, trying to relight his pipe, when he spotted Oscar entering the chapel. He thought it strange he was still on campus, and wrongly (and annoyingly) assumed that he'd been burning the midnight oil, something he'd most recently advised him against doing.

"I know he thinks he ought but I wish he'd take a hint," the professor muttered to himself. However, he didn't give it much further thought, as he had his own travel arrangements to make, but for some reason, it wrangled and lodged in his mind. Doddy turned and made his way back to his rooms to collect his already packed clobber. He was off on his traditional Easter walking and sexual sabbatical in the Lake District!

The professor, together with his fully-ladened rucksack, walked the ten minutes from the college to the Central bus station on Drummer Street. He was catching a National Express coach – this was by far the most convenient and cost-effective way to travel. He didn't drive and throughout his time at King's, he'd never had the cause, craving or inclination to do so. He didn't even have a bicycle, which of course many of the staff did. Doddy was often heard to say, "I prefer to use my own legs and the action of walking as a means of conveyance – Shank's' Pony, less complicated but immediately to hand – or foot!"

The coach would drop him off in Keswick, where he would be met by his friends of many years standing. He enjoyed the coach journey, taking with him his own prepared sandwiches and a thermos of coffee. He put the travel time to good use, reading his students' end of term papers. He would then be free to enjoy everything he knew the Lake District had to offer.

The professor's programme for his ten-day stay never varied, neither did he want it to. Having been picked up in Keswick by the Pilkingtons, Doddy would spend the first night with them, enjoying fare of roast beef and Yorkshire pudding, followed by apple crumble. The evening spent catching up on the latest scuttlebutt and a reasonably early night was the order of the day after all the travelling. He would present Eunice with a large box of her favourite chocolates and the latest classical CD for Wilfred.

The next morning would see all three of them walk the lake. As always, Eunice would remind Doddy that Bassenthwaite was the only lake to be officially called a lake. Doddy would nod as if hearing and learning something new and it became a standing joke. After the first morning, he would be on his own and all three of them knew why, though not a word passed their lips. Despite being pillars of the church and extremely pious, they were not prudes and had long known and accepted the professor's longstanding 'bit on the side'.

On Doddy's first stay, Eunice, being the caring and thoughtful type of woman that she was, had arranged that someone would come in and do the necessary tidying up for their guest. Following a few enquiries, a small but large competent lady who cleaned at the village pub (*The Poacher Inn*) had been recommended. She had agreed to pop in each morning and flick a duster around. Although tiny in stature − five feet four inches, she was definitely large in size, and could be likened in build to that of a non-fasting lumberjack. She could quite easily have flicked over any rugby front-row forward, judging by her enormous hams of arms. However, what had not been foreseen or expected by the kind and forward-thinking Eunice, is that the larger-than-life cleaning lady would become Doddy's bit on the side, and what an absolute windfall it was for both parties.

At the time of their first meeting, Dunstan Falcon Dodderington was 40 years old, with Violet Eileen Mowbray (nee Eckersley) ten years his junior. Violet had married at eighteen and separated before her 22nd birthday. There were no children, or any further sighting of Mr Mowbray, who had apparently disappeared off the face of the earth (well, certainly Bassenthwaite), with apparently a younger and presumably slimmer model. Violet had not pined and had no desire whatsoever to set eyes on her no-good husband again. Though legally separated, she had never got round to getting a divorce, for one reason or the other, and had retained her married name. She had returned home to live with and look after her widowed mother in the lower end of the village.

The lower end of the village, as it was known and referred to by all, was not meant in a nasty, demeaning or derogatory sense, although it wasn't as nice as the upper end of the village. She worked each morning in *The Poacher Inn* (the only drinking hostelry within ten miles), and in any of the holiday homes when called upon. Eunice had kindly made the cleaning arrangement on behalf of the professor, who would never have thought to have asked.

It would not be too unkind or scurrilous to describe their sexual relationship as odd, as unusual it certainly was, both physically and mentally. Doddy was six feet tall and only a smidgeon shy of twenty stones in weight. It was only his height that deceptively allowed him to carry his obesity with a BMI bordering on 30, Violet, on the other hand, was 10 years his junior but matched him stone for stone! Her small size but undeniable weight meant she resembled something akin to a miniature bouncy castle.

He was a highly intelligent and deep-thinking professor, who knew much of subjects that Violet had no understanding of or desire to do so. She, on the other hand, was a simple lass but with a vibrant personality, boundless energy and a love of life. Yet, for some strange reason or quirk, these two unlikely people established an immediate rapport and chemistry for one another. It certainly was not a case of love at first sight, more a case of honest lust.

Alas, Doddy as an academic bachelor, had spent years in the sexual wilderness, and at a complete loss as to how to promote or pursue his physical attraction for the lady who had unexpectedly appeared literally larger than life. He needn't have worried. Violet with her womanly intuition had read the signs and the look in his eyes, decided to take the law into her own hands. This she had so done after two days of pussyfooting around, making coy suggestive innuendoes to each other, similar to children experiencing their first date and suggesting they meet behind the bike shed. Or wherever the youngsters of today met and did.

The next morning, back from his traditional five-mile walk with the Pilkingtons, he'd one hell of a surprise awaiting him. There, lying in his bed was certainly not little Red Riding Hood, but one very large pink and bare lady named Violet Mowbray, as naked as a Jaybird – well most definitely naked!

Not many things shocked or surprised Dunstan Falcon Dodderington. His cossetted life of academia within the safe and refined confines of King's College, allowed him a controlled and well-organised way of life. Any minimal shock or surprise normally came in the guise of some intellectual discovery by one or some of his new undergraduates, which enabled him to cleverly devise programmes in order to get the very best out of them. He greatly enjoyed the control and independence that being a bachelor afforded him. His life remained one of contentment and satisfaction, the montage of photographs on his wall a visible testament, and that was all the reward he sought. What more could he wish for? He already had Wagner and poetry, plus his annual sabbatical to Cumbria.

It would, therefore, be fair to say, that when he opened his cottage bedroom door, he was indeed both shocked and surprised – but pleasantly so. There to find occupying his bed, an undressed cleaning lady, not that this was readily apparent, with a white spinnaker of a sheet pulled up and held firmly under her many chins. Doddy's years at King's College, honing and refining a highly developed intellect and quick-thinking agile brain, enabling him to both respond immediately and appropriately.

"Good afternoon Violet, or may I call you Vi? Please forgive me, but not wishing to appear utterly dumbfounded or to sound completely daft or obtuse. To what do I owe this delightful but unexpected pleasure?"

"Doddy, now stop all that college twaddle, you know well enough. Have I got this right, or have I got this right (over the years, Violet had developed an amusing habit of repeating herself)?" A voice came back in her coyest Cumbrian accent. At the same time, she slowly and seductively lowered the sheet to reveal the two most enormous breasts possessing brown nipples and surrounding the size of beer mats. He approached the galleon with its lowered sail, revealing two large crows' nests! Doddy rubbed his large plates of hands together, as if preparing to put to sea, or was she inviting him to enter harbour?

"You've got it absolutely right, my dearest Vi, absolutely right, my dearest Vi (mimicking her habit), as well you know it. I think we both secretly knew there was some unique chemistry between thee and me; I think they call it lust! What I believe exists between us is a refreshing honesty of two people who would like nothing better than to enjoy each other's bodies, without the unnecessary preamble or complicated label called love. Would it, therefore, be too presumptuous or coarse of me, to suggest that we would both enjoy a good old-fashioned shag – for want of another word?"

"Actually, I've been waiting here hoping you'd say that you'd very much like to fuck me." Doddy roared with laughter, the expletive was just the invitation he needed. Without further ado and with not another word spoken, he hurriedly undressed and joined her in what was now a very crowded bed! They really were two giants and not a couple to be viewed amorously on a cinema screen. So what? There was no one else around to judge or pass comment on what was surely the most unlikely pair of lovers one could ever wish to cast eyes upon. As he climbed in beside his expectant siren, he chuckled out loud and jovially pleaded, "Please be gentle with me."

They went at it like rabbits – very large rabbits. Their lovemaking was honest, hasty and raw. It was perfunctory; short, sharp, shuddery and sweaty, with much longer periods of required rest and respite. Doddy had only one brief previous sexual encounter, and not satisfying or memorable; this was far better. Violet loved it, and in time, she came to appreciate the accompaniment of Wagner and attempted to time the crescendos. Doddy had aptly named her two breasts K1 and K2, as they were mountainous in size and weighing at least a kilo each. They were his base camp before making yet another demanding ascent.

For two huge masses and despite the excessive flab, Doddy somehow managed to fumble and find his way through the moving tectonic plates, mountain passes, folds and crevasses of flesh with determination and ingenuity. There then followed a short period of frenetic 'activity', enjoyed by both the mountaineer and the mountain. Later, whilst Doddy took a shower, Violet cooked and served him dinner, before returning home and always before the evening was out.

The following morning, he met up with Wilfred and Eunice, and off they would go with not a word said, for there was no reason to say anything. The new 'arrangement' was evident to the Pilkingtons; the look on Doddy's face was enough. They both smiled, considering it to be a fait accompli. Meanwhile, Doddy and Violet must have thought all their Christmases had all come at once. Having discovered the wanton lust of each other's large bodily forms, they couldn't get enough of each other. Two things had to give – the time spent cleaning the inn, and the time spent on the daily walk around Bassenthwaite Lake. The landlord in the lower part of the village was not privy to the latest goings on in the upper part of the village, as was Wilfred.

On one of the morning walks, Wilfred had mischievously remarked, "Doddy, you seem to have an added spring in your step. Our fresh Cumbrian air must clearly be doing you the world of good?"

Suffice to say, both morning commitments were completed with a sense of purpose, a hint of urgency, if not undue haste. The time saved allowed Violet to call earlier at the cottage at the upper end of the village and complete her other chores! It also enabled Doddy to be back in the cottage to help in any way that he possibly could.

With Wagner doing his level best, these two honest and lustful folks enjoyed each other's company with a refreshing honesty, as if it were the first day that sex was no longer rationed. They would fondle, flay, fornicate and finally flop exhausted alongside each other. Certainly not the prettiest of sights but two heavyweights who repeatedly went the distance, with neither prepared to throw in the towel. By early evening, they were a spent force, contentedly so but happily so. Whilst Doddy disappeared to have either a shower or a bath, and change into his pyjamas and dressing gown, his mistress would cook his dinner. It was a labour of love, as she would never join him, needing to get home and cook supper for her mother and herself. Then she would be back in the morrow – what a service! It was to be an enduring relationship that prevailed year upon year with no further communication throughout, merely a tacit understanding and acceptance that next Easter was always less than a year away.

What would Doddy have thought, whilst lying next to his lady friend, if he'd known what his star pupil was about to get up to many miles south?

Chapter 14

The distance from Cambridge to London is around 65 miles, not much more than a gentle two-and-a-half-hour car journey at most. This meant they could all catch a few hours' sleep first, not needing to set off until three in the morning. This is what they did. Not that they slept that well, which was hardly surprising; either for fear of oversleeping, or what they later intended perhaps playing on their minds? In fact, Oscar hardly slept at all, the prospects of what they were about to do weighing heavily, with more than the hinted stage nerves.

They met under the cloak of darkness with not another living soul around, save that of a sleek and sinister looking black, green-eyed cat out on its nocturnal mission. It paused to give the three humans a cursory look before slinking off to continue its prowling. It was a cold and still night, or rather − early morning, the college asleep. The car park deserted apart from Oscar's Yaris, the only remaining vehicle. Even the ubiquitous Fred Turnbull's familiar old Vauxhall had disappeared; the college indeed was deserted, apart from one feline with its own agenda. It was 2:55 am with each suitably attired in jeans, jumpers and anoraks, all carrying two bags. The first contained their disguises and 'equipment', which now included a hammer and a couple of long screws and a pair of tweezers, the second containing their holiday togs. Both Horace and Raffer had been horrified at the initial suggestion of perhaps using a snake, and the repugnant idea had immediately been squashed. After mumbled greetings, nothing further was said; they all remained quiet with plenty enough to think on.

The small, crowded, well-packed Yaris drove the short distance to Oscar's lock-up, where the Citroen car had sat for the past three weeks. Encouragingly, if somewhat surprisingly, the Citroen fired into life at the first turn of the ignition, a good omen, even though the car looked to have seen better days. It was a Citroen C2 1.1i VT silver in colour, automatic transmission, with 106,000 miles showing on the clock and bearing the number plate f-AA- 229-11-oo. It had two purposes: get them safely to London and as a red herring in the form of a French left-hand drive vehicle.

It was agreed that Oscar would drive the Citroen, with Horatio and Raffer following in the Yaris – a single journey, a convoy of two. Oscar had chosen an automatic for reason of it being a left-hand drive. He'd found it easy driving the short distance to the dock area in Calais, now he was on 'our' side of the road. It was best not to complicate matters with a gear stick to contend with. The drive south down the M11 and onto the M25 was uneventful, with the mood in both cars markedly different. They sensibly stayed in the nearside lane and drove conservatively, with an unexpected high level of traffic passing them. Where were so many people going in such a hurry at such an unearthly hour of the night, or as the radio suggested early morning?

The driver in the Citroen was far from being relaxed. The whole thing had been Oscar's brainchild and obsession, but now he was the one having second thoughts. Were his concerns and apprehensions merely rational and natural jitters (as Raffer had said), of what would happen in a little less than 12 hours' time? Or was he now considering the dreadful consequences if it all went wrong and they were caught. What then? What would Doddy think? What would Fred Turnbull make of it? What would the other students think? Lastly and not least, what would his parents think and what would become of him? He tried to allay these fearful thoughts with the knowledge that they could always abort at any time; wasn't that the beauty of it all and the contingent safety net of the whole enterprise? Yet, try as he might, he could not entirely convince himself. Repeatedly, he would check his rear-view mirror to ensure his convoy of one was still following.

The mood in the rest of the convoy was paradoxically different. Horatio and Raffer were in ebullient high spirits and clearly looking forward to the drama that lay ahead. Horatio – the would-be anthropologist – was totally relaxed and philosophical about the whole escapade, assuring Raffer that it was meant to be, and a challenge that they were intellectually up to. He had no thought whatsoever of failure or any such misgiving, neither had his companion Raffer. His was a simple desire to play out a part, his love of acting, as this would be his first major role as a thespian. He'd welcomed the opportunity to dress up and apply makeup not only to himself but to the other remaining members of the cast, be it only two in number. The drive and the time together alone gave Horatio the opportunity to quiz his good friend on his sexuality.

"Raffer, you've been very open about your bisexuality and I wonder if you'd be at all offended if you would enlighten me as I really don't get it. I'm a complete ignoramus as to what makes you and others like you tick; and as part of my studies, I'd really like to know more and be better informed. If you don't want to tell me, just say so, and I'll mind my own bloody business."

"Not at all, old bean. I couldn't give a fish's tit as it fails to embarrass by a single jot (this was typical Raffer language). Let me tell you how it works with me and how I feel. You know me, I'll be totally honest, and I promise I'm not at all upset at your asking. I just don't see what all the fuss is about and it's really no big deal," he replied. "It's true, most people such as you, can't fathom a sexuality in which individuals are attracted to more than one gender. You can test the water, but you eventually must pick a side the thinking often goes. But we bisexuals don't need a label, a science, or the approval of those attracted to only one gender, to prove that we exist. In my case, I first noticed a lovely girl in sixth form. We were both fifteen. She was attractive, vivacious and made me laugh and I so enjoyed being with her. She became my sweetheart and together we found love. We eventually found our way into my bedroom for our first-ever sexual rendezvous. I gave her my virginity and I took hers, and we enjoyed every minute of it.

"The following year, I met Karl and was instantly attracted to him and I simply asked him out. Kissing him, my first male experience of erotica, it was cosmic and pure ecstasy. Did I enjoy his touches more than my sixth form sweetheart? No. They were both equally as enjoyable in their own different ways. And so, the most common question I get asked is, are you sure, and am I? The answer is short and succinct – yes, and you tell me." Horatio nodded, impressed with the candid way in which Raffer was explaining himself.

"There is such a load of stuff and nonsense with unnecessary confusion made about the concept of bisexuality. Many are 100% gay or lesbian; in other words, they are sexually and emotionally attracted only to parties of the same sex. Others are completely heterosexual, such as you, bonding in sexual and intimate relationships only with people of another sex. What about everybody else? There are a significant percentage of people such as myself, who do not fit into either of these categories, because we experience sexual and emotional attractions and feelings for people of different genders."

"Do you find me at all attractive then?" Horatio asked.

"Sorry, old bean. No, you're not my type at all. Don't get me wrong. I like you as a friend but not at all sexually desirable," Raffer replied, almost apologetically. Horatio was slightly disappointed almost miffed with the answer but couldn't understand why; an odd and curious but not an uncommon reaction, or so Raffer tried to reassure him.

"Being intimate with someone of the same sex doesn't mean you're gay, just like being intimate with someone of the opposite sex doesn't mean you're straight. It just means I fall somewhere in the beautiful fluid spectrum of sexuality. Many just don't get it and it can be quite tiresome trying to explain one's behaviour, current company accepted of course, old bean. By the way, we are not automatically more promiscuous than any other person – gay or straight. Admittedly, being attracted to more than one gender does provide more potential partners, but it doesn't necessarily increase one's likelihood of physically or emotionally connecting with them. Just because you have a refined and eclectic taste for wine, it does not make you an alcoholic. By the same token, being bisexual does not make one greedy. Furthermore, being attracted to both men and women doesn't have anything to do with commitment. I have a healthy sexual appetite and imagination, but I still define myself as a bisexual even though I have currently chosen to be with Damian. I'm also sexually attracted to Caroline, both of them in the same study group, which I must confess is a problem. So, whatever you may think, we have our own standards, and we are not so-called tarts. Like it or not, us bisexuals are here to stay. Does that help at all?" Raffer ended.

"Yes, it does, it helps a great deal and I thank you for your candour. What do your parents think?"

"Well, this is one area where I'm not quite so honest. I think they would be absolutely devastated to learn that I'm currently bedding a darn good rugby player! They know I'm a bit arty farty, but put it down to my theatrical leaning, so for the time being it's best kept a secret. I know my sister, Rosemary, is suspicious, but as we don't see each other that often I can continue to live a double life. At least for the time being, I intend to keep it that way."

Horatio had found Raffer's explanation and frankness most enlightening. Up until then he'd no real comprehension of what he'd so openly admitted. To him, the very thought of being in bed with another man was quite abhorrent and not at all natural or desirable. However, he'd listened, and he'd learnt. After all, it was he that had asked the question, and only right and proper that he tried to understand his friend's odd sexuality as best he could, which now he did – somewhat.

After a period of silent driving, Raffer then confessed his real dilemma and concern: should he ever marry, to whom and what gender? However, for the time being he was content and determined to make his way in the world of thespianism. For the time being, playing many parts seemed to him the most natural thing in the world.

Horatio was impressed by the logical pragmatism espoused by Raffer, and the way he had clearly come to terms with his sexuality, seeing it as an asset rather than a liability. He'd only met Raffer on a few previous occasions and was amazed anyone could be so open to an almost stranger. He then saw Raffer for what he truly was: an intelligent, confident, good-looking young man who accepted and used his bisexuality to his advantage, genuinely feeling blessed in having the best of both worlds. What he did off stage was his business, as long as he performed well on it, with not too many asides.

"Well, now you know all about me, what pray does the aloof and rather distant Horatio Benedict Charteris get up to behind locked bedroom doors, I wonder?" Raffer jokingly asked in a good-natured way.

Just then a police car went screaming past with blue light a flashing. Was this a good or bad omen, but more likely a motorway accident? Raffer had been discerningly accurate in his question-come-statement. Horatio was, without a doubt, an enigma, an unknown quantity and noted throughout King's for his private and reserved modus operandi. He was the sort of person you could spend an entire evening with and learn little. He was neither rude nor forthcoming. He came across as someone who rarely expressed an opinion, as if fearing being dragged into an unwanted conversation.

"Well, for a start, I'm heterosexual and I've never had the slightest inclination to kiss another man, let alone fancy him. Mind you, Raffer, with that French outfit and makeup on, I've bedded less attractive women. That said, my libido and sex life is not mundane but rather boring by comparison from what you've described to me. Yes, I've got a girlfriend. It's a protracted relationship which isn't going anywhere. We've long had regular sex, but not that good, exciting or particularly satisfying. To be honest, our relationship, if one can call it that, has only perpetuated by my being away at Cambridge and seeing each other on term breaks. I'm sure it will fizzle out when I graduate and clear off on my world travels. I don't see Rebecca as part of my long-term plans, not that I've told her so, but she must surely have guessed. Anyway, she has her own future to pursue as a doctor; an aspiration which she has admitted is proving increasingly demanding and difficult. I'm sure that the parting of waves will be good for both of us, but we'll see.

"I currently have my eye on Helen Williamson…yes, the one in your drama group. Perhaps you could put a good word in for me? …No, I haven't asked or approached her as yet, with this being our last year and all that. I thought it best to get this little adventure behind us first, but I do like her. When this is all over, you could casually introduce us, maybe? Well, that's sorted us two out, what do we make of our leader?" Horatio ended.

"Well, old bean, I don't think Oscar has a girlfriend, well, not to my knowledge, but I do believe he's straight. His mind seems set on finishing at King's and going onto Harvard. No doubt we'll see and hear of him in years to come as a highly successful barrister, or alongside us in prison," Raffer joked.

"Raffer, that's not at all funny, will you please resist jesting about it! I'm only here because we made the plan fool proof or as near fool proof as possible, with always the option of bailing out if things go awry, which I'm sure they won't. Remember, it was me that initially poured cold water on the whole enterprise, and then it was both of us who identified the obvious weaknesses, before coming up with a better plan. It was only then that I was persuaded it would be a fun wheeze. Remember, we still have the critical task to do of selecting a suitable drop point when we get down there. As Oscar rightly pointed out, it's a once-in-a-lifetime opportunity to do something really outrageous and daring, then to store it in the back of our memory banks for the rest of our lives. If I thought for one moment that we'd end up being caught and in prison, then I would not be sitting here in this car I can assure you of that," Horatio replied emphatically.

As planned, they turned off the already busy M25 and into the short stay car park at Terminal Three of Heathrow airport, finding a quiet row furthest from the entry and departure entrance. The time was 5:45 am, everything was going to plan. Oscar had earlier thought of stopping at a service station, if only for a comfort break and perhaps some hot liquid refreshment. He'd wisely decided against it. They could have been spotted and remembered, no matter how unlikely. Anyway, it was not part of the agreed plan. *We must keep strictly to the agreed plan*; he admonished himself for even thinking of such a deviation; he had regained his calmness and composure.

Separately, they made their way into the terminal building. They had sensibly decided against the slightest of risk of being seen together. They had picked the arrivals area as a suitable place to while away the hours up until lunchtime. There in the spacious concourse they could allow themselves the luxury of sitting having a tea or coffee together, or separately. No one was interested in them; everyone had their own agenda.

Arrival terminals are bustling, light, air-conditioned venues for happy reunions and drivers holding up cards with names of a passenger they are meeting. People continually wander some vacant looking with trolleys and suitcases in the hope of finding the right desk or person. The occasional businessman will hurry past with a briefcase and suit over his arm, striding purposefully and knowing exactly where he is going. Everyone is different, each with their own reason for being in such a place; even the little black lady with her trolley and assorted mops, buckets and cleansing agents, going into one of the numerous toilets. None are the slightest bit interested in the three young men talking with expensive polystyrene cups of coffee in hand; they were not part of their world.

The morning passed uneventfully but oh so slowly. They had drunk three cups of either tea or coffee, spread sparingly over the dragging hours. Once more, and for the very last time, they had slowly gone through every step of what would happen. Once the deed was done, they would all go merrily on their separate ways to hopefully enjoy the rest of the Easter holiday. Meanwhile, the terminal now provided the ideal facility for their change in identity and persona. Raffer was the first to depart to the toilet to make the required transformation. He reappeared fifteen minutes later and was quite unrecognisable and highly attractive. Both Oscar and Horatio had to smile as they noticed a number of men turning their heads in obvious admiration. Not only did 'she' look like a French mademoiselle, but she walked like one. Raffer looked absolutely stunning! Without so much as a single sideways look or a hint of acknowledgement, 'she' made her way down the concourse to yet another Costa facility.

"Follow that if you can Horatio, or should I say, Miss Heathrow?" Oscar whispered.

"I'll try," replied Horatio as he too made his way off to the 'changing room'. When he too had reappeared, Oscar was duly impressed. Clearly, the rehearsals that Raffer had insisted upon had paid dividends. The clothes, the shoes, the wig and the lipstick would have fooled even a second and closer look. It would only be later in the Citroen that Raffer would apply the finishing touches to the makeup to both Oscar and Horatio. It was important that eyeliner, mascara and foundation creams were correctly applied, and which would pass the test of any discerning eye. Miss Heathrow disappeared to an empty bench alongside the newsagents WH Smith.

By the time Oscar appeared, it was time to make their way back to the cars, all walking and taking a different route. Back in the Citroen, Oscar congratulated them all on their wonderful and impressive appearances. The excitement and adrenalin had begun to flow, the game was on! The next 15 minutes was spent with Raffer applying the professional touches to the required makeup. He was in his absolute element; it was like being backstage waiting for the curtain to rise. All three had commented how hot the wearing of a wig was, and how did women cope for hours on end − many out of necessity. So far, they had been careful not to be seen or noticed, apart from some evident unknown admirers.

One last check on the time and it was time to go, with all the bags now in the Yaris. The hammer and screws in the front passenger floor well. Earlier, they had agreed on a change of plan as regards leaving the Citroen. It was decided to leave it in the Birnbaums driveway with two flat tyres. It would give a convincing impression that the car had picked up punctures at the worst possible time and place, forcing the gang to abandon it and make their getaway on foot. It had been Horatio's idea and agreed by all and would eliminate the problem of having to dispose of it later on. All they had to ensure was that no DNA or fingerprints were left − fingerprints and DNA of people for whom the police had no record. For some unaccountable reason, they all shook hands, with Raffer mischievously giving them both a kiss on their cheeks, which didn't seem wrong or out of place. Oscar wondered what Freud would have said on the subject.

Chapter 15

They were in position and ready to go. A small wastebin had been decided upon as the drop point. It was ideally situated near to the corner of West Heath Avenue and North End Road, only a matter of some 30 yards from the house in question. The Yaris was parked in a nearby cul-de-sac, hidden from view. The three French-looking mademoiselles sat nervously in the Citroen parked further down West Heath Avenue. It was now a matter of waiting for the departure of Mr Birnbaum. They had been in position for the past 20 or so minutes, spending the time going over the plan one last time.

During the earlier drive from Heathrow to Golders Green, Oscar had had time to reflect on what they were about to embark upon, at the same time as concentrating on the busy late Saturday morning city-bound traffic. He had never driven in London, or for that matter, anywhere near the capital, and it was certainly a different style of driving and an acquired skill, especially by the many weaving cyclists. Everyone, well, it seemed like everyone drove as if they were late or taking part in some car rally. Many times, the convoy would be split, and he'd had to pull over and slow until the Yaris regained formation. The fact he was driving a left-hand car seemed to make life all that more difficult.

He began to think of the consequences, heaven forbid, should it all go tits up. To extort a person's wealth or means of livelihood was no minor misdemeanour, especially when it involved frightening some poor old lady half to death. If apprehended, he knew they would automatically be passed from a magistrates' court, after presumably a brief and cursory hearing, onto a Crown Court to await trial. A magistrates' court carried a maximum tariff of a one-year prison sentence. The crime of kidnapping, abduction and associated blackmail rated considerably higher up the tariff of serious crimes, deserving of lengthy prison sentences which could only be meted out by a Crown Court judge.

Many months earlier (it now seemed a lifetime away), when first toying with the idea, he'd looked up the pertinent definitions; abduction, kidnapping, extortion and ransom. He wanted to know and get a feel for what each precisely meant and how they were seen from a legal viewpoint. This curiosity, he logically ascribed to his law studies; or was there also some macabre subconscious thinking at play? Whatever it was, he was not surprised by what he discovered: 'To abduct is to force someone to go somewhere with you, often using threats or violence'. He thought that more or less covered what he had in mind, until reading the definition of kidnapping. 'To kidnap is to steal, carry off, or abduct by force or fraud, especially for use as a hostage or to extract ransom'. He now knew that if caught they would be charged with kidnapping. 'To extort is to get something by force or threats, especially money or other property. A ransom is an amount of money that is demanded in exchange for someone who has been taken prisoner...'

He'd concluded that kidnapping with the aim of extorting a ransom seemed to fit exactly the bill for what he still planned to do! At the time, the definitions hadn't frightened, only confirming that what he had in mind was no game and the consequences would be devastating if caught. But he had no intention of being caught and decided not to share this knowledge with the others.

Two minutes past midday, Mr Birnbaum was seen lifting the metal hoop holding the wide three-barred oak gate in place. He stepped through and carefully replaced it. He then placed his black briefcase on the ground whilst he straightened his tie and checked the silk handkerchief in his suit top pocket. He then picked up his briefcase and set off towards the main road and Golders Green tube station. Mr Birnbaum was clearly a man of habit and routine. Five minutes and West Heath Avenue was empty and silent – presumably most other Jewish occupants were observing their religious demands?

The Citroen slowly approached and stopped, Raffer jumping out and opening the gate, allowing the car to drive in, then closing the gate. Almost immediately, Horatio was out and banging a long screw into each of the two front tyres. A few seconds later, they slowly deflated, the hammer back in the rucksack. They quickly looked around there was no sight or sound of anyone.

The three French-looking mademoiselles walked up the gravelled driveway to the front door, Oscar with a small bag in hand. The door opened almost immediately; perhaps Mrs Birnbaum had thought it was her husband returning having forgotten something? Horatio immediately jammed his foot in the door and forced his way in past the startled Mrs Birnbaum (in the normal course of events, she would have immediately replaced the security chain after her husband had left, but as she would soon be off on her shopping errand and had not bothered). The other two quickly moved inside and the door was closed. The approach and entry had all been completed in less than a minute.

Raffer and Horatio hustled the diminutive and clearly shocked Mrs Birnbaum into the lounge and placed her on an upright chair. The look of terror on her face now plain to see, as she was manhandled by three women! It was now Horatio's turn to do the talking in his best practised French-Pidgin-English.

"We will not hurt madam if she comply, comprendre?"

The trembling woman nodded, her small hand shaking and her lips quivering, the outward and evident signs of fear. Horatio indicated that she take off her rings. She was wearing two: one a wedding ring and another rather ornate one on her right little finger. She duly tried to pull them off but without success. Oscar produced his bottle of *Fairy Liquid* and this did the trick.

"Where is your insulin, Madam?"

"In the kitchen, but please, not my insulin, as I shall need it soon," she spoke for the first time.

Raffer appeared with both insulin and syringe, as Mrs Birnbaum started to cry.

"Madam, please hold like so." Horatio held his gloved hands out with palms up, as if begging. This she did, as rings, syringe and insulin were placed on them. Oscar, on his mobile, then photographed a crying Mrs Birnbaum sitting slumped in a chair with trembling hands.

"Madam, your husband's telephone number?" Horatio asked with his fingers to his face mimicking a phone, in what was good French.

"I don't know, I can't remember, it's in the book," she mumbled, pointing to the hallway table. Three numbers were found for the jewellery store, including a mobile. All three were called and the same message and photographs sent through twice, just for good measure. With the long and detailed message duly sent, all they could do was to wait for a favourable response or reaction.

1. MR BIRNBAUM YOUR WIFE HAS BEEN KIDNAPPED BUT IS SAFE AND UNHARMED. HOWEVER, YOU WILL ONLY SEE HER AGAIN IF YOU DO AS INSTRUCTED AND

IMMEDIATELY. BRING YOUR COMPLETE REPEAT COMPLETE STOCK OF RAW AND UNCUT DIAMONDS BACK TO GOLDERS GREEN. PLACE THEM IN THE SMALL WASTE BIN FIXED TO THE LAMPPOST OUTSIDE NUMBER FOUR WEST HEATH AVENUE. THEN PROCEED BACK TO THE SYNAGOGUE ON NORTH END ROAD AND AWAIT FURTHER PHONE INSTRUCTIONS.

2. IF AND WHEN WE HAVE COLLECTED THE DIAMONDS, YOUR WIFE WILL BE RETURNED UNHARMED TO YOUR HOUSE. YOU WILL THEN RECEIVE A SECOND CALL TO RETURN HOME.

3. YOU CHEATED ON YOUR DAUGHTER OVER HER FAKE RING, DO NOT BE FOOLISH ENOUGH TO TRY AND CHEAT US.

4. DO AS WE SAY AND DO NOT CONTACT THE POLICE AND ALL WILL END WELL.

5. FAILURE TO COMPLY WILL RESULT IN THE CERTAIN AND UNNECESSARY DEATH OF AALIJAH AND ENTIRELY DOWN TO YOUR ACTIONS. IF YOU HAVE ANY DOUBTS, THEN SEE PHOTOGRAPHS ATTACHED.

6. THE CLOCK IS ALREADY TICKING, BEST YOU GET MOVING AND ACT NOW AND DO EXACTLY AS INSTRUCTED.

Without another word said, Mrs Birnbaum was hustled outside and into the back seat of the Citroen. They had first paused to check the coast was clear and also to allow her to see the car and its French number plates. She was then helped into the car. It was time for Horatio's next party piece.

'Sacré bleu, pneu a' plat,' which roughly translated meant, 'bloody hell, flat tyres'. A fact he made abundantly clear by gesturing and pointing wildly towards them. It was a most convincing demonstration and one that poor Mrs Birnbaum could not possibly have missed.

The three women quickly went into a rehearsed and contrived huddle, with Mrs Birnbaum looking on from within the car. By now, she would (hopefully) have had time to have noticed a few things for herself, such as the left-hand drive, the French cigarette packet in the door side pouches, and the two A to Zs.

As if forced to make a change in plan, she was then unceremoniously pulled out of the car and escorted back into her house. This time, she was returned to the same chair and bound firmly to it by yards and yards of grey gaffer tape. Oscar was careful to ensure that it was secure but not painful in any way. An electric tie was affixed to her wrists, which firmly held the hands together. Initially, they had thought to cover her mouth with tape, but had decided against. The next-door neighbours were so far physically removed and would never hear any cries for help. Furthermore, with her diabetic condition, they didn't want to run the risk of the poor woman having trouble to breathe. What was the definition for murder?!

As it was, she did look a frail and pitiful sight. Was Oscar already having misgivings − it was too late for that now. Then for the first time, a look of steely defiance appeared in her eyes and she held her head up in act of what seemed bravery and resolve. Horatio thought of all the suffering the Jews had suffered and endured over the centuries; perhaps Mrs Birnbaum was trying to show that they would never be beaten or cowed.

"Madam we wish you no harm or ill. Your husband will be home shortly, let us hope he has done as asked." Oscar then placed his copy of the *Diamond Dealers* magazine on her lap and under her tied hands. It was open at the page and the paragraph highlighted where Mr Birnbaum had boasted of diddling his future son-in-law. Perhaps it was a lasting but deliberate memento, just on the off chance that she had never been made aware of his despicable deed and possibly the reason for todays' attack.

Oscar took one last look around to check they hadn't left anything, no clues, fingerprints or DNA. He noticed the dining room table still laid up with the candles on display. He'd read about the Jewish Shabbat being observed from a few minutes before sunset on a Friday evening until the appearance of three stars in the sky on the Saturday night. The start of Shabbat is ushered in by lighting candles and reciting a blessing. Tonight was likely to be a hive of Metropolitan police activity, with no thought given or time to go stargazing.

The three left, Mrs Birnbaum glaring after them as they hurriedly departed. Oscar locked the Citroen taking with him the keys − no point in making their task any easier, leaving the car deliberately abandoned inside the drive. They walked slowly back to the waiting Yaris. There to wait and see if Mr Birnbaum was going to do as asked.

20 minutes passed, by which time the three French mademoiselles had disappeared. The clean wipes had removed all traces of makeup and a comb had sorted out the hairstyles, now replaced by three men in jumpers and jeans. However, it was still a long wait. Then Mr Birnbaum appeared, looking hot and walking hurriedly. In his hand, he had what looked to be a small package wrapped in newspaper. He looked to check the house number and then at the lamppost receptacle, into which he carefully placed the parcel; at the same time looking round to see if he was being observed. He then turned in the direction of North End Road and towards the synagogue. It appeared as if he had done as instructed.

They waited a further five minutes before stopping a few yards past the bin. Raffer quickly retrieved the gift and away they drove – slowly. They had no way of knowing whether they had been observed or would be followed. That was in the lap of the gods.

Chapter 16

On receiving the threatening text – thrice over – Mr Birnbaum's immediate reaction was to press the panic button – but he didn't. This the direct link to the nearest police station, which just happened to be Scotland Yard. This hotline facility had been installed on the advice and recommendation of the police; it also helped in reducing his exorbitant insurance premiums.

He had read the text in a shocked and alarmed manner. He'd been in business for many years, and thought he was a good judge of character as to whether someone was bluffing or not. This one of the reasons why he was such a wealthy man – knowing when to put up and when to shut up. This message had a chillingly sinister and cutting edge to it, implying it meant what it said. How did they know about the engagement ring? Yes, he loved his wealth, but did he love his Aalijah even more, or dare to do anything that would jeopardise her safety?

He disappeared into his office and opened his private safe – its very existence and whereabouts known only to him. He'd learnt and decided very early on in life that somethings are better not shared. The hidden safe contained a number of official-looking documents laid on top of two small dark blue velvet corded pouches. Each pouch contained a small fortune in raw uncut diamonds 30 small-sized diamonds in the one, 22 much larger stones in the other. He removed ten of the larger diamonds, which he added to the other purse. He then replaced the pouch with the 12 remaining diamonds back into the safe and swung the dial. He carefully wrapped the demanded ransom of diamonds in two sheets of yesterday's copy of the *Metro* newspaper.

On reaching the door, explaining to the staff that he had to nip home for an hour or so, he had a change of heart. He returned to his office and opened the safe and quickly emptied the remaining diamonds into an envelope, which he then hid in a concealed desk drawer (another secret), replacing the now empty pouch back into the safe and locked it. He then left without further explanation, clutching his valuable paper-clad parcel.

Having deposited his package in the designated waste bin, Mr Birnbaum turned and headed for the Synagogue, exactly as instructed. His only slight deviation from the exacting texted instructions was to quickly glance up and down the avenue. There was no one in sight, apart from a solitary car parked further down the avenue and a cat that was on its way home. The sweating Mr Birnbaum had been in the synagogue but a few minutes, when, true to the texted message, he received a short simple missive: *'Merci, maintenant de rentrer á l maison'* (thank you, now go home). He rightly guessed what the French words meant.

Ten minutes later, Mr Birnbaum entered his home to find his wife bound and slumped in the chair. She looked to be asleep, the chin down and resting on her chest, if not asleep then certainly drowsy and in need of her next insulin injection. The look of relief in their eyes said it all. Released and injected, Aalijah Birnbaum looked another person, appreciably brighter and more with it. Mr Birnbaum then telephoned the police and waited…

Three minutes later, he received a call to say that a police team would be with them shortly.

As good as their word, four minutes later, they arrived. Detective Chief Inspector Brian Younger introduced himself, "I'm the investigating officer and will be leading on this one…"

Mr and Mrs Birnbaum looked at each other thinking much the same, as Mr Birnbaum quipped, "In name and looks also."

The DCI smiled, giving them one of those polite but tired old-fashioned looks, as if to say, how many times have I heard that before.

"Firstly, can we go into a room that the intruders didn't visit, there I can hear your first-hand account of what happened…yes, the dining room would be fine." They moved three chairs away from the candle-set table.

"Right, Mrs Birnbaum, if you will, from the very beginning. When we've finished, I'll need you both to come to the Yard and then record it all again."

"It will have to wait until Shabbat has finished, you understand?" Looking at her husband for support.

"I understand." Clearly, the DCI knew of the strong Jewish community in and around Golders Green, probably why he was such a young DCI!

Both the DCI and Mr Birnbaum sat attentively as Mrs Birnbaum related her story from when the intruders had forced their way in… "So in conclusion, all I can tell you is that they were three French women, one wearing a purple thong, which I noticed when she bent over. After they'd shoved me into the back seat, their discovery of the flat tyres came as a real surprise, and I could tell that they were not at all happy. That's when they bundled me back into the house, thank God. Apart from that, there isn't much more to tell, except they all wore expensive foreign-looking gloves and attractive masks that you sometimes see in films or on television. So, I didn't get a really good look at any of their faces, but they were all young and attractive from the little I could see."

"Thank you, Mrs Birnbaum, you've been extremely helpful, and that will do for the time being. If you will let us know when you are available to come and give a full statement, I will send a car for you and your husband. In the meantime, I've arranged for one of our recovery vehicles to collect the Citroen, which hopefully might help us with our enquiries. In the meantime, our forensic team will continue with their work in the hope of finding some fingerprints or DNA, although I'm not hopeful from what you have told me. Can I also have your mobile phone, Mr Birnbaum, and I have one further request. I hope you won't mind if we don't make this public with either the press or the media. The less information the kidnappers know the better… Yes, we'll also be giving you a 'Crime Reference Number', Mr Birnbaum, in order that you can inform your insurers. May I ask, strictly in confidence, did you hand over all of your stock of diamonds, and can you remember precisely how many?"

"I handed over my entire stock, and yes, of course I know exactly how many there were. I had thought for one brief minute of keeping some of them back, but my wife's safety was the most important thing to me, and so I decided to do exactly as they instructed. You will let me have my mobile back once you've done and extracted everything that you possibly can; it's an expensive one?"

"Yes, of course, Mr Birnbaum. You did the right thing as this sounds to be the work of a ruthless and professional ring of women operating from the other side of the channel. We've already informed all ferry ports and airports to be on the lookout for them. It all depends on how much of a problem the punctures and the lack of a car has had on their plans. With luck, they may still be holed up somewhere in this country."

Chapter 17

Arriving home for all three was a very different experience, each handling the day's traumatic events in their own particular way.

Horatio had caught the tube to Waterloo and the next mainline train to Ramsgate. He was spoilt for choice, with various options available, St Pancras, King's Cross and Charing Cross, all providing a regular service to the south coast, for a less than two-hour journey. It was early Saturday evening when he arrived home. The euphoria and excitement of the day's adventure already replaced by a feeling of emptiness, together with a puzzling mixture of anti-climax, guilt and disappointment.

It was always good to see his folks again but staying at home now held little attraction. His parents knew this and fully expected that this would be but a fleeting visit. His brother had moved out. Tristram had taken to county cricket like a duck takes to water, although he wasn't looking to score many ducks! He now shared a house with three others of the team's regular first 11 players. It was true that it had all gone exceedingly smoothly with no real slip ups or deviations from the plan. Yet, throughout the journey home, the thought of the frightened and pitiful Mrs Birnbaum, sitting trussed and bound, niggled, weighing heavily on his mind. Thankfully, the family had cheered up the so-called budding and brilliant anthropologist, as they now ribbed him. Perhaps after a goodnight's sleep, he would feel a lot better, and ready to enjoy the rest of the Easter break.

Horatio's parents had thoughtfully invited a few friends around for a barbecue the next day, with his longstanding girlfriend, Rebecca, amongst them. They both knew their relationship was withering on the vine, and he had no intention of having his wicked way. This would be taking unmerited and selfish advantage – both as physical and mental release valves – in more ways than one.

Having only been home a matter of hours, and already he wished himself back at King's, absorbed in the fascinating subject which he had so enjoyed studying. He wondered whether the subconscious spectre of the Golders Green ghost would persist, as he progressively and increasingly felt uneasy and ashamed of what they had done. Now, thinking back, he'd only been finally persuaded by Oscar, when at the time he remembered saying, 'against my better judgement'. Both he and Raffer had only been won round and lulled into being convinced it would be something to remember in years to come when in their dotage. On reflection, and in the harsh light of day, it had been nothing more than a dastardly deed, conceived and carried out by three self-opinionated university brats. It was a crime committed for own grandiose intellectual superiority, with scant regard to the feelings of their victims.

There also remained his doubts regarding the French language used in the follow-up text messages. Would this be seen by the police as a slip up, or just another clever ploy? Thinking about it, it did seem a rather odd thing to have done, having given such detailed instructions in English. Anyway, it was too late now, the deed was done. It was going to be a long Easter recess, Horatio thought, at the same time wondering what his family and friends would think if they knew what he'd been doing. Indeed, how would he react if placed in their shoes? Before retiring for bed, he remembered to look out his passport.

Raffer had also taken the underground back into central London. They had both agreed to proceed independently, a logical ploy – safety in a lack of numbers. He was lucky, having only five minutes to wait before catching the next Paddington to Penzance West Country service, which stopped at Plymouth and Truro. It was late Saturday evening before he finally arrived home.

Unlike Horatio, he had had no such qualms about the day's adventure. It had provided the opportunity to do a little play-acting and no one had got hurt. From the article which Oscar had shown them from the *Diamond Dealers* magazine, this Birnbaum was a bit of a shit and perhaps he'd got his rightful come-uppance. Furthermore, there remained the added attraction of a visit to Amsterdam in the not-too-distant future; that's if all three going wasn't considered too risky. He certainly didn't experience any guilt or disappointment. As far as he was concerned, it was another tick in life's box and a thing of the past.

His parents must have been pleased to see him, not that it was readily apparent or obvious; they were by nature a quiet and undemonstrative couple. They could just be tired, having had a very busy day in their garden centre in keeping with the start to the Easter holidays. However, his sister, Rosemary, entered into the spirit of her brother's homecoming, with her own show of mischief by introducing him to her best friend, Susan. To which there was a predictable – not interested cold shoulder.

The following day (Sunday), he phoned a couple of his chums who worked backstage in two of London's West End's biggest and longest-running productions – *War Horse* and *Les Misérables*. Both friends had promised him that he could come up and see what went on behind the scenes and witness first-hand how things really worked. And if he promised not to get up to any hanky-panky, he could doss down in their flats for a few days.

That, Raffer thought, would take care of the first few days. He would then return home to spend a few days with his family, just to show willing. Something else would crop up, it always did. Raffer was one of those types of people around which things seemed to happen.

Arriving home for Oscar was a traumatic experience. As his trusty Yaris entered the long private road, over a hundred yards in length, accommodating five large and impressive houses, he could see two parked police cars! His immediate reaction was one of panic. For some inexplicable reason, he thought they were waiting for him! He calmed down and logically concluded this was impossible and there must be some other reason.

His parent's house was his mother's pride and joy, and his father's status symbol. As he approached the front door, the scene was one of utter devastation. He was met by his father and a senior-looking police officer.

"Hello, son, we tried to get hold of you on your mobile but there was no answer," his father began.

"Hi, Dad, what the devil's happened?"

"The house has been completely ransacked, and the bastards that did it, then left the taps running! The house is a complete wreck," a distraught and angry Mr Ormsby-Waite vented.

"Could I have a private word with your son, sir?"

"Yes, of course, officer, by all means."

The uniformed policeman (Oscar thought an inspector, although not sure), guided him back down the red-gravelled driveway, whilst a despondent-looking Mr Ormsby-Waite stood, gazing at his ruined home.

"Can I explain what's happened, sir, as I'm afraid your parents are not really up to it at the moment. Apparently, they've been down in London for the past two days, some special treat, from what I can understand, seeing a couple of shows and doing the normal sightseeing. When they arrived home this lunchtime, they found the house under water and burgled! Unfortunately, this is the familiar departing trademark of a professional gang that has been operating successfully throughout the Midlands for a number of years. Not only do they clean out properties, always at the upper end of the market, they then vindictively let them flood. When they've taken everything what's wanted, every basin and bath plug are inserted, and all taps turned full on. It doesn't take long for ceilings to collapse, with water continuing to fill the house. As you will shortly see, it's a real mess and any chance of finding any fingerprints is absolutely zilch, as is the realistic prospect of nabbing them.

"Number Eight has also been burgled but for some unusual reason it's been spared the 'water treatment'. Be assured, no one is going to be living here for quite a long time to come," the messenger of doom concluded.

"Thank you, Officer. I'd better go and find Dad."

"Where's Mum?"

"She's next door with Mrs Willcox, who has very kindly offered to put us up for the next few days until I can sort out other alternative accommodation. Her husband's away in Norway on a business trip and won't be back for another week or so. If the truth be known, I think she is looking forward to having our company," his father replied, still in shock.

Next door was not exactly next door. It required a 20-yard walk further along the road and up a lengthy driveway to another large, secluded property, hidden by a barrier of fir trees on three sides. Oscar had briefly met Mrs Willcox once before, and that was when they had moved in. He'd never met Mr Willcox, who apparently spent half of his time commuting backwards and forwards to Stavanger and Bergen. He was some senior executive for one of the oil companies. It was a well-paid position but with a far from satisfactory home life.

"Dad, how come you and Mum were both away, I can't remember the last time. I really can't."

"You're right, son, and now you can see why! We knew you wouldn't be arriving home until tonight, as you'd already kindly informed us so a few weeks past. Not many sons are as thoughtful or as well-organised as you, Oscar. So, I decided to take the rare opportunity of treating your mother to a couple of days down in London. She's always wanted to see some of the shows, and we could take in the usual sights at the same time, which we've never seen or done. I splashed out somewhat, well, we can afford it, staying at the Ritz and making a real do of it. It all went splendidly, and we had a great time, both shows were amazing, until arriving home this afternoon to be met by this lot. We opened the front door to find utter chaos and destruction, a high price to have had to pay for two enjoyable days away. Your mother's vowed never to step foot inside the house again, and that's not counting the irreparable damage done with the loss of so many personal items. Yes, we can replace the furniture and carpets but not the family jewellery and photographs, presumably which they nicked because of the solid silver frames they were in − the bastards!"

Oscar listened to his father's sad story, thinking that the fickle finger of fate has on occasions a funny way of throwing the dice or dealing the cards. What were the chances of their son committing a robbery-come-kidnapping on the very same day that his own house was also being broken into? Most self-respecting bookmakers would lay odds in excess of a million-to-one. Oscar couldn't get his mind around the double event, despite not being able to share his incredulity with either his father or the police officer! It was not the happiest of home comings, and after the earlier event, it left Oscar bemused and feeling inwardly guilty.

Oscar made the solitary walk to next door, leaving his father to fester and fume, only to find his mother in a dull state of despair. Earlier, Mrs Willcox had phoned the local health clinic, asking that the on-call GP pay a visit, even though it was an Easter Saturday. Having had the situation explained, the duty locum agreed to come to the house. In the event, some suitably strong sedatives had been prescribed, which one of the constables had been despatched to collect. Having consoled her with a hug and a kiss, there was little more he could do, apart from thanking Mrs Willcox for the offer of a bed. He, therefore, re-joined his father to add a willing hand, not that they could do much.

Mr Ormsby-Waite had tried as best he could whilst wading through water, to try and compile a list of items taken, but it was a hopeless task and best abandoned. The house had been virtually cleared, reflecting the workings of a professional gang including jewellery, television, computer, laptop, ornaments, alcohol, furniture, Chinese carpets, Persian rugs and even clothing. It was by now getting dark as too was the house. The water had ingressed into the electrics, shorting everything out. Oscar had sensibly suggested his father's time would best be spent arranging for a skip and a clean-up gang to come the following morning – double time for Sunday work should be sufficient enough inducement.

His father nodded dutifully and disappeared off to make the necessary calls. This gave the police officer the opportunity to advise Oscar on what happened next.

"Sir, the first thing we need to do is allocate a 'Crime Reference Number' (presumably in exactly the same way Mr Birnbaum would have been given one!). You will also be given contact details of the investigating officer, who will provide regular updates whilst the investigation is ongoing. You'll need to give your crime reference number whenever you get in touch. But not wishing to be too pessimistic, I have to warn you that the chance of any recovery is slim to remote. I shouldn't really tell you this, but I think it's better you know the facts, rather than your family get up any false hopes. The way in which the house has been systematically cleared strongly indicates the work of the professional gang I mentioned earlier."

"Thank you, Officer, I appreciate your candour, it's what I thought you'd say, and I agree, it's far better to know the true position. I'm up at Cambridge in my final year of studying law, and we've had lectures on this very subject and more importantly the worrying aftermath. From what we were told, about a quarter of the victims subsequently move house and over half of them never feel secure in their homes again, taking at least seven or more months to return to some level of normality – if ever. As expected, the loss of sentimental values is the most distressing, as they are irreplaceable. Also, the feeling that your home and space has been violated or in some way tainted can make for some never feeling safe again."

"Sir, you've got it absolutely spot on, in fact what you've just said is virtually a textbook answer. It's true, the emotional upset at being the victim of crime causes most outpouring of grief. The loss of sentimental goods far outweighs the loss of practical items, including money. Photographs and family heirlooms prove the most distressing items, as you've intimated."

"Thank you, Officer, you've cheered me up no end." To which they both laughed at Oscar's half-hearted attempt at trying to make light and show some spark of humour.

It was gone 10 pm when the police finally departed, with father and son returning next door, only to be greeted by Mrs Willcox, saying that she had put Mrs Ormsby-Waite to bed. Apparently, the prescribed sedatives had done the trick and she had not resisted the advice that a good night's sleep would do her the world of good. This turned out to be good advice for all. Oscar began to feel the pangs of guilt.

Meanwhile, at t'other end of country, the situation was a far happier state of affairs. Doddy had duly arrived and was thoroughly enjoying his Easter walking and sexual sabbatical (perhaps it should be sexual and walking); with his feet now firmly under the table – and in bed!

Having been met at Keswick by the Pilkingtons, he'd partaken of his customary welcoming meal of roast beef and Yorkshire pudding. Later, over a coffee, and in a patently false and over-casual (far too casual) and somewhat coy manner, he'd asked, if Violet was and would be still available for cleaning duties.

The Pilkingtons of course knew exactly what the 'arrangement' was and the long-established status quo that existed. However, these churchgoing, lovely but far from prudish paragons of virtue, enjoyed playing devil's advocate and going along with Doddy's so-called secret.

"Dunstan, I do believe you've got me there and I'm not sure that I know. You'll need to enquire at *The Poacher* when we finish our walk in the morning," said Eunice.

Pilkington had responded with delicious devilment in a glib but plausible white lie. Needless to say, all concerned knew, apart from Doddy, that Violet would be next door when they returned home.

"Yes, I'll do that," Doddy replied, a little disappointed.

It was midday when Doddy entered his cottage, his first walk of the year around Bassenthwaite Lake complete. The Pilkingtons had enjoyed the walk, knowing full well what surprise lie in store for their long-time and much adored cerebral guest. The landlord at *The Poacher Inn* had played along with the game and was not sure what Violet's arrangements were outside of the pub.

Violet was hiding in the kitchen with a hot cup of tea to welcome him back. The look of sheer delight on Doddy's face was a picture. This and the considerable thoughts he'd had over the past few weeks had been well founded. He'd come to realise that he missed both the Lake District and Violet more than he had realised.

After a hurriedly drunk cuppa, the reunion-come-union was hurriedly completed. It was almost a dead-heat as to who was undressed and in bed first – it was time for Doddy to go mountaineering! He, fondly, in both senses of the word, reacquainted himself with K1 and K2, before eventually finding his way into basecamp!

After a short but thoroughly exhausting session of lovemaking, they both lay still, recovering from their physical exertions. Well, after all, it had been a year since the last time. It was then that Doddy shared his deep and measured thoughts with Violet. Her squeals of delight and surprise must surely have been heard all around Bassenthwaite Lake, which by the way is the only lake…Whereupon she placed one of his very large hands back on K1 or it could have been K2!

Needless to say, the Pilkingtons were absolutely dumbfounded but delighted with what Doddy had to say. Furthermore, the accompanying offer was one they could and would not wish to refuse. By the time Doddy had returned to King's, he'd achieved far more than he'd ever have thought possible.

"We've been in touch with Aunt Gertie, and she's magnanimously agreed to put all three of us up until we get ourselves sorted with something more permanent," his mother said the next morning.

Oscar didn't like his father's sister, few did. She was one of those people that seemed to irritate and annoy, probably why she was such a miserable old bat of a spinster, his father often said.

The word 'permanent' inferred a move and meant a new home elsewhere. His mother had made it abundantly clear that she would never step inside this house again, and that was that – end of debate. Oscar had in the meantime luckily retrieved his passport.

Chapter 18

Without having planned or previously considered it, all three arrived back at King's on the Sunday. This being a full two days before the final Easter term officially began on the following Tuesday (26 April), completing on Friday the 16th of June. The award ceremony for the degrees would take place the following Friday. Then it would be out into the big wide world – perhaps. So, what better place to have a private powwow than out on the Cam?

Horatio automatically took the pole and punted them out into the centre of the river, which was exceptionally busy. It would seem that a fair percentage of students had returned to the college early for a number of reasons; lack of cash, time to prepare for the next term, or complete work which should have already have been completed. This was also partly true of Oscar, Horatio and Raffer, but this rendezvous was not to discuss law, anthropology or drama.

Oscar began by explaining the shock at returning home and the subsequent course of events. One night with Aunt Gertie had been quite enough, who he compared to a rottweiler, and a nasty rottweiler at that, and had made his excuses to visit friends, leaving his poor Ma and Pa to suffer her continual nagging and moaning.

"But it did get me to thinking of the upset it had caused to my family and what we in turn had done to Mrs Birnbaum. I must confess to feeling more than a tinge of guilt. A guilt which has not gone away, in fact it's increased, I'm sorry to say."

"Don't feel sorry, Oscar, I've been very much of the same disposition and mind," replied Horatio from the till.

"Well, I'm damned if I do, old beans. I think that Birnbaum chap was a right shit and I bet his other half was not that impressed to read of his daughter's engagement ring scam," Raffer said with feeling. "Anyway, I've not heard a single blip in the media or a single printed word. So, we achieved what we set out to do and committed the perfect crime. Once we've been to Amsterdam, the charities will benefit. So, we can now get on with our studies and put it behind

120

us as one hell of a wheeze. I must say we all did look the part. I saw at least half a dozen fellas giving me the glad eye and at you two also," Raffer concluded.

"I'm not sure it's as simple as all that, Raffer. What say you, Horatio?"

"I tend to agree with you, Oscar, but obviously Raffer doesn't have the same hang up or conscience that we two seem to have, which makes what I'm going to propose all the more difficult and possibly unpalatable and hard to accept or swallow for Raffer here," Horatio added.

"What are you trying to say, old bean? You're both making me feel a teeny-weeny bit nervous, I hope I don't smell cold feet and the like," Raffer added.

"What I'm saying is that Oscar's home experience and the damaging affect it's had on his mother and Mrs Birnbaum, for that matter, does not sit at all comfortably with me."

"That's only because you're up to your neck in all that anthropology nonsense. It'll wear off in a matter of weeks, you see if I'm not right, old bean," Raffer enthused, whilst inwardly alarm bells were ringing.

"I'm not sure that it will," added Oscar. "Go on, Horatio, what were you going to say?"

"I suggest that we use the next 12 weeks to complete our studies and review how we feel about our crime, and then decide what to do for the best."

"What do you mean, what to do for the best? Surely, it's as plain as the nose on your face. We curtesy and collect our degrees, say thank you King's for three glorious and fruitful years, and I'll say cheerio to my numerous boyfriends and girlfriends, and then we'll all poke off and get on with the rest of our lives. Well, that's certainly what I intend to do," Raffer almost shouted.

"I'm afraid I'm with Horatio on this. I know it was my brainchild in the first place and I'm prepared to accept full responsibility. I'm not sure I can live with the guilt, that's all I'm saying," said Oscar.

"That's all you're saying. Hand yourselves in, do not collect 200 pounds and go straight to jail! They'll throw the keys away on you two. I am telling you one thing, I'm not confessing or going into any prison, it would kill me and probably my parents. It would ruin your lives and for what? Whatever you two old beans decide I'm out and I can assure you the next 12 weeks will not change my mind one iota. If it's still your intention to throw away successful careers, that's entirely up to you. I, for one, will make sure that I have alternative arrangements in hand," Raffer said, with finality.

It went very quiet in the punt, with none of the three looking at all happy. There was no point in pursuing the discussion further, it seemed fairly clear which way the wind was blowing for all three, with one of them blowing hot and in quite a different direction.

Doddy had also returned to King's on the Sunday, as was his custom. This year it had been more of a wrench to leave Cumbria, the foothills and slopes of K1 and K2. However, this time all would be different, and he'd left a very happy Violet and indeed Pilkingtons back in Bassenthwaite. His first and immediate task had been to slip an invitation card under the doors of all his students, requiring their presence in his rooms at 9 am on Tuesday for a final term 'Way Ahead Get Together'.

Cometh the hour and cometh the day, all nine law undergraduates were assembled in his room. It was clear that the previous term and the recess had not been completely uneventful for some. Two had bronzed faces, the result of exotic holidays spent further afield. Then there was Marie-Jo with a definite bump! She proudly informed them all she and Sebastian (unashamedly holding her hand) were engaged, and they would both be returning to the United States after graduation.

"My father is going to take on Seb in his law firm, and they've been wonderful about everything." Everyone clapped, even Doddy, who didn't necessarily approve of the order in which things seemed to occur in modern times. Oscar decided not to regale them of his parents' burglary or of his successful kidnapping and ransom, and that in his room he had a velvet purse containing a large number of raw uncut diamonds of many sizes.

"Well, whatever you've all been up to, you now need to focus 100 per cent on the next 12 weeks. The small light at the end of the tunnel I mentioned two and a half years ago is now much nearer and larger. What you don't need is to be hit by a train or get derailed at this late stage. Apologises for the poor play on words, but my mind has grown lazy whilst walking in the Lake District.

"I also have some news for you all, which I'm now at liberty to divulge having spoken to the vice chancellor and senior members of the staff." The mention of the vice chancellor was the spur for all of them to look up and listen attentively. This was something not always akin to undergraduates – paying attention.

"This too will be my final term at King's. I've decided at the age of 60 to call it an academic day. I'm going to retire back to the Lake District with my photographs, visitors' book and music collection. There I will enjoy Wagner without the worries of the likes of you lot. Who, I have to say, have been a marvellous bunch of scallywags." They all cheered and clapped spontaneously. It was a genuine show of affection and deep respect for someone who was liked and admired throughout the college.

"Therefore, lady with child, and gentlemen, we require that all of us to give it our best in this final dash to the finishing line. There, you will receive your well-earned and deserved degrees and we can all then get on with the rest of our lives, down whatever paths they may lead." Oscar smiled to himself, not at all sure of what path down which he would be heading.

Back in Birmingham, Oscar's parents were slowly coming to terms with the disaster that had befallen them. 'Mr O-W' had tried to placate and reassure his wife that it could have been worse. If they'd been lying in bed asleep, they could have had their heads bashed in or even killed (he knew this line of reassuring was far from the truth, as the police had told him that the house would have been watched). Mrs O-W remained true to her word and had no intention of returning to her once wonderful home. In the meantime, the few remaining possessions had been removed, dried and placed in storage. The house would need to dry out before a complete redecoration was undertaken with new ceilings and so forth. It would then be placed on the market for circa £1.8 million.

The elapsed time allowed Mr O-W to return to his jewellery business whilst Mrs O-W went house or bungalow hunting. The urgency with which she went a lookin' was surprisingly met with Mr O-W's approval. He wanted to spend the least possible amount of time with his sister. Fortunately, they found (she found) the quintessential chocolate box bungalow-come-cottage not far from the Malvern Hills. Admittedly, it meant a longer commute to work for Mr O-W into Hockley and his firm, but it could only be a once or twice a week visit.

"Alfred, it's called delegation," his wife, Winifred, would advise, with more than just a subtle hint.

To their credit, the police had kept them informed, if only to inform them that no progress had been made. "In the meantime, we can only suggest you go ahead with your insurance claim."

"What price do you put on a family photograph?" she asked, but not unkindly. Although it was painful to pass by their 'old house', they did so in order to visit Mr and Mrs Willcox. They'd taken them a beautiful bouquet of flowers, a crate of decent champagne and a selection of very expensive liquor chocolates. It was a small thank you for a neighbour who was no longer one, but who had come to their rescue in their hour of need. Mr Willcox remarked that he'd missed all the fun. Fun it certainly had not been, although the poor unfortunates at Number Eight had decided to remain put. At least they'd been spared the water treatment.

In no time at all, they'd purchased the chocolate box and moved in. It gave Mrs O-W the excuse or indeed necessity to refurbish completely. The shopping spree to end all shopping sprees was a great panacea and it was amazing to see how such painful memories slipped to the back of Mrs O-W's mind. Mr O-W's only stipulation was no more trips to London – well, not in the foreseeable future.

In 14 West Heath Avenue in Golders Green, all was not well. It was very far from well. The traumatic experience Mrs Birnbaum had undergone had been handled by a strong-willed and very determined woman. No Type 1 insulin-dependent diabetic or kidnapped victim was going to be beaten or get the better of this Jewish matriarch.

In fairness, the Metropolitan police had done all that was reasonably expected and could not be faulted in anyway, as they had had little or nothing to go on. This, however, was not entirely the case with Mr Birnbaum, who certainly could be faulted or at least questioned!

The Birnbaums were not a happily married couple and it had long been anything but, rather a case of a respectable veneer when viewed from the outside. In truth, it had never been a happy marriage, and like so many, it had endured for the sake of their daughter. Except her daughter was no longer at home, having married her longstanding boyfriend and they had gone to live back in Israel, in the attractive part of Haifa. Mrs Birnbaum was shortly to join them! Not that Mr Birnbaum was aware of her intended geographical move.

It had not been the kidnapping or the paying of the ransom in diamonds that had broken the already brittle marriage, but rather the *Diamond Dealers* magazine left by the French Mademoiselles. She was incandescent with rage to learn what her husband had done to their own daughter. He'd put his own financial gain and greed ahead of any family consideration or priority. How dare he!

Well, he could enjoy Golders Green and his Hatton Garden jewellery business all on his own. She'd had enough of his blatant avarice and had accepted the genuine and loving request by her daughter and son-in-law to join them. She could have her own annex and…

Mr Birnbaum's troubles didn't stop there. Both the police and the insurance underwriters were suspicious of the exorbitant claim for loss of diamonds that he was now seeking. The problem remained, who could prove or disprove it? Only one person could, and that person had the diamonds (untouched) hidden in his sock drawer in King's College, Cambridge.

How little did Mr Birnbaum realise at the time that an idle boast that he had once foolishly made to a journalist would have such long-term ramifications and devastating effects on his life.

Chapter 19

Back at King's, Doddy had employed the services of a reputable lawyer firm based in Keswick (on the recommendation of the Pilkingtons) to sort out Violet's marital status, having explained the reason for both secrecy and expediency. At last, his many years of teaching the finer points of law could now be put to his own personal advantage – and of course Violet's.

By the end of the first week of his final term at King's, he'd completed all of his outstanding tasks. He could now sit back and wait for the fruits of his labour to ripen and drop. In the meantime, he still had Wagner and Byron to enjoy. He also noticed he was slimmer and fitter, having shed over a stone in weight during his time in the Lake District. It must have been all the walking!

During the final term, the three ex-mademoiselles saw very little of each other. Indeed, Raffer made a point of deliberately being elsewhere, with Horatio and Oscar meeting only twice to sound out each other's views. In the meantime, there had been no mention of the 'Golders Green Heist', as the police later called it. The police had stated that the trail of three French women back to France had gone cold. In truth, it was sub-zero from the word go. The subsequent police investigation was thorough, or as thorough as it could be with little or nothing to go on. Mrs Birnbaums recollection was somewhat cloudy, probably due to her needing her next dose of required insulin and being tied firmly to a chair! Her only clear and lucid recollection had been in describing the three attractive women, even down to their shapely ankles and one 'accidental' purple thong.

The police acknowledged the fact that she could still remember the registration number, which they could confirm as they still held the Citroen in their compound. Unsurprisingly, no fingerprints or DNA was found; it appeared to be the work of professionals. She did, however, think their accent came from the Normandy area, but could not be sure. Overall, the police were impressed with her honest, if limited, report.

They were, however, less impressed with the detailed report submitted by Mr Birnbaum. The amount of diamonds he claimed to have handed over was in the hundreds, which seemed an awful lot for his size of store, and his hasty insistence on being given a Crime Investigation Reference Number, in order to get onto the insurers. Perhaps Mr Birnbaum had overlooked the fact that the police would check all the other stores and gauge what the average holdings would reasonably be. It wasn't accurate, of course, but it gave a rough rule of thumb. The exact number of diamonds (held and untouched in a student's sock drawer) had dramatically increased to a fabricated number, threefold in avarice and perjured terms. The insurance actuary had agreed with the Mets' joking remark that luckily Mr Birnbaum's statement had been taken before the number and value went any higher, possibly to the value of the Koh-I-Noor! However, the police had still to take the claim seriously, in view of the kidnapping and accepting the perpetrators had been clever French whores no longer on these shores. It was his word against the authorities and impossible to disprove no matter how questionable.

Fate had also helped Oscar and Co and in a way that could not possibly have been foreseen. It was a terrorist attack carried out the very next day in the heart of London, resulting in a number of deaths. Needless to say, the emphasis and resources immediately switched from diamonds to dead bodies. Everyone deserves an element of luck, even the best laid dastardly plan.

Later, Oscar was to recount to Horatio the now famous words spoken by President Franklin D. Roosevelt [the 32nd president of the United States] at his inaugural address: '…the only thing we have to fear is fear itself'.

It was on the last Monday of term that the students were unofficially-come-officially informed of their attained degree results. The good news was that everyone had passed: as a tangible air of relief seemed to sweep through every nook and cranny of the college. Oscar and Horatio had both attained a first with honours, the word honour not lost on either. Raffer was totally content with his 2:1, as he and everyone else had long predicted.

It was the day of reckoning, the day that all three had agreed that a decision would be made, a decision that was irrevocably − firm and final. The outcome to a large extent was like Raffer's degree − predictable, if not the ensuing course of events.

Both Oscar and Horatio had been of a similar mind and affirmed their intention to make a clean fist of it and hand themselves in, but only after the graduation ceremony and having had time to give their parents the devastating news. They both logically argued and felt that by giving a full confession and the return of the diamonds, the mitigation would be strong and persuasive. They also undoubtedly knew and accepted the fact that they would be given a substantial prison sentence, but hopefully minimised with time off for good behaviour. After which they could then rebuild their lives and reputation with some measure of self-respect. As intelligent young men, they knew it would not be easy, but preferable to living under a constant cloud of guilt. They also intended to visit Mrs Birnbaum and publicly apologise, if it would help. As to how their parents would react was quite another matter.

Raffer was mortified at what he was hearing, as he listened in stunned silence, not uttering a word. After what seemed an age of tense silence, he spoke whilst looking at them with a penetrating stare.

"I had a feeling this would be your answer, old beans, even though I'd hoped and prayed that common sense would prevail. Evidently not! Well, you won't be surprised to learn that I haven't changed my mind or my view either. So, I guess we all have to do what we all have to do." With this short, succinct and prophetic statement, Raffer solemnly shook both their hands and left the room. It was typically Raffer, dramatic and with telling effect. It left Oscar and Horatio nonplussed and flatfooted, as if at a loss and what to say or do next. There was clearly no point in chasing after him, after all, hadn't they all stated that their decision was final and binding?

The following morning, Raffer missed both tutorials, with a fellow student volunteering to go and enquire after him, as to whether he was ill or indisposed for some other unknown reason. They found his room stripped bare and empty of all his personal possessions. All that was found was an envelope addressed to his parents. His tutor asked Damian (all in his syndicate appeared to know of their special relationship), if he would be so kind as to contact Raffer's parents in Truro.

His parents were totally surprised to receive such a call and completely unaware of anything untoward, instructing the college to open and read them the letter, which they duly did.

My Dearest Parents,

What I have to say will shock, sadden and disappoint. However, it needs to be aired as things are already afoot and are moving fast − I have little time.

A few weeks ago, on Easter Saturday, I was one of three who committed the Golders Green Heist (I'm sure you will hear more in the fullness of time). Since then, the other two have been subsumed by a guilty conscience and intend immediately after the graduation ceremony to hand themselves in to the police. They will go to prison of that there is no question. For my part, I cannot allow myself to be incarcerated in such an institution, for many complex reasons (Sis may have guessed). Therefore, I have no option but to make myself scarce. I believe I have the knowledge and guile (if not the wisdom) not to be found. The only downside is that I will miss you all and denied the opportunity of saying farewell properly to a wonderful family who have been so good to me and mean so much.

Selfishly, can I plead that you still attend the graduation ceremony, despite my absence (I got a 2:1, as you forecast). It is highly unlikely that I will ever be able to return home. I can only hope that in time the hurt and shame will abate sufficient for you all to think kindly of me from time to time.

I now set off down a quite different path of life than that I had hoped or indeed originally envisaged.

Your ever-loving son…
Rupert
25th April 2017

PS: Please let Rosemary have first choice of my book and music collections, which I know she has always secretly admired.

All the Fordhams could say in response was that they would of course be attending the graduation ceremony.

Raffer was never seen again. In addition to the letter to his parents, there were two other letters, one addressed to Damian, the contents of which were never made public. The third to his tutor, asking that he make his apologies for his absence at the graduation ceremony but asking that his name still be read out.

His bank account had been emptied the previous week, together with his Halifax savings; together they totalled the grand sum of £18,024. His passport had gone.

Following the usual guesses and enquiries, there was not the slightest clue or indication as to where he may have gone. Raffer enjoyed drama and he was playing out his first major starring role. Where and to whom his appreciative audience were no one knew, not even to this day. The sudden disappearance of Raffer merely added to both Oscar and Horatio's pervading sense of guilt.

Raffer may have thought his parents were only West Country yokels and not aware of the sexual goings on by their son. Well, he was wrong and wrong by a long chalk. They had been cognisant and only too fully aware of his bisexual orientation for a very long time, as was Rosemary. They had chosen not to bring it into the public domain. What good would it serve? They hoped that the career he wanted to pursue would suitably mask his physical diversity.

For Oscar, the guilty conscience had begun almost immediately on returning home. The catalyst had been witnessing the terrible effect their own burglary had had on his mother and the family. It would be an exaggeration to suggest it had ruined their life, but it had certainly resulted in dramatic consequences.

Having returned to King's, he'd wrestled with what they had done, whilst accepting that he'd given little or no consideration to the hurt and harm suffered to others. This part of the equation had been lost in his obsessive desire to plan and commit the perfect crime. How then could it be so perfect if he now felt so wretched and Horatio experiencing the same misgivings?

As the weeks passed, he tried desperately to concentrate on his studies. Yet at the back of his mind, he knew that in giving himself up – to rid and clear his conscience – would have a dramatic and adverse effect on his aspiration to practice law. The legal system demanded intelligence, honesty, integrity and ethical observance from its practitioners. It therefore made eminent sense that there were restrictions on who could apply. Ergo: to be admitted as a lawyer, required a person of good name and character. That did not mean every candidate should have a squeaky-clean background and being in trouble with the law did not mean immediate disqualification, accepting that any criminal record would need to be disclosed. It would then depend upon the nature of the offence, how long ago the offence was committed, and at what age and circumstances at the time. A minor road offence such as speeding was likely to be overlooked, but probably not kidnapping with ransom demands!

He'd also done his homework, which was now second nature to him, and had contacted the Honourable Society of the Inner Temple and the Bar (for £100, you could acquire a lifetime membership of the Inn). The Inn would then still consider applications from people with previous convictions. However, the process takes longer, as the application has to go before the Master of the Bench on the Admission and Call Committee. They, in the fullness of time, decide whether you can be admitted to the Inn. You must also complete an additional form which will ask for more details about the offence.

Oscar knew that he would need two references; he had in mind Doddy and the vice chancellor, both had known him for almost three years. He was also under no illusions, knowing that to become a barrister was going to be a formidable uphill struggle. It was a small and competitive profession. And so, it was best to be realistic, but if determined, which he was, as he was still convinced that he could yet succeed. His plan, if accepted, would be to undertake a mini-pupillage, court visits (he'd already been in one), and as much other legal experience, possibly working unpaid in a solicitor's firm or Citizens Advise Bureau and so forth.

In short, he knew the chances were slim and prospects poor, but not impossible. At least he would have something to strive for, and at least he would have regained his self-respect and cleared his nagging guilty conscience. The other major hurdle would be the anger, shame and hurt experienced by his parents when told. This he intended to do before the eve of graduation day – the fateful day. He looked forward to telling his parents a lot less than walking into the police station. It would be one occasion when he could well have done with some of Raffer's acting ability.

All of these thoughts, together with how the other two would think and react, had constantly filled and occupied his overworked mind in the days and weeks leading up to his final examinations.

Whilst Oscar had adopted a typical lawyer-type methodical brainstorming approach to the dilemma, Horatio, on the other hand, had been quite audacious in his course of actions, once having made the decision to confess. He too had suffered with a guilty conscience, whether his studies in anthropology had any bearing is impossible to say, but possible. It was also true that he had enjoyed the prank. The term prank was something the law would not agree with, especially the frightening of an old woman nearly half to death with the sole aim of extorting money. The afterthought of giving the money to charities would not wash, not at all. Abduction or kidnapping was not a prank in anyone's book. Even so, this is how Horatio had seen it. Moreover, he did not consider himself to be a criminal or a bad person, and an unavoidable stint in prison was more of an inconvenience. It was viewed by him as a mere hiccup and certainly not a terminal illness.

At least this was the impression he recited to Oscar. As to how much of it was bluster and bravado and face saving to the person who had sown the illegal seeds in the first place, is a matter of conjecture. However, it had not taken Oscar long to convince him of the right course of action, after they had graduated, that was the key timing.

With this scenario in mind, Horatio had boldly approached the head of his faculty and candidly explained, in confidence of course and hypothetically, what he had in mind. To his delight and somewhat amazement, the response was more than encouraging. At least he had a way ahead. But he too had still to feel the stings and arrows of his family.

Preparations for graduation began on the Wednesday with a full-dress rehearsal. After the rehearsal, there was a special evensong in the chapel followed by dinner in the hall. It was during the dinner that Oscar and Horatio finalised and agreed their immediate plan of action once the graduation ceremony and the buffet lunch party in the Provost's garden was over. Like would-be surgeons, they needed the amputation to be swift, clean and effective.

Chapter 20

For the parents of Oscar, Horatio and Raffer, the graduation was like the curate's egg – good in parts. The initial delight experienced soon turning to shock and despair. For the Fordham family, it had been one of despondency from the time of leaving Cornwall, knowing full well that their beloved son had disappeared off the face of the earth. They were only here to honour a plea made and in the hope of confronting his accomplices.

In the event, this is exactly what took place. Oscar and Horatio bravely arranged a tri-family eve of graduation dinner in their favourite Cambridge restaurant. This type of convivial evening very much in keeping with what many students planned. This they thought would be a suitable venue and familiar territory on which to declare all. At least the prisoners would leave on a full stomach!

The three-course dinner was eaten with little small talk, the absence of Raffer never mentioned, with two sets of parents quite oblivious of the timebomb that was shortly to explode. It was over coffee that Oscar and Horatio performed what can only be described as a double-act, explaining to a stunned table what they had done and their somewhat belated decision to confess. As the story unfolded, so the look on the parents faces changed from one of disbelief to that of anger and then to looks of agonising hurt. Initially, Horatio's father thought it some huge students' prank, until seeing his son looking shamefaced and nodding assertively. The magnitude of what they had done clear to see on both of their bowed heads and crestfallen faces. Oscar swallowed hard and tried valiantly to lead for the defence.

"We know that to even try to say sorry to you all at this stage is totally inappropriate and futile. We also accept there is little or no point in either of us trying to explain or excuse what we have done. We have had three months in which to realise the crassness of it all. It was my stupid idea in the first place and therefore I'm the most culpable and take full responsibility. We now hold our hands up and intend to take what punishment is meted out.

"Raffer made it clear that going to prison was something that he could not cope with under any circumstances. He therefore made his own decision and he's gone, with no one having a clue where he is. On our honour, we can honestly say that we don't know his whereabouts, on that we swear. Not that our honour counts for much at this moment. I know that you have now been given the letter he wrote," Oscar looked at the two Fordhams, "and so there is little more we can add. It is our intention to receive our degrees tomorrow, and then go directly to Great Cambourne and hand ourselves in at the Sackville Way Police Station. This is not how we wanted to end our time here at King's, but I'm now in danger of stating the blindingly obvious." Horatio patted Oscar on the back as he sat to a silent table of ten.

It seemed an age without a word being spoken or any movement made. It seemed that each person was slowly absorbing the dreadful information they had been given by two articulate − criminals! In reality, it was probably no longer than 20 seconds, when Oscar's father took it upon himself and stood up and responded. Mrs Featherstone (there at the family's insistence) put her arm around Mrs O-W − an act of instinctive comfort.

"Our proudest moment as parents was when Oscar received his letter of acceptance to King's, and we have fed and lived off that feeling of pride ever since. We arrived here, thrilled and excited to witness the culmination of his three years of hard slog. And what have you done? You have destroyed the very fabric of common decency and let yourself, Feathers and we your parents down in the worst possible manner. So much so, one of you has found it necessary to depart in fear of going to prison, where you two will undoubtedly go and deservedly so. I can only speak for myself, but I will not be attending the graduation ceremony, as I have not the stomach and no longer wish to call you my son. I'm at a loss to describe the hurt and shame I feel at this moment. So, if you will all excuse me, I will settle the bill and leave. Are you coming too, Winifred?"

Mrs O-W looked questioningly around the dumbstruck faces, as if seeking support or at least guidance.

"I'll be along shortly I have a few words to add." As she spoke, looking directly at her son, she continued to wipe the tears that were now running freely down both cheeks. "I have to agree with what Alfred has so cruelly expressed, but I will be there to see you graduate. I will not deprive myself of that privilege no matter how painful it now will be. I can only presume that you all feel the same having made the journey." Everyone nodded. " I'm afraid the enormity of it all is too much for me to take in and fully comprehend at this time. I thought being burgled and my home destroyed was the lowest point in my life but that pales into insignificance compared with what you have said and done. I suppose there's no point in asking why; it's too late for all that?!"

"I'm afraid it is, Mother. You best go and join Father and I'll see you all briefly tomorrow." It was the first time in her life that she turned away and rebuffed his offered kiss. It was only then that Oscar knew how deep the knife had gone in, if not fatal then damned close to the heart.

"I think enough has been said," added Mr Charteris.

By now, the restaurant had gone perceptibly quiet, with many of the tables and their occupants staring in the direction of Oscar's table. Many of the tables were the same, with parents and students enjoying their pre-graduation dinner together. They were now unwitting witnesses to a tragic melodrama that was unfolding nearby. The faces of both Horatio and Oscar were evidently familiar and known to many of the other students in the restaurant. The raised voices and the look on their faces was more than enough to tell them there was trouble at mill. Even the waiters and waitresses had stopped and were now staring at the source of the Shakespearian styled tragedy. Had it been Stratford upon Avon or a West End stage production, now would be the moment the curtain should have dropped, and the applause begin. This, however, was neither a Bard's nor a West End play, but real-life drama without cause for clapping, cheering or any encore, nor a happy ending.

As they stood to leave, Mr Fordham turned to Oscar and Horatio and bravely quipped, "I was hoping to say that it was nice to have met you two bright blades, but somehow that would be somewhat disingenuous, don't you agree, gentlemen?" He turned and left without waiting for a reply, for which there was none forthcoming. The hubbub of noise in the restaurant returned to its original level, with tables now deep in conversation. There was no prize for guessing what the general topic of was around the crowded room.

As she turned to leave, Feathers put a hand on Oscar's arm in a kind and almost reassuring way and whispered, "At least you've done the right thing, and I'm sure some good might eventually come of it all."

Oscar and Horatio walked back to the college to complete their packing of personal effects accrued over three years. They knew that in the morning when they walked down King's Parade, they would not be returning.

The graduation ceremony began early at 8.45 am, when the students gathered outside King's College Chapel in the bright morning sunshine. The 119 students (one noticeable absentee who was named as Rupert Archibald Fordham reading Drama) wearing the college gown of black and white, walked in procession out of the college, down King's Parade and into the Senate House.

As graduates about to receive an undergraduate degree, they wore the academic dress that they were entitled to before graduating; for example, most students becoming Bachelor of Arts wear undergraduate gowns and not BA gowns. Having duly arrived at the Senate House, they were presented college by college, in order of foundation recognition by the university, except for royal colleges.

The congregation of over 300 were already seated, amongst them sat three doleful families. Their solemn and glum demeanours an accurate testament to how they must have felt. It was paradoxically in total contrast to the happy expectancy that clearly enthused from the people around them. The sad ones had had a whole night to dwell and fester on what had been revealed to them. Today would see the final act of what had been a traumatic and devastating 24 hours.

Programme
The University of Cambridge Graduation Ceremony in the Senate House
Friday 23rd June 2017
This brief explanation is respectfully included for the guidance and benefit of visitors not accustomed or familiar with the protocols, Latin language and terminology used during today's ceremony, which will last two hours. Guests

are also reminded that photography is not permitted inside the Senate House and mobile phones and pagers must be switched off or muted.

—o—

The ceremony will be conducted here in the Senate House, which is now mainly used for the degree ceremonies of the University of Cambridge. It was also formerly used for the meetings of the university's Council of the Senate, and originally intended to be one side of a quadrangle, however, the rest of the structure were never completed. It forms part of the 'Old Schools Site', and it is a Grade One listed building.

The ceremony commences when the vice chancellor's procession enters, led by the Esquire Bedells – a junior ceremonial officer involved in the conferment of degrees. The title was first used in 1473 and formally recognised in the University statutes by Edward VI in 1549.

All stand.

When the vice chancellor and his deputy reach their place on the dais, the audience sits. The university officers, by tradition, remain standing. The ceremony itself begins when the proctors cross the house and take their place on the dais, leaving their Statute Books.

After welcoming visitors, the Senior Proctor proposes any special graces relating to individual graduands (a person who is about to receive an academic degree). After each grace, the proctors allow a pause to permit any member of the Regent House present to call a vote, which is done by saying, *'Non Placet'* ('It does not please'). If this does not happen, the Junior Proctor indicates the tacit approval of the Regent House by saying, *'Placet'* ('It pleases'). All formal proceedings thereafter are in Latin.

—o—

The Senior Proctor gives the following grace:

Supplicant reverentiis vestris viri mulieresque quorum nomina juxta senaculum in porticu proposuit hodie Registrarius nec delevit Procancellarius ut gradum quisque quem rite petivit assequantur.

(Those men and women whose names the registrary has today posted in the arcade beside the Senate House and which the vice chancellor has not deleted beg your reverences that they may proceed to the degree for which each has properly applied.) If there are no objections, the Junior Proctor says, *"Placet"*.

One of the bedells then leads the vice chancellor to the chair at the front of the dais and the presentation of graduands starts. When any candidates for higher degrees and candidates by special grace have graduated, the praelector presenting the graduands holds the candidate by his or her right hand, saying:

*Dignissima domina, Domina Procancellaria et tota Academia praesento vobis hunc virum (hanc mulierem) quem (quam) scio tam moribus quam doctrina esse idoneum (idoneam) ad gradum assequendum (*name of degree*); idque tibi fide mea praesto totique Academiae.*

(Most worthy vice chancellor and the whole university, I present to you this man (this woman) whom I know to be suitable as much by character as by learning to proceed to the degree of (name of degree); for which I pledge my faith to you and to the whole university.)

--o--

The graduand's name is called and they step forward and kneel. Clasping the graduand's hands, the vice chancellor saying:

*Auctoritate mihi commissa admitto te ad gradum (*name of degree*), in nomine Patris et Filii et Spiritus Sancti.*

(By the authority committed to me, I admit you to the degree of (name of the degree) in the name of the Father and of the Son and of the Holy Spirit.) The new graduate then rises, bows to the vice chancellor, and exits through the Doctor's door to receive their degree certificate.

--o--

When any candidates for higher degrees and candidates by special grace have graduated, the presentation of graduands by colleges begins. By custom, candidates from King's, Trinity and St John's Colleges are presented first, following by other colleges in order of foundation or recognition by the university. The praelector may present candidates groups of four. He does this by holding his right hand out and each of the four then grasp a finger. The candidates then kneel one by one before the vice chancellor. They put their hands together in front of them (as if they were praying) and he then covers their hands with his saying, *Te attium*…The candidate then stands, steps back one step and either bows or curtseys, leaving the Senate House via the side door.

After the first group has been presented for the same degree, abbreviated formulae will be used; the praelector saying:

Hos etiam praesento et de his idem vobis praesto.

(These I also present and of them I give you the same pledge.)

The vice chancellor in turn saying:

Te etiam admitto ad eundum gradum.

(I admit you also to the same degree.)

--o--

After the last graduand has been admitted, one of the esquire bedells calls the congregation to order with the word *'Magistri'* (Masters).

--o--

All stand.

The vice chancellor dissolves the congregation with the words *'Nos dissolvimus hanc congregationem'*, and leaves in procession led by the esquire bedells and followed by the registrary, the proctors, the pro-proctors and the university marshal. Other present remain standing until the procession has passed out of the house and may then also leave.

--o--

On completion of the ceremony, the new graduates will briefly be joined by fellows, staff, family and friends on the Senate House lawn, before returning to their colleges (photography and mobile phones are permitted).

The three families, minus Mr O-W, emerged back out into the sunshine and onto the provost's spacious lawn; after having sat for over two hours the opportunity to stretch the legs welcomed. However, their immediate concern was to try and see if Oscar and Horatio were still anywhere to be seen, they were not. Disappointed, they walked back to King's, but none wished to stay for the lavish spread laid out. Under any other circumstances, it should have been a fitting conclusion and culmination of years of endeavour, but sadly not the case.

Outside, Oscar stood, waiting for Horatio. They then slipped quietly away whilst the congregation continued to watch the closing minutes of the ceremony. Later, at four pm, that same afternoon, two new now disrobed undergraduates presented themselves at Sackville Way Police Station, where Oscar returned the diamonds.

Chapter 21

Having agreed to stay long enough for a cup of tea, they were approached by a large gentleman bedecked in his flowing gown, resembling a black and gold spinnaker. It was Professor Dodderington; he had clearly sought out Mrs O-W having asked around.

"It is Mrs Ormsby-Waite?" Doddy ventured, offering an extended large right hand. "I'm Professor Dodderington and delighted to make your acquaintance. I was desperately hoping to have a final word with Oscar. You probably didn't know it, but he really was my last and final star pupil, I need to congratulate him and bid him a fond farewell. You see this is also my last term at King's, I've decided to retire to the Lake District. He fully deserved his first with honours and really did produce the most exceptional results. You must be extremely proud of him, and I foresee a bright future ahead of him, no doubt as an eminent barrister. Where is Oscar, by the way?"

"I'm so glad to have met you at long last, Professor, Oscar has so often spoken of you and always with deep affection and admiration. I'm afraid he's already left; he had a further pressing commitment to meet."

"What! What could possibly be more pressing than his graduation day spent with his family?"

"Yes, you would have thought so, but sadly it's not the case. You'll probably find out in due course, but now is neither the time nor the place."

"Well, I'm really sorry to have missed him; we spent many enjoyable hours together. Will you please convey my very best and in all his future endeavours? Tell him that I've decided to take early retirement. I think he'll be surprised to learn of my premature leaving."

"Wait, Professor, I've just had a thought. Would you like to be our guest for dinner tonight as a final farewell, where I will tell of Oscar's other more pressing meeting?" replied Mrs O-W with a quickness of mind.

The professor rubbed his chin thoughtfully, before answering, "Ordinarily, with all my packing to do, I should decline, but I cannot think of a nicer family with which to spend my last night in Cambridge. So, the answer is yes, I would be delighted to join you – thank you."

"That would be absolutely marvellous. Shall we say seven o'clock in the lounge bar of the Clarion Hotel? It's where we're staying," Mrs O-W responded, glad that she had made the suggestion.

"Seven it is. I'll see you there and be sure that Oscar is in attendance. So, if you will excuse me, I must go and say hello and cheerio to my other students – sorry, I mean graduates." Doddy then disappeared, unaware of the developing drama.

Back at the hotel, Mr Charteris and Mr Fordham found Mr O-W in the lounge bar reading the local paper. Mr O-W had resolutely stuck to his guns in stating he would not be attending the graduation ceremony. It was a defiant gesture taken with a reluctant and heavy heart, wanting so much to be part of his son's visible recognition of all that he had achieved. He knew it would be a long time before he could bring himself to forgive him, if indeed ever. He was that type of person and his determination and stubborn pig-headed obduracy were traits he was only too well aware of, but he couldn't change. It was perhaps one of the reasons why he'd made such a success of his jewellery business, starting from virtually nothing.

"How went the ceremony?" Mr O-W politely asked, in what could be termed a half-hearted way.

"It went extremely smoothly, as you can well imagine, after all, they've had years of practice," Mr Charteris replied. "We met Oscar's tutor, Professor Dodderington, and your dear wife has invited him to join us for a farewell dinner tonight. So, I think you need to grin and bear it and make the effort."

"Yes, of course I will, if only for the rest of you," Mr O-W replied, putting on a brave face.

Over dinner, it was left to Mrs O-W to do most of the talking. It was clear she had a sharp and retentive memory, informing the professor almost word for word what Oscar and Horatio had confessed (her detailed account and list of what had been stolen from her house had also been nigh on perfect).

"Well, I have to say this is a shocking state of affairs. Whoever would have thought it? But all is not lost, and things are never quite as bad as they first appear. The fact that they have handed themselves in is more than a step in the right direction. There are also factors of mitigation and exemplary provisos to be weighed. As you can appreciate, my entire adult life has been spent emerged in the field of law, which is therefore, not without its many advantages. What we now need to do, and as a matter of some urgency, is to ensure they are both given the finest of defence barristers. I know of a few who I will now undertake to contact. I must warn you that their fees are exorbitant in the extreme. But in the end, you get what you pay for."

"Money is not the problem," Mr O-W remarked (obviously, he was slowly coming around).

"Well, I had planned to travel to the Lake District early tomorrow, having bid my fond final farewell to King's. However, I will only go once I have spoken to all three of the finest legal brains in the land in the hope that at least one of them will consider taking on the case. I will then phone you with their telephone numbers, including mine. If you don't mind, I'd like to be kept in the picture and help in any way that I can. It would be such a waste to see two lives ruined by one stupid act of folly. I also feel that I have a moral responsibility being Oscar's mentor for the last three years. I couldn't have done a very good job, could I?" They all knew this was not the case – hadn't Oscar attained a first with honours?

"Presumably, you've not heard from your son?" enquired the professor of Mr and Mrs Fordham. They both shook their heads in a negative manner, visibly more in an agitated state of turmoil than the other two, not having a clue where their son had disappeared to.

"No, I'm afraid we haven't, and it seems unlikely," as Mr Fordham passed the professor Raffer's farewell letter.

Raffer had soon got the vibes that both Horatio and Oscar had decided to give themselves up, their guilty consciences apparently being too great a burden to carry. He certainly didn't feel anywhere near to the same amount of guilt, in fact, he'd quite enjoyed the dressing up and playing the part of a French tart. After the dreadful scam that Mr Birnbaum had pulled on his own daughter and future son-in-law – he bloody well deserved it. Anyway, he'd get his diamonds back and his wife had only been shaken up a little.

The trouble was he knew that the other two would have to say who the other mademoiselle was. This left him no option but to depart King's and Cambridge before the graduation and their confession. Where would he go and with what funds? These were the two major issues that Raffer then addressed; at least he'd had the foresight to pick up his passport when last at home.

His research indicated that there are 33 countries with which Britain does not have an extradition treaty. These range from the unattractive Afghanistan, Armenia, through to Qatar, Iran, China, Japan and not forgetting of course, Russia. The country that caught his eye and imagination was that of Madagascar. It sounded sufficiently exotic with an unknown charm; well, that's what Raffer decided. And so. he researched a little deeper and how he could get there and what he could then do.

Three days later, Raffer left England, bound for Nairobi aboard an Air Kenya ageing Airbus. He had on him his worldly assets amounting to £33,241, a passport and his collection of his written drama work completed at King's. In the departure lounge, he wisely invested in a money belt, which he secured about his person under his clothes like a precious umbilical cord.

He was not sure how much of a useful reference his bulky drama notes would be on the other side of the world, but he couldn't possibly leave the visible fruits of his labour behind. It was bad enough having to leave his family in such a shocking manner, but as he saw it, he had no option. Why couldn't they just have let sleeping dogs lie and let the whole thing die a natural death?

There were direct flights from Nairobi to the capital of Madagascar (Antananarivo), but he decided on a cheaper option. He therefore spent the next fortnight cadging lifts and the occasional train down through Kenya, Tanzania, eventually ending up in Mozambique. There, he caught the ferry across to his new home of Madagascar. He checked into the one-star hotel called the 'Charmah', the star being presumably being awarded by virtue of there being a reception desk, if little else. King's College, Cambridge it certainly wasn't, but Raffer, ever the optimist, declared it was better than prison!

Professor Dodderington was as good as his word. He'd immediately made contact with an old friend, Sir Peter Thornbury QC, a highly respected and successful barrister and an old King's boy himself. Having explained the story from beginning to end, as best he knew it (without a single interruption from Sir Peter), Doddy waited for a response.

"Well, from what you have articulated, all may not be as dire as it first sounds. These things never are, once you've had time to analyse them in the cold light of day. That is why we charge such exorbitant fees, before reaching our valued judgements. Yes, I will take the case; I've just had three months touring the Amalfi coast in Italy. I need to get my brain working again and this sounds to be an ideal case in question. Let's call it a farewell favour for your imminent retirement DD, but it will cost them dearly."

The duty desk sergeant, a Sergeant Makepeace (with such a name, surely he was destined to join the police force) was enjoying a quiet Good Friday picking out the long odds winners for Saturday's race meeting at Newmarket. It was not going to be a quiet or a good day after all!

Now, standing in front of him stood two graduates, presumably from one of the colleges. They hadn't as yet uttered a single word, but he knew they were graduates.

"Good afternoon, gentlemen, and what can I do for you two on this bright Easter afternoon?" the sergeant offered in a relaxed and good-natured manner. "Don't tell me, someone's gone and nicked your expensive bicycles."

Then the roof fell in!

"I'm afraid it's a little more serious than that, Sergeant," Oscar being the first to speak. The demeanour of the sergeant changed in an instance. His years in the force had taught him to recognise the big one when it came along. For the vast majority of his working week, the tasks were humdrum, routine and predictable in the extreme, but not this one he suspected.

"Before you say another word, can I just be sure that this is not some graduation day prank dreamt up for you to have a laugh at my expense?" the sergeant enquired, almost in the hope of hearing words in the affirmative.

"I'm afraid not, Sergeant. We committed a serious crime some three months ago. We also believe that we got away with it but in our planning, we had not taken account of the subsequent guilty consciences we now experience. So much so, we need to confess in order to restore any self-respect and take whatever punishment we have coming to us." This time it was Horatio that had answered, with Oscar nodding his agreement.

The desk sergeant remained hesitant and unsure of himself. His intuition told him that they were indeed serious, but he still needed to be convinced he was not being taken for a ride. They were after all a couple of highly intelligent and well-spoken young men and easily capable of pulling the wool over most gullible police eyes.

"What is it that you claim to have done?"

"We held a Jewish jeweller's wife against her wishes in her own home and then demanded her husband hand over his complete company's stock of raw and uncut diamonds, which he duly did. There was obviously more to it than that, but that was the crux of the crime. We believe it's become known as the Golders Green heist," Oscar explained slowly and explicitly.

"You say this took place in Golders Green, down in London and not up here in Cambridge?"

"Yes, that's correct, Officer," Horatio continued the double act.

A look of relief then appeared to spread across the sergeant's face, as if a great burden had been lifted or removed from his clearly overweight shoulders.

"Will you both please follow me into the interview room and take a chair whilst I make a number of phone calls." The first call was to his station superintendent, who agreed with what the sergeant had explained and proposed. The second call was to Brent Cross Police Station in North London, apprising them of the situation and requesting their guidance and instructions.

"Right, gentlemen we have a plan of action. Because the crime was committed in and around the Golders Green and Brent Cross locality, it is necessary and appropriate that the nearest police authority handles the case. And as we speak, two plain-clothes police detectives are speeding their way here. How's about that for an efficient service?" the sergeant beamed with relief. Perhaps it was going to be a good Friday after all.

"Before they get here, you can spend the next two hours writing out a preliminary statement on what you claim to have committed. In the meantime, I'm happy to offer you a cup of tea or coffee. We have two empty cells at your complete disposal, so you will not be interrupted or be able to share in any note taking."

"Thank you, Sergeant. We'd like a coffee…white in both, but no sugar. I hope we're not putting you to too much inconvenience. I couldn't help but notice you studying the racing form. There's an outsider running in the three o'clock race at Newmarket called *Guilty as Charged,* which is too much of a coincidence not to be worth having a couple of quid on," Oscar replied in a cheerful way. At least they now knew what was happening. In fact, they were not surprised by the turn of events. Administratively, it didn't make any sense for the Cambridge police to get involved, it merely complicated the matter, best it be dealt with by the appropriate force. At least one desk sergeant agreed with the rationale.

The London officers arrived almost on the two-hour mark, which seemed to indicate a rather speedy journey north. In the meantime, both Oscar and Horatio had completed numerous pages of two-sided A4 sheets of foolscap. They had been allowed one telephone call each and both had informed their parents at the Clarion hotel. They both thought it only right and proper that they knew what was happening. What neither of them knew was that their parents, in conjunction with Professor Dodderington, were already arranging a defence brief to act for them.

It was almost ten pm when the two cell doors closed on Oscar and Horatio. The journey back down to London had been a silent one; this was at the behest of the two affable detectives; having been advised that there would be time enough for talking once they were formally interviewed. In the meantime, it would help if they could sort out in their minds the entire course of events. Both Oscar and Horatio looked at each other and shrugged. Hadn't they just spent the past two hours doing exactly that and then putting it down on paper?

The Good Friday evening was spent in Brent Cross Police Station being formally interviewed. Not that far away, in a quiet suburban avenue in Golders Green, Mrs Birnbaum lit extra candles − but for whom?

Chapter 22

Oscar and Horatio were to spend the rest of the extended Easter weekend occupying separate cells, although it would be fair to say that the duty officers didn't treat them as common criminals. In fact, they were well looked after in the way of refreshments and meals and provided with an ample supply of reading material. They were both given small portable televisions, which seemed a generous act. Therefore, you can well imagine the all-round surprise and pleasure as they watched *Guilty as Charged* romp home as a 40-to-one outsider. They were later informed by the duty night sergeant that Sergeant Makepeace had indeed placed a fiver each-way bet on Oscar's off-the-cuff throw away tip.

The weekend spent alone gave them the time and the opportunity to sit and reflect on what they had done and what the future possibly had in store. Both had secretly hoped to have received a phone call from their families, but none came. Perhaps they too had spent the weekend cogitating, whilst regretting what their brilliant but stupid sons had done.

It was early on the Tuesday, the day following Easter Monday that they were officially charged with kidnapping and extortion and would be presented at magistrates' court that very morning. Sitting in the back of the black windowless police van, they were driven to Bow Street Magistrates' court. It was Horatio who broke the silence.

"Oscar, my dear fellow and partner-in-crime, what with your legal background and all that, you must know all about this sort of thing. Please enlighten me, so at least I'll know what to do and expect – forewarned is forearmed as they say."

"Horatio, amazingly as it may sound, I've never actually been inside either a magistrates' or a Crown Court, despite having spent three years studying law. We were scheduled to visit both during our second year, but for some reason, it never happened and never got revisited. I must have a word with Doddy about

148

it, as I'm sure he would like to include it as an essential part of the course. But, yes, I do know most of what to expect."

"To begin with, virtually all criminal court cases start in a magistrates' court, with more than 90 per cent ending there. The other more serious offences, such as ours, are passed automatically on to the Crown Court. Where, once tried, we – the defendants, having been found guilty and sentenced; having experienced the full and legal weight of the law before a judge and jury, will go to prison.

"Basically, magistrates deal with three main types of cases, the first being summary offences. These are the less serious, such as motoring and minor assaults, where the defendant is not usually entitled to trial by jury. These are generally disposed of in a magistrates' court. Next there are the 'Either Way' offences, which as the name implies, can be dealt with either by magistrates or before a judge and jury in a Crown Court. Such cases could include theft and handling stolen goods, where a defendant can insist on their right to a Crown Court. Magistrates can also decide that a case is so serious that it should be dealt with in the Crown Court, which can impose tougher sentences if the defendant is found guilty. Lastly, there is the category that we fall into – Indictable – only offences, such as murder, manslaughter, rape, robbery and demanding diamonds with menaces! These must be heard by a Crown Court. In our particular case, I guess the magistrates will decide whether to grant bail. This, by the way, is most unlikely. They may also consider other issues such as reporting restrictions, before passing us onto the next available Crown Court."

"Bravo, Oscar, you certainly know your stuff," Horatio answered, impressed by his friend's in-depth knowledge.

"I bloody well should do."

"So, tell me, who are these mysterious magistrates?"

"Magistrates or Justices of the Peace, as they are also known by, are local people who volunteer their services. Interestingly, they do not require any formal legal qualifications, but will certainly have undertaken a training programme, including court and prison visits, to learn and develop the necessary skills. There are of course plenty of built-in safeguards. Because they do not need to have legal qualifications, they are advised in court on matters of law, practice and procedure. This advice is provided by Justices' Clerks and Assistant Justices'

Clerks. You'll immediately recognise them as they are the only officials to wear black gowns, everyone else, including the bench, wear mufti.

"Normally, magistrates sit in panels of three, both mixed in gender, age, ethnicity and so on, wherever possible to bring a broad experience of life to the bench. All three have equal decision-making powers, but you'll notice that only the chairman will speak and preside over the proceedings. The two magistrates sitting either side are referred to as 'wingers'.

"Our case will be brought to court by the Crown Prosecuting Service (CPS) but there are other prosecution agencies such as the RSPCA, the Environment Agency, Department of Work and Pensions, and English Nature and others who I can't recall right at this moment. After pleading guilty, we'll be sentenced; as simple and as quick as that. As I mentioned earlier, a magistrate's sentencing powers include the imposition of fines, community payback orders, probation or a period of not more than six months in custody, with up to a total of 12 months for multiple offences. None of which is appropriate or covers our serious misdemeanour," Oscar concluded.

"I'm a little confused, so please excuse my ignorance. Are there any advantages at all for our going to Crown Court, as there doesn't seem to be?" Horatio quizzed, worryingly wanting to know more.

"Yes, of course there is," Oscar replied, "not that we have any option or say in the matter. There is a much higher acquittal rate as jurors are notoriously more likely to accept political and mitigating defences and less likely to believe the police. For some reason, rightly or wrongly, the general public still have a suspicious disposition that many police officers are bent, or if not bent then at least not entirely straight. This in truth I do not believe to be the case, as nowadays there are so many checks and balances, but it's still a perception held and difficult to dissuade otherwise. Also, if we are acquitted − which we won't − and the CPS appeals and wins − perhaps say on a point of law, our acquittal cannot be overturned. I give you that as a crumb of hope and useless information, but in all honesty, I'm afraid it's not worth a candle."

"So, what are the disadvantages, there must be more?"

"Crown Court cases generally involve a lot more lengthy hearings: ergo, more visits and travel required at ones' own personal expense. Cases can drag on some may take up to a year or even longer. Not in our case. Ours will be short, cut and dried with a fairly stiff and lengthy sentence. I won't bother to explain the full nine yards of the trial procedure as it will become self-evident. First, we need to concentrate on today."

When they arrived in the holding cell, they were somewhat taken aback and surprised to see an immaculately dressed grey-haired and suave looking gentleman waiting to greet them. The man had one of those friendly looking faces that people warmed to. Oscar thought of his 'horns or halo' rule of thumb. This is where he instinctively decided within the first 30 seconds of meeting someone, whether he liked them or not. Of course, it was neither a scientific nor a fool proof method − but it worked more times than not. The affable and confident stranger definitely wore a halo.

"Good morning, gentlemen. I'm Sir Peter Thornbury, Queens Councillor, and I've been asked to represent you, the request coming from both of your families and Professor Dodderington. I must say that once the background had been explained to me, my interest was whetted, and I could hardly refuse; and also the fact that the professor and I go back a long way together.

"As time is short, I'd appreciate it if you let me do all the talking and you all the listening, as what I have to say may ease the painful experience you are shortly to undergo, and make no bones about it, it will be both painful and to some extent quite frightening." Oscar and Horatio exchanged worried looks, not at all sure of what to expect from their unexpected knight in Aquascutum.

"As you know, having already pleaded guilty to what are serious charges, your appearance here today is a mere rubber-stamping formality before being placed on remand and in custody prior to a full-blown Crown Court trial. This means you will go immediately from here to Belmarsh Prison, and hence the real reason why I needed to see you and to prepare you as best I can for what will surely be an unpleasant ordeal. Please allow me to explain what you should expect and what not to expect." Oscar and Horatio were immediately impressed by Sir Peter's concise and straight talking, making it appear abundantly clear that such a briefing was indeed necessary. How right he was.

"After sentencing, in your case being placed on remand to await trial, you will be brought back down below the courtroom and to this cell. You will not be able to see any friends or family before being whisked away to prison. The timing of this transfer will be unspecified, and you'll get no indication of how things are going. At some point, I will be allowed to talk to you in a holding room. There we can discuss the sentence and what it means, or possibly an appeal, but that is most unlikely, and you can pass me any last-minute messages.

"So, let's go through the process, one step at a time. You've been sentenced and now you're facing your first night in prison. Understandably, it's a daunting prospect." Both Horatio and Oscar nodded, as if in agreement. "Particularly as you are unfamiliar with the prison system and have no idea what to expect." Both nodded.

"When you arrive, you'll have a formal interview and assessment. During this interview, you'll be informed of the prison rules, and given information about how the day is structured and what is expected of you. You will also have your rights explained to you. After this initial interview, you'll be told about the various courses and educational sessions on offer. I don't think they cover Law and Anthropology." Horatio and Oscar looked at each other and smiled, realising that their unexpected saviour had a sense of humour and that he'd also done his homework. "Your general physical and mental health will also be assessed to make sure you receive the correct healthcare whilst you're in prison. Around this time, you'll receive your prison number, and will also be issued with an identity card, which you need to carry on you at all times. As part of the process, you'll also have any property you've brought with you taken away and stored somewhere safe. This will be returned to you when released.

"You can also expect to be strip-searched, to ensure you're not concealing any weapons or drugs. This may involve a finger up the bum or being asked to sit in a special chair which assesses whether or not you're hiding any electrical or phone equipment in your body, that's if you've got a large rectum! This doesn't sound at all pleasant, and I'm sure it isn't, but it's important to remember – every inmate has to go through it and the prison staff are used to carrying out strip searches. This means they're generally efficient and get the job done as quickly as possible.

"After which you'll be given a PIN number, which you need to enter before making any phone call; it's permissible to make one call. However, be aware that you only have a maximum of two minutes to talk, so plan what you want to say beforehand to avoid wasting the precious time allocated. And be warned – if it goes straight to answerphone, it still counts as your phone call, and you won't be permitted to try again.

"These days, it's generally recognised that arriving in prison can be a nerve-racking ordeal. Consequently, it's likely you'll be placed in a special induction wing for the first week or so. Serving any kind of prison sentence isn't easy and the first night is often the hardest. It's important to remember that your family and friends are still contactable and on your side. It's therefore beneficial, and which I strongly advise, that you both seek out their support rather than trying to get through the unknown prison experience on your own. I must say, having met and spoken with your families, I can assure you that they have your best interests at heart, otherwise I wouldn't be standing here.

"Now, a few words, as we still seem to have time, on what to take into prison. Good, I can see you've got your toiletries and changes of underwear, although some items they may not let you have because they can be purchased on the 'canteen' arrangement?"

"What is the canteen arrangement?" Oscar interrupted.

"A prison commissary or canteen is a store within prison where inmates may purchase a limited range of products. These are items you buy for yourself on a weekly basis. The choice is limited to basics, such as hair shampoo and deodorants and simple treats such, as chocolate or biscuits. It is via the canteen sheet that you have money credited to your phone account.

"Where was I? Take as many as eight sets of underwear and as many books as you can read, stamps, writing paper and envelopes as well. How much money have you both got on you?"

"I've got fifty pounds," replied Oscar.

"I've got a hundred," added Horatio.

"Oscar, here's another hundred, just to be on the safe side," Sir Peter said, extracting a number of notes from an amply stocked wallet.

"Sir Peter, we've only brought an extra three pairs of underpants."

"I'll bring in another half dozen each on my first and earliest visit," he answered. It was becoming very apparent that they had struck gold in the way of a defence barrister. *Presumably down to the efforts of good old Doddy*, Oscar thought to himself.

"You will probably also meet someone from the probation service who will mostly be checking your mental state. If they offer you food, take it, as you won't know when the next is coming.

"When you get to the prison, don't be surprised if you end up staying in the van within the gates for a while as they process others. It depends on how busy the prison is. You will then undoubtedly be moved from one holding room to another, in between times, you will be called to various places so that officers can take details from you (several times at least). At some time, you will be given your prison clothes and your bundle of blankets and plastic cup and plate, etc. You will be seen by the prison doctor and allocated a cell and asked any questions about particular issues you may have in the prison.

"It will then be a case of hanging around until they take you to your cell. Do not expect the cell allocation, in terms of your cellmate, to be thought through. Consider yourself lucky if it is, but I do know the governor and I will endeavour to get you into single cells, as it is most unlikely you will be paired together. Therefore, it's best to be safe than sorry and go for the single option. Otherwise, you could end up with some great hairy moron of a sexual deviant who doesn't care who he climbs on!

"By now, it is probably pretty late in the day, and there has been no time for any induction or anything else for that matter. So, you will be locked in a cell with absolutely no idea of how anything works. And you will (rightly) feel like you are now expected to just get on with it, as the next time your cell door is opened, none of the guards will even realise that you are new. So, you will have to work out if the door is opening for exercise – a walk in the yard, to use the showers or get food, etc. Just follow everyone else and do what they do.

"One last thing to remember, once you've settled, you may get moved to a new cell several times and a cellmate may change. This is always a nervous time as it's almost like starting over again, so it is best to be prepared for any such eventuality.

"You may be told when I might come to see you, and when you can make your first phone call, or when the induction process will be. These can all be wrong. Be warned and do not be surprised that any instructions or advice given, could well be wrong by a matter of hours in either direction – and should set the tone for things to come. So, the earlier you learn to roll with it, the better, even though this is incredibly tough. Rolling with it will be harder than you think.

"The major culture shock of being imprisoned comes from being so out of control of what happens to you. Many try to compensate by focussing on key expectations or milestones, such as what might happen and when, from showering, food and telephone calls. Attempting to do this might seem like a sensible strategy, but you'll soon find out that events won't occur as you expect, and the result is that life can seem like the end of the world. However, you are both highly intelligent young men and should have the wherewithal, intellect and mental strength to cope, as you have now been forewarned.

"Obviously some things do have an uplifting effect, such as when you receive and get to go through your property. Being reunited with your books and toiletries, and having something to read and clean yourself with, you'll find ridiculously exhilarating. But this could be on day one, two or day ten, irrespective of what it officially says. So, don't try to expect too much.

"Don't expect to be told what's going on or given proper advice on induction into how it all works. It's a case of fending for oneself. In fact, any induction programme could take a few days to get on, and in that time, you have to be prepared to have absolutely no idea of how anything works. You'll have to figure it out as you go along. Again, you will see posters on the walls telling you what happens for induction, and you'll have guards telling you that it will be the next day − don't bank on it. And when you finally get on one, remember who the target audience is − the most vulnerable and needy, not graduates who have recently attained first class degrees with honours.

"It may feel like a useless health and safety course, telling you about self-harm and only to use the emergency bell in emergencies. It will not tell you useful things like how to find out if you're getting a visit from your family or me or moving to a more open prison. The main reason for all this uncertainty and things not going as planned is because these institutions are large, complex, funded at the margins and dealing with a variety of difficult to manage people. If they were all like you two, then it would be a doddle and there would be no shortage of prison guards, but I won't go down that route.

"You will gradually work out which guards know a lot, and which know very little, and starting a rapport with the right one may help, but initially you won't have a clue.

"The immediate loss of contact with the outside word will also hit hard and you will be focussed on all ways to achieve some calls or visits. It is one of the hardest things to achieve in prison. So be prepared to fail in all your efforts over the first few days, albeit that's not a reason for not trying. I promise that I will visit you both at the earliest opportunity, if only to bring in a dozen pair of small-sized underpants. I promise, so have faith in me. Just bear that in mind, I have a fairly good idea of what you'll be going through and experiencing.

"They've just called your names. I'll be here when you get back, which will be in very short order. Good luck."

Their appearance in Bow Street's Magistrates' Court was over before it had begun. For any disinterested bystander, the journeys undertaken by the three families to be present would hardly have seemed worth the effort. But there again, any stranger would not know the full background story and were not the loving next of kin.

The courtroom was three-quarters full of all those attending already seated. The front row was occupied by the subdued and still despondent family members. Behind them sat Professor Dodderington, alongside other friends from King's and a number of strangers. At the rear was the usual gaggle of reporters; not forgetting of course – the four men in the dock. The slight and diminutive figures of Oscar and Horatio were flanked by two large and visibly tattooed uniformed guards. One could easily have been forgiven for thinking the guards were standing in the wrong place! There appeared to be only junior advocates for both the prosecution and the defence with no sign or presence of Sir Peter or his opposite number.

A brief look and a nod of recognition passed across the courtroom from Oscar and Horatio to their parents, who raised their hands in moral support. It was the first time they had seen their sons since receiving their scrolled, rolled up and ribbon-tied diploma degrees. When would they see them next, they wondered.

The professor had been the last person to be seated, having completed a necessary errand to the rear of the courthouse to one black windowless police van. He'd given the driver a 20-pound note to see if he could see his way clear to giving the two bags to… The driver had said he'd do what he could, but no promises. Doddy got the feeling the driver wouldn't let him down.

A side-door opened, and the three members of the bench entered, everyone stood as protocol demanded. The chairman was an attractive lady in probably her late fifties or early sixties, who wore an expensively tailored two-piece navy blue cashmere suit. This was completed by a simple (but again expensive) white silk blouse and colourful neck scarf. Oscar's first impression was of a professional woman who was confident in her appearance and comfortable in the present surroundings (he later learnt that she had been a Justice of the Peace with over thirty years of experience). The other two were men, equally smartly turned out in blazer and flannels. This appeared to be an accepted civilian uniform befitting the occasion, but still eclipsed by the chairman, who had clearly been a stunning beauty in her earlier years and was still attractive and pleasing on the eye. This was evident by the approved asides that passed along and between the rows of male reporters – who did not look as smart.

Oscar almost expected one of the blazers to hold the chair for the chairman, but they didn't! The chairman nodded to the gowned court official, as if tacitly indicating that the hearing may commence. Behind her on the oak-panelled wall the Royal Coat of Arms appeared to be resting on her head, not unlike a halo. Well, that's how it looked to a certain professor. The official (another lady) standing below the bench read out the charges.

"Oscar Ormsby-Waite, Horatio Charteris and Rupert Fordham absent, you are charged with committing the act of kidnapping and extortion on the 19th of April 2017 in the North London district of Golders Green. How do you plead?"

"Guilty," replied Oscar.

"Guilty," replied Horatio, to which the chairman immediately responded.

"This case is too serious to be heard here and I am sending it to Woolwich Crown Court. Bail has not been requested and in view of the absent third party, it will not be given. The accused will, therefore, remain on remand in Belmarsh Prison until the trial. Take them down." Without further ado and almost in a seamless motion, the three members of bench then stood and left the room; shortly followed by the four men in the dock. The courtroom went from silent to noisy the moment the main actors had left the stage. It was as if someone had turned up the volume control from zero to maximum.

Oscar and Horatio's appearance in Bow Street's magistrates' court had been a brief but necessary stepping-stone in the legal process. The whole performance had lasted no more than three minutes. It was just long enough for Oscar to notice and admire the huge size of the diamond adorning the chairman's third finger. Clearly, diamonds still featured in Oscar's psyche.

Once outside and away from the courthouse, the professor finally approached the three families. They had just agreed they all needed a cup of tea or coffee, or perhaps something even a little stronger. They eventually found their way into the lounge bar of the nearby hotel. Without exception, they all ordered coffee.

They were to be joined later by Sir Peter Thornbury QC, after he had given Oscar and Horatio his final words of advice, as he promised he would.

Without preamble, Professor Dodderington explained the short and almost non-existent court appearance.

"I expect you're all thinking that it was a long way to come for such a short hearing, but I suspect you knew this would be the case. That was why the prosecuting and defence counsels were represented by junior bar members, it being a mere formality. However, no matter how short today's hearing was it served a number of useful purposes which you should all be aware of and at least appreciate. Firstly, it would have done both Oscar and Horatio the world of good just to have seen you here today. They may have executed an elaborate and skilful crime, albeit an act of madness, but they are not hardened criminals and are now paying heavily for their act of folly. That said, it is no good crying over spilt milk. It is now Sir Peter's task to look after them and get them off with the lightest of sentences, bearing in mind they have already pleaded guilty.

"Let me try and give you some comforting thoughts to travel home with. As Sir Peter and myself well know, there is extenuating and exemplary mitigation which will go heavily in our favour, come the day of reckoning, which I fear will not be for at least a further four months. Sir Peter's staff have already checked with the Woolwich Crown Court and at the present trial schedules, ours is likely to be at the end of August or early September, depending on how the other trials progress."

"Professor, can you explain more about the mitigation?" Mrs O-W responded.

"When a court imposes a sentence, it also takes into consideration a number of principles regarding the sentence. Should it be increased or reduced to account for any relevant or mitigating circumstances relating to the offence or the offender. Mitigating factors are subjected to a finding based on a balance of probabilities, and not beyond a reasonable doubt. Pleading guilty and cooperating with the investigation are frequent examples of mitigating circumstances that would tend to reduce sentence, as is the existence of remorse or regret – mitigating circumstances often relate more to the offender than to the offence.

"This means that Oscar and Horatio now have to spend the next few months incarcerated in Belmarsh Prison. I will not lie to you; it will not be a pleasant time or experience. Belmarsh is home for some of the country's nastiest and most vicious hardened criminals, with many of them serving full life sentences. Sir Peter is, as I speak, explaining to them what to expect from here on in. But it is our fervent hope that the time now to be spent on remand will be sufficient to satisfy the judge and the sentence." Then, as if on cue, Sir Peter arrived, having had a final brief word with his two clients before wishing them all the best.

"Thank you, Sir Peter, firstly for taking on the case and taking the trouble to explain where we all stand. This is not something we're familiar with and would like to know if you require any payment to be made up front," Mr Ormsby-Waite offered.

"Thank you for your offer, Mr Ormsby-Waite, but that won't be necessary or how it works. First, let me do my professional utmost to ensure that these two bright young gentlemen do not have their futures ruined by one moment of madness, which by the way, many of us are in private admiration as to their ingenuity and cunning.

"Professor Dodderington and I were at King's together and he's asked me to be his best man. So, what with this late in life request and the fact that Oscar was his last star pupil, puts me in an invidious position and behoves me to do my best, although I won't be waiving my entire fee. I will of course keep you all informed of any progress and developments, as Doddy has volunteered to be the communications conduit. Finally, I also wish to announce that I too now have a personal interest as I am a board member of the Kent County Cricket Club and have a certain admiration for Tristram Charteris, who has proved a fine captain. You must be extremely proud of him?" Mr and Mrs Charteris' day had suddenly got a lot better.

It was then Doddy's turn to say his piece.

"If it makes you all feel any better, I've given both Oscar and Horatio some post-graduation work to do on behalf of King's. I thought it was payback time and at least it will keep them occupied and away from the rest of the inmates. Now if I could have all of your addresses and telephone numbers, I will do Sir Peter's bidding."

Sir Peter was right, they were back in the underground cell before you could say guilty as charged! They only had a few minutes to ask Sir Peter to tell their parents not to worry, not the most sagacious messages from two Cambridge graduates.

Sir Peter had not been completely right. Rather than be kept hanging around as he'd implied might happen, they were told they would be transferring to Belmarsh within the next few minutes. Sir Peter had only enough time to reassure them that all was in hand and he would see them again in the next few days. To wit, the two guards arrived to collect their charges. Without further ado, Oscar and Horatio were bundled into the back of the police van, compliments of the two bouncers in blue! There, on the floor, in addition to their rucksacks containing their personal effects were two large Sainsbury's plastic carrier bags. The professor, a 20-pound note and the driver had all done the trick. They were puzzled by the bags but now was not the time to examine the contents as the van moved away and began its short journey across London to Belmarsh Prison.

Belmarsh Prison was built on part of the former Royal Arsenal in Woolwich and became operational in 1991. It is adjacent and adjoined to Woolwich Crown Court and as such the prison is used for high-profile villains, including those that extort raw and uncut diamonds. As a Category A Prison, it holds 910 prisoners from all over the United Kingdom. Accommodation at the prison is a mixture of approximately 60% multi-occupancy cells and 40% single cells, distributed mainly across four residential units. This was to be Oscar and Horatio's home for the next three, four or five months. They'd made their bed and now they had to lie on it, but hopefully in single cells, if Peter Thornbury QC had worked his governor magic.

Chapter 23

The arrival procedure for being admitted into Belmarsh Prison was laboriously slow, as Oscar and Horatio were soon to find out, being two of another eight prisoners being processed. The earlier briefing provided by Sir Peter proved to be invaluable, at least preparing them for what, by and large, eventually took place.

It was 8:30 pm when they were finally escorted to their cells, which was to become their refuge or home for the next 125 days. The timing coincided with lockdown as other prisoners left the corridor and disappeared. Their arms and hands were full, carrying personal effects, blankets, plastic knife, fork, spoon and mug, and of course a full (heavy) Sainsbury's bag.

At no time had they been offered or given any food. Supper had finished, but neither felt hungry. Presumably, the day's events had placed new and exacting demands on the brain, which in turn had cleverly switched off or overridden the normal demands of the stomach. They had been warned that the first night in prison could be the worst, and so both had resolved to make the best of a bad deal and brazen it out. Their cause was greatly helped when told they had been assigned single cells (it would appear that Sir Peter had indeed worked his magic with the governor).

They were in adjoining cells on Wing C of residential House Block Four, which accommodated vulnerable, drug-free and remand prisoners. Home was now a room six foot wide by ten feet long. Surprisingly, there was a 14-inch television on a plastic desk (with chair) in one corner and a metal toilet and washbasin in the other, and of course a bed. A typical student's room at King's it was most certainly not! In fact, inspection was completed in a lot less time than was customary when entering a typical holiday hotel room. Here, instead of a balcony and view of the beach with its rolling sea, there was in lieu a small mesh window, which looked out onto a solid and unmoving brick wall.

The first striking impression to hit Oscar was the number of gated doors that had to be accessed; he counted 15. Each one having to be locked before the next one was duly opened; it was a time-consuming ritual which the warders (screws) did routinely and almost without having to look to see which key was needed.

Having familiarised himself with his new home and surroundings, which had taken all of 30 seconds, he sat on his hard but functional bed and opened the Sainsbury's bag which had mysteriously been delivered to the police van. Inside were a number of books and a great deal of writing pads, pens and a letter. Oscar recognised the writing and the immaculate hand of dear old Doddy.

Before opening the letter, he quickly removed and looked at the title of the books: Poems by Lord Byron, The UNICEF Handbook; Lord Denning's *The Discipline of Law,* Bill Bryson's *A Short History of Nearly Everything* and a pristine Bible. Oscar thought it quite a strange eclectic mix, but that was typical of Doddy, never expect the expected! He opened the familiar high-quality cream-coloured envelope and read.

My Dear Oscar,
Lakeside Cottage Bassenthwaite
Nr Keswick Cumbria
25 June 2017

I thought I'd best refrain from the usual Ormsby handle, now that you are no longer one of my students, merely a friend in need.

Suffice to say, I am aware of all that has gone before and intend (not wish) to help in any way that I am able and allowed.

My understanding (from Sir Peter) is that you are likely to be in Belmarsh for the next three, four or possibly five months. We therefore need to ensure that both you and Horatio do not have a scintilla of time in which to become morose or downhearted. Be aware and assured, there are many willing to help you, but you in turn need to do likewise, hence my remedial bag of goodies.

One of the many notable attributes you displayed at King's was your attention to detail and the ability to cover all relevant points most comprehensively (almost to the point of becoming tedious). Therefore, I am proposing you employ this meticulous talent to compile a new handbook for student's considering King's as their college of choice. May I suggest a title: 'Preparing for King's?' May I also suggest that you use yourself as a typical example? As you know, we already have a pamphlet which we send out, but hardly adequate or good enough, well, according to you! It needs to be more personal and informative and cover all aspects from… I'm sure the task will keep both you and Horatio mentally employed for a good many hours and weeks.

Lord Denning's tome I'm sure you will find absorbing and fascinating reading, in which he gives a personal account of his contribution to the changing face of the law in this century (that's my last tutorial, I promise). I've also had the temerity of popping in a bible. As you know, I am not a deeply religious person, but I do know that when I look out of my cottage window, I know that no man could have created what I see. It is probably the most singular and ideal opportunity in your life where you have both the time and inclination to delve inside its pages, not that I'm suggesting you read cover to cover – but it's just a thought. I know Bill Bryson is one of your favourites, so I've enclosed just one. If you want more (and can find the time), let me know. Finally, I've left possibly the most important one until last, the UNICEF handbook and contacts.

When this whole ghastly episode is behind you, which hopefully will be sooner rather than later, you will need direction. You've probably already realised that any driving aspiration (remember – acres of diamonds) you had to become a barrister will sadly have been greatly diminished. Therefore, what I'm suggesting is possibly a new tack, a fresh and completely different direction and approach; a job or task that will give you a renewed, reinvigorating, meaningful dimension and purpose to your life.

In your confession statement, you mentioned giving any money to charity. Well, why not go abroad and use your not inconsiderable skills and legal brain working for UNICEF? They have a pressing need for bright, thrusting legal lights such as the likes of you that can help desperate children throughout the world. In other words, it would provide a worthwhile opportunity to rehabilitate and set out a new and laudable stall for a certain Ormsby-Waite. You'll find a number of useful contacts and addresses, should you wish to pursue my suggestion and I leave it to you – it's just another thought.

On a personal note, don't worry about your parents. They are more resilient, understanding and loving than you'll ever know – your father is softening by the hour. In the meantime, I've given you enough to read, write and ponder and would welcome any comments.

Don't you think life is odd and continues to confound? As I start my retirement and relative freedom, so you start your incarceration!

Stay true to yourself and I'm confident that all will be well in the end. When you get out, please come and visit me in my new home as indicated above, where you can sign 'our' new visitor's book.

Yours as ever…

PS: The police have said you can now have the Citroen back. Please let your parents have the necessary instructions, Doddy.

Oscar sat and reread the warm and encouraging words of someone he realised was now more than just his once mentor and revered tutor. Doddy had clearly gone to a great deal of thought and effort and the sincerity of his words and offered advice shone through. He then stopped to think what must have been in Horatio's bag of goodies, which he would find out the next morning during his first visit to the exercise yard, when he told of his own surprise package.

He liked the idea of *Preparing for King's*. He'd often banged on about how inadequate the joining brochure had been and didn't really address the points that needed to be addressed. Now he and Horatio had the opportunity to give something back to King's. The compilation of which would also occupy a great deal of their cerebral skill and more importantly – time. In fact, on reflection, the content of one Sainsbury's carrier bag was not nearly as eclectic as he'd first thought.

Doddy, in his inimitable and clever way, had covered all points of the compass: a written task, a legal lesson from the past Master of the Rolls, some light but informative reading in the form of a fact-cum-novel, a bible that hitherto would never have been opened, and last but certainly not least, a possible way ahead in the form of overseas work using his legal knowledge where a new start was possible. Not such an odd list after all and an invitation to visit the Lake District to meet his new wife – who would have thought it. He needed to write to his father, to ask for his forgiveness and to ask him to dispose of the Citroen for whatever he could get, rather than be charged rent by the Metropolitan Police Force. But first, a banana and a Kit-Kat he'd wisely packed.

After a surprisingly decent night's sleep, he woke and watched the morning television chat show, until he heard the cell doors being opened, it was 7:30 am, the first full day on remand. It was to be a further hour before five warders escorted the entire wing to the exercise yard. It was then that Oscar and Horatio were able to compare notes and check on how the other had faired.

"How did you sleep AA7640?"

"Not bad at all," replied AA7640. "We must get our prison numbers to Sir Peter as soon as we can, as apparently it has to be used in all contact references."

This was the beginning of an in-depth conversation between the two as they walked the perimeter of the yard, in exactly the same way as most of the other inmates. They were, however, only two of about eighteen wearing their own clothes. The majority of the other 100 or so wore standard prison issued uniforms which consisted of a grey shirt, a grey jumper and grey trousers (jogging bottoms) and an assortment of trainers.

The exercise yard was about the size of Wimbledon's Centre Court, perhaps a little larger. But instead of a centre net there was a peripheral 24-foot-high strong wire-netted fence. Groups of inmates were already congregated in well-established groups. The foul language and preponderance of tattoos was the first thing to hit them. Oscar could see one prisoner using a mobile phone, although not permitted. It would seem the warders turned a blind eye in order to keep everything calm and under control.

Before they could even get onto the subject of carrier bag contents, they were approached by a noticeably round-shouldered and stooped elderly gentleman, who shuffled over with the aid of an ornate walking stick.

"Good morning, gentlemen. I take it you are new?"

Horatio was about to make some sarcastic remark about being 22-years old next birthday, but his politeness and kind enquiring face made him bite his lip.

"Yes," replied Oscar, "we arrived last night and we're on remand. Is it that obvious?"

"I'll say it is, wearing your own clothes and not a single tattoo between the pair of you." A hand left the security of the walking stick and was feebly offered. "The name's Norman Jenkins and more than willing to answer any burning questions you may have. Presumably, you haven't been told anything yet? To be perfectly honest, it would be an absolute godsend to have a decent conversation with folk that don't say fuck as every other word."

"Are we really that obvious?" Horatio asked.

"I'll say. Remanded prisoners can wear their own clothes and those that have earned and obtained a higher enchanted reward level, for being well-behaved. And have a look around you, how many do you see without tattoos?" It was true, Oscar had a real dislike of tattoos and immediately downgraded his assessment of someone so adorned, an automatic stigma of something lacking.

"By the way, and before you ask, I'm in for having the fingers in the till. The till belonging to a large reputable bank with a black horse, who, not unreasonably, took exception to my many unofficial withdrawals over a period of five years. I knew I'd get caught in the end, but it was fun whilst it lasted. I got the same five years. I've done over two, so only a few more months to go." Prisoners are released as a matter of routine after serving half of their awarded sentence, unless they have been naughty one way or the other. "My real punishment is this wretched parachute I now have to carry around," pointing to his back, "the doctors call it osteomyelitis."

"That's very kind of you, Norman. So far we've been told the square-root of absolute zilch."

"Let's find somewhere to sit and out of the way of the circling rabble," he said (in a whisper and behind the back of a frail hand). "My back can do without the exercise."

"Well, for starters, could you run through the daily routine," Oscar replied having helped Norman into a sitting position against a prisoner-proof wire fence.

"Unlocking times are from 7:30 am to 12:15, and 2:30 pm to 4 pm. The only difference is the weekend, when it's an hour later at 8:30 am. The most important event of the day is association time between 5:45 pm and 8:30 pm. This is when all prisoners are let out for recreation. They may play pool, table tennis, use exercise bikes, watch television or just sit around and chat. It's the only time when all prisoners from a block are out and together in one place and it always makes the screws nervous. This is a time when other prisoners can wear their own clothes and also at the weekend.

"The period now and up to 11 o'clock can be spent here in the exercise yard, the education block or the library, but visits to the library are limited to 20 minutes at a time. At 11 am, it's back to the house block for mealtime. We can't say 'feed' anymore because that's what you give to animals. We're supposed to call the cells rooms, but how many rooms do you know where you get locked in! We're normally taken in groups of six to collect food and then return to our cell to eat it.

"At 12:15 pm, everyone is locked up until 2:30 pm, whilst the warders have their protracted lunch break, then unlocked time from 2:30 pm until 4 pm. This is when prisoners can do jobs or work on their own activities or hobbies. Then it's locked up time before recreation."

"What about meals?"

"There are usually five or six main course options available, plus a vegetarian and Halal. When you collect your dinner — known in prison as tea — you will collect your breakfast. This never varies and consists of a single portion of cereal, a small carton of UHT milk, four tea bags, a couple of sachets of jam and pats of butter for a roll. Don't feel you have to give someone your cereal or whatever, just because some will ask. They will always try it on and are used to being told no, but just do it nicely.

"Lunch is always a sandwich, usually cheese, and a packet of crisps. A couple of times a week, we are given half a small pork pie, which we jokingly call 'porkpieicicles', as they are usually still frozen. Meal sheets are issued a week in advance. Failing to get the form returned to the wing orderly means you receive the default meal, which is the vegetarian option.

"Now one valuable tip I will give you. Get to know the chaplains. It doesn't matter if you're not religious, they won't mind or care. Ask to have a chat with them for pastoral reasons as soon as you can, they can't refuse you. They are good to talk to because your mind will be full of questions and worries, which they've heard all before. More importantly, if you need help or a favour, they are in a good place, but they won't break the rules for you or for anyone else. But they do seem to exercise common sense more than the others are able. You'll soon get to see why none of the warders have made it through the qualifying heats for mastermind!"

Oscar and Horatio were both beginning to enjoy listening to Norman, who was also clearly enjoying talking to two exceptionally bright young men, which was exceptionally rare given where they were sitting.

"In bang-up, the chaplains also have the benefit of being pretty accessible. If you spend some time outside your cell and in the corridor of the wing, you'll see them at least once a day wandering around. Now, do you know anything about the canteen?"

"Yes, our barrister mentioned the basic rudiments."

"The important thing to remember is that you are allowed to initially spend £15 per week and you'll also get paid about £1 a week for the pleasure of being here. So, don't spend it all at once. Another good tip is getting a subscription to a newspaper, and you get to know what's going on in the outside world. Arrange it through your barrister, they'll need a cheque or a postal order, your name and prison number."

"I've forgotten mine already," Horatio quipped.

"It's the one number you'll never forget throughout your entire life, believe me, young sir."

Just then a prisoner suddenly screamed, both sides of his face pouring with blood. Amazingly, there was now no one near or around him. Two vigilant warders walked hurriedly towards him, quickly escorting him away, one providing a handkerchief to help stem the flow of blood. It later transpired (via the jungle grapevine) that someone had used a SIM card from a mobile phone as a Heath Robinson razor blade to terrible effect. The scarred victim was unable to say who the assailant was, being known as a grass was worse than having a scarred face!

"That was most unusual," offered Norman, "but welcome to Belmarsh. By the way, what did you say you were both in for?"

"We didn't, and we'd rather not say," replied Oscar, but he said it nicely! "Perhaps, another day we'll reveal all, but at the moment, we'd rather keep a low profile and feel our way in."

"Fully understood. Now, would you be so kind in helping a broken old man to his feet?"

Once alone, they told each other about their letters and books and what Doddy had proposed. They both welcomed the proposed task with genuine relish, agreeing to have a stab at producing draft chapter headings. Each day, they would meet and agree what the day's work should be and convene again during recreation time.

They then swapped letters, which they read in silence whilst walking the perimeter, with not a ball boy in sight! They both agreed to reply and do as suggested.

Dear Horatio,

Human, Social and Political Sciences (HSPS) – Social Anthropology Faculty

King's College, Cambridge CB2 1ST

Professor Dodderington has asked me to send you some appropriate reading material. I'm afraid I'm at a complete loss as to know what you've already devoured on the subject such was your rapacious appetite for knowledge. Therefore, I've sent you a few which may be new to you (hopefully). Please return them when you eventually take up your position as previously discussed and agreed.

I'm also aware of the handbook assignment suggested by DD, which I look forward to reading. In the meantime, I'm sure you will gainfully employ your mind before returning to King's. My colleagues also send their best and look forward to hearing you recount your intriguing but exciting aberration.

Yours…
Dr Michael Appleby
26th June 2017

Chapter 24

"Well, I do have to say and I say it with all sincerity, that it's been a real privilege and indeed a pleasure meeting you both. I shall miss our daily téte-a-téte, but not the rest of the days!" This was Norman Jenkins saying his last farewell to Oscar and Horatio in the exercise yard, an event he greatly looked forward to.

In the ensuing four months, it had become a daily morning ritual of meeting in the exercise yard. It was something which the younger men had not tried to avoid, displaying compassion and understanding. Without a doubt, the short but overt rendezvous was the highlight of Norman's day, when he could converse with intelligent human beings and help him put the world to rights. Tomorrow he was being released, having completed exactly two and a half years of a five-year sentence. His sister, Ethel, was picking him up, she having decided that blood is still thicker than water and he was to live with her – and make no bones about it, as yours are crumbling by the day, she had brutally reminded him. At least he would be able to pay his way, as he'd managed to ferret away some of his Black Horse ill-gotten gains!

The timing of his release was absolutely perfect, as tomorrow they would go on trial at Woolwich Crown Court. Oscar thought it a lucky coincidence, whereas Horatio was more profound and philanthropic.

"Oscar, don't you ever stop to think, that perhaps there might be some far greater power that ultimately decides when things happen and that everything we do is orchestrated and done for a reason. Aren't we just a miniscule part of some majestic universal master plan?"

"I'm not sure that I've ever thought about life and what we do in such a way. But I can fully understand why the faculty of social anthropology at King's are so keen to have you back," Oscar answered his sage friend.

The 125 days spent in Belmarsh Prison had passed quicker than both Oscar and Horatio had ever dared or hoped for. It had been an experience – not a pleasant experience – and not one to be recommended to friends, but it had opened their eyes to another world and other types of people. These were definitely not the type with which to share a punt on the Cam. Fortunately, a real blessing in disguise, was that they had not been overly pestered or intimidated, having been labelled by most of the wing as a couple of lightweight la de dah intellectuals! It was a label they were more than willing and prepared to live with, as it at least provided the luxury of relative interference-free privacy.

In all prisons and for all inmates, the number one enemy is the interminable dragging of time. This proved not to be the case for Oscar and Horatio, who had more than enough to occupy their time. The task proposed by Doddy had been a brilliant one and was just what the doctor-come-professor had ordered. They both agreed and decided that the finished product should be a work of art – *par excellence* – and worthy of standing up to any scrutiny by the King's College Administrative Department. The result was precisely that, as modestly and humbly owned by both. It was exactly what any prospective student wanted to read.

In addition to *Preparing for King's,* they also had other volumes of reading, and of course the tactful writing of the weekly letter home to the family. In fact, there was little time to watch television, preferring to devour each and every word of the daily newspaper. Horatio received *The Times,* Oscar – *The Daily Telegraph,* which they duly swapped. Sadly, there was not enough time to open the Bible, which remained untouched – it was ever thus.

Sir Peter had visited them on three separate occasions. The first visit was after three days, when he brought fresh changes of shirts and trousers, in addition to numerous pairs of pants. He acted as a willing postman and general errand boy – an extremely well-paid errand boy.

In addition, they both had one other unexpected caller, for Oscar, it was Professor Dodderington, and for Horatio, it was Doctor Michael Appleby. These visits were totally unexpected and unannounced, and therefore received with evident displays of surprise and delight, and certainly a novel experience for the distinguished visitors.

Doddy had decided to make a weekend of it, having bought Violet down with him, intending to show her around London and take in a West End show. For Doctor Appleby, it was a day-return train journey from Cambridge. For both, it demonstrated how kind and thoughtful people can be, and also went to show that they were not considered to be pariahs of society. On the contrary, everyone sent their best wishes, with a danger of them becoming celebrities, although this is not what either wanted. It remained their fervent desire to put it all behind them – but when?

They had no other visitors and by choice. Both sets of parents had repeatedly asked to visit but had been refused, as gently explained in their weekly letter home. Belmarsh was not a place that they wanted to be identified or remembered by.

What you don't see won't hurt you, Oscar had written to his mother. *Please, let's just wait until we know the outcome of the trial, then perhaps we'll see*. It had been a similar message to the Charteris family, which both had reluctantly accepted. Both Sir Peter and the professor had also been in regular contact with them and were able to explain the dilemma more fully which had helped. By now, Mr O-W had buried his own excavated hatchet and had unilaterally forgiven him. He'd already lost one daughter and he surely didn't want to lose his only son, as Mrs O-W had repeatedly reminded him.

The second visit was to report on an unexpected journey Sir Peter had made to the Bay of Haifa situated on Israel's Mediterranean coast. This being the new home of Mrs Birnbaum, now living in a self-contained annex next to her daughter, Athalia (God is exalted) and Avi Rosenberg, the son-in-law, in their well-appointed house.

"I tried to call on Mrs Birnbaum at Golders Green, at a time when I knew Mr Birnbaum would be at work, hoping to explain your desire to apologise, quite unofficially, you understand. There was no one in, but as I was leaving, I met her neighbour, a widow by the name of Mrs Cohen. This was another fine Jewish lady, in the form of a little, stooped white-haired individual dragging behind her a wicker basket shopping trolley, ladened only with two bagels after a synagogue visit.

"I respectfully but candidly explained the reason for my call and asked if she could help.

"To which she boldly replied, 'I can, but I suspect I shouldn't. But, as a creaking 92-year-old, having lost both my parents and seven brothers in Auschwitz II, I consider I've earned the right to decide what I can do and what I cannot do. I was only spared because I was considered to be a freak, having been born without any finger or toenails', holding out a small parchment-wrinkled hand as if needing to prove it. This, she declared defiantly with a smile that looked as if it had emanated from her very inner core or soul.

"'I'm still in touch with Aalijah, that's Mrs Birnbaum, and we write to each other every other week. The telephone is far too expensive, you understand. I'd been on at her for years to leave that wretch of a husband, even though I knew it was not my place, but we are close you understand. Then, out of the blue, she suddenly finds the courage to leave him, which gladdened my heart, whilst at the same time sad that I was losing a dear friend. You must think me awful speaking so badly of someone, but he really is the meanest and most miserable son of a bitch – excuse my language – that I've ever had the displeasure of meeting, and he's still my next-door neighbour, worse luck. So much so, I'm seriously thinking of selling up and joining her in Dallyat at-Rawha, that's where she now lives. I'm going to persuade her that we should find somewhere else to live together and give the youngsters more space to themselves. As for him', pointing a nail-less finger in the direction of the house, 'I'm quite sure he hasn't got a friend in the world; only his precious diamonds and he still wouldn't be satisfied, even if he had an acre full. What good have they done him?'

"'First, he lost his daughter and now he's lost his wife and serves him damn well right.'

"She gave me Mrs Birnbaum address, stating that what you both had in mind was a noble gesture and therefore worthy of such an indiscretion. I then left, agreeing it would remain our secret, as neither the police nor the judiciary would approve, citing collusion and all that sort of thing. She kissed me on both cheeks and waved as she said shalom (peace and goodbye) and trundled off."

"You can, therefore, imagine Mrs Birnbaum's dumbfounded surprise when I called on her at her new Haifa home. I also met the daughter, Athalia, who was in the process of applying for a job. Her husband had already secured a managerial position in the nearby oil and petroleum refining and chemical processing plant some ten miles away. Apparently, they had known all along about the father's shoddy ring scam, but had decided not to say anything, just to keep the peace, even though mother was oblivious of the deplorable deed. I must say, I found Mrs Birnbaum to be a delightful, strong-willed person, who seemed to be enjoying life being away from her miserable and miserly husband, as she described him, 'He thinks of nothing but making more money and hasn't got a friend in the world. I've put up with his avarice for far too many years, and in a funny sort of way, the intrusion did me an enormous favour. I've already filed for divorce on the grounds of his unreasonable behaviour, which I suspect he will not contest, as it would cost him money!'

"I then asked her for an account of what happened, which she did, also informing me that she had been advised that she would be called to appear at the trial. Interestingly, she referred to it merely as an intrusion by three French women, of that she was positive. She was adamant that the shapely ankles, the makeup, and the hint of an expensive perfume were totally convincing. The purple thong was the clincher, thinking how typically French. And so, gentlemen, your ruse was indeed remarkably successful. So much so, she would have been prepared to testify and swear under oath to the fact that you were definitely women. This deception I understand was largely down to the skills of your absent friend.

"She also thought that she had been handled with care and consideration. Even when tied, it was apparent that you were careful not to be rough or hurt her in anyway. I mentioned that when her husband found her, she had her head down on her chest. She explained she had dozed off, having not had a good night's sleep, which I know, as one gets older one rarely sleeps through. All in all, she'd coped well with the ordeal; in fact, far better than her husband was now having to do with both the police and the insurers.

"She said she was quite amenable to your calling and respected the sincerity of such a visit. I left with the distinct impression that Mrs Birnbaum was a stronger and more independent person than Mr Birnbaum ever imagined. However, how living in the pockets of her family would work out had yet to be seen. My experience is that it seldom does – space is needed by all concerned.

"So, the idea in mind by the indomitable Mrs Cohen could prove to be beneficial all round. And as I've already stated, she did agree that my visit remain our secret, as she did not wish to complicate or muddy the waters, as she so put it. Athalia then kindly drove me to the airport, for what really had been a flying visit, which of course, you two gentlemen will ultimately be paying for. It was a visit well worthwhile, as I now have a reasonable reassurance that her testimony and appearance in court will not reveal anything of an adverse nature. If the truth be told, she doesn't want to appear, as it means an unavoidable meeting and possible confrontation with Mr Diddle-me-daughter, as you so aptly nicknamed Mr Birnbaum."

The third and final visit by Sir Peter was to give them the news of the trial date, starting next week.

"Gentlemen, we have an hour, so let's not waste time explaining the short notice. Suffice to say, the present trial finished early due to an 11th-hour change in plea to that of guilty, something you've already done." Oscar and Horatio exchanged glances, having again been reminded of their own guilty plea.

"The trial will be heard at Woolwich Crown Court; not a stone's throw from where we are now, on Monday commencing at 10 am sharp. And in view of the guilty pleas, it is likely to be concluded within the week. I have, therefore, already taken the liberty of informing all interested parties, which of course includes your families, Professor Dodderington, Doctor Appleby and the administrative department of King's. The Fordham family have expressed a wish to be present, even if their son isn't! I now require to be reminded of exactly what happened from beginning to end, starting with the letter of invitation. Don't hold anything back or omit the smallest of details. I know and accept it's all written down in your statements, but I need to hear it again in your own words. I need to know every answer to every question, even those unasked. We barristers are a funny lot, you should know that, Oscar. We should never be found wanting, and we certainly do not like surprises. It is also axiomatic that we only ask questions to which we already know the answers. Is that not correct?"

"Absolutely," Oscar replied, as Horatio realised that Anthropology was by far a more rational subject.

"The case for the prosecution is, to all intent and purposes, cut and dried – as easy as falling off a log. For them, it must seem money for old rope. However, my aim is that neither of you end up swinging from one, if only to coin an old-fashioned phrase."

"Of course," they both replied in unison, as each recounted their own versions of what had happened…

Sir Peter was greatly impressed with the almost verbatim accounts articulated by both. He went on to explain how he would try and guide the judge down the suggested path that surely time on remand was punishment enough, vis-á-vis the extenuating and the exemplary mitigation.

"I can also tell you that a certain Mr Birnbaum was more than surprised when you handed yourselves in. So much so, he now has to explain himself and his numeracy to both the police and insurance company. So be sure your sins will find and catch you out. My skill is to persuade both judge and jury without trying to tell them how to do their business. Judges have a habit of being at best displeased or at worst visibly annoyed, which can have an adverse and counterproductive effect. It's a very fine line to tread and that's why I get paid such vast fees.

"The judge is Rufus Willmott QC, who does not take prisoners. Well, actually he does! He has a reputation for banging them away for as long as legally possible, with a liking for the maximum of sentences on offer. He was the judge who sent down the Hatton Garden gang, so at least you have something in common. Not forgetting the fact that he also went to King's, where he was the college chess champion. So, there are no stalemates in his court, only inmates!"

Both Oscar and Horatio could see that Sir Peter was clearly in good spirits and an amusing frame of mind, and possibly looking forward to the imminent trial?

"The one area, where I must confess, I have no idea of what the outcome will be, is in the sentencing of your absent friend. What's his full name again?"

"Rupert Archibald Fordham, whereabouts unknown," Horatio replied, knowing full well that Sir Peter knew.

"And you haven't heard from him since he disappeared into thin air."

Sir Peter asked, again already knowing the answer. This time, it was Oscar who noted this habit.

"No one has, not so much as a word," answered Oscar. "I thought, at the very least, he would have contacted his parents or his sister, Rosemary, or even us. Not a blip, which must be very hurtful to his family, who really do think the world of him."

"I would only add," Horatio opined, "if anyone was capable of pulling a switch, or turning a new chapter in life, then it would be Raffer. He has this rare ability of being able to compartmentalise his life and his activities, be it sex, gender, work, play or whatever. So, if anyone is capable of starting over, then it's Raffer – the old bean."

"I agree," added Oscar. "As well as being bisexual, I wouldn't be at all surprised if he isn't bipolar also."

"Well. I must confess I have no real feel for what sentence the judge will pass in your friend's absence, except to say, it doesn't help your cause one iota."

"We guessed as much," Oscar replied.

"Purely as an aside, I must tell you that I was recently offered the exalted position as a Circuit High Court judge, which I graciously refused. Oscar will explain to you the monastic and restricted life it entails, whereas I prefer to watch my cricket and play my poor golf. I digress; I need to brief you on what happens when we get to court and the attending procedures. I want you both to feel comfortable, if not exactly at ease, then at least aware of what to expect and knowing what goes on around you at all times."

The hour spent, with Sir Peter doing most of the talking and they doing most of the listening flew by. By the time he had bade them his cheerful goodbye, they both felt considerably more cheered. It was clear to see why he was so successful and respected throughout the legal profession. It had been an honest, no nonsense, or hidden agenda type of exchange. At best, he was cautiously optimistic. He stressed that what he hoped would happen might not agree with what the judge decreed would happen!

Sir Peter was also requested to become their postman. Would he please post a further letter to Doddy? In it, Oscar stated that he and Horatio had completed the masterpiece of a handbook – *Preparing for King's*, which Sir Peter would be hand-carrying the fruits of their labour. In which, he also confirmed his intention to take up his visionary idea of UNICEF, but still hadn't given up all hope of eventually becoming a barrister, even though the prospects were bleak.

Sir Peter then surprised them by revealing the fact that Professor Dodderington had been his best man when he had married in King's chapel. Now and more surprising, Doddy had asked him to return the compliment. His old sparring partner was a diehard bachelor, whose only two loves had been Wagner and poetry. Apparently, on his annual walking sabbatical to the Lake District, he had been smitten by some Cumbrian lass. She had been doing more than just cleaning, it would appear.

"I believe many of the King's staff will be attending, including invitations to all of his latest tutorial class. Unfortunately Oscar, you may miss it, being currently indisposed, but the rest of the congregation know why!"

When Sir Peter had left, having promised to keep them in the picture of any development, the two men were escorted back to their cells. Without further ado, Oscar sat down and wrote a second letter to Doddy, congratulating him on his forthcoming marriage, and would dearly have loved to have been in attendance. He then sat down and compiled a shopping list of things that he needed to do in order of importance and priority. He decided that a letter to his parents came first to tell them how much he loved them and to ask for their understanding, no matter difficult that may be. He went on to explain Sir Peter's visit, the trial and that he was most encouraged by what he had said. Privately, he did not completely share in his optimism.

Many thousands of miles away in Madagascar, Rupert Archibald Fordham was starting a new life. On arrival, he had sensibly assumed a new name, to be revealed later, but became known to all as 'Rab'. His invented moniker and abbreviated 'handle' being accepted without question by all whom he met, why wouldn't it? There remained the problem of his passport, but that was something to work on. At least he could remove his umbilical cord, start a bank account and look for work.

Despite Horatio's assessment that Raffer could cope with starting a new life, it was never going to be quite that simple. True, the logistics and practicalities had been fairly straightforward and the decision and wherewithal of finding a new destiny was within his compass and capabilities. It was the emotional and the far-reaching consequences that still had to be conquered. He too suffered from a guilty conscience, not for the crime, but the way he'd been forced to leave his family and friends.

It was after three weeks that he hit on a plan that would at least ease the persistent nagging in his mind. A guest in the hotel was flying to Paris for a business convention. He agreed to put local stamps on the three letters that he'd written, once in the French capital and onward post them. This the businessman duly did, and the letters reached their intended in the course of the next few days. At least his family and his two friends would know that he was alive and kicking.

Sorry for everything, and please do not think too badly of me, Raffer had signed off. As to his true whereabouts, none had any idea, but had guessed that Paris was not where he was. It was to be the last time that Raffer ever signed off using that name. He later contrived to claim that his passport had been stolen (by a mysterious and fictitious robber, who was patently never apprehended), thus enabling him to obtain a new one in which he kept his Christian name.

Chapter 25

Contrary to the ongoing trials and tribulations elsewhere, back in Bassenthwaite, all was sweetness and light, honey and roses, with love positively pervading the Cumbrian air. Horatio, the anthropologist-come-philosopher would merely have said it was a simple case of cause and effect. In reality, for Doddy and Violet (and others), it meant announcing and planning for a wedding, a cottage refurbishment; to say nothing of the coming together of the lower and upper parts of the village.

Once the initial euphoria experienced by all, on learning of the forthcoming marriage, had sunk in and the excitement had begun to wear off, the accompanying but necessary practicalities had to be faced. Doddy, with his legal hat on, considered the overriding priority was in obtaining the required confirmation of Violet's divorce. The subsequent matter of getting married could then follow, with little to-do. Not so with Violet, she considered, or rather demanded, the makeover for their new home to be of paramount importance. Violet won!

The first decision was to name their bijou or love nest 'Lakeside Cottage'. Violet thought the name absolutely perfect and how clever of Doddy to have thought of it. Doddy, for his part, was acutely embarrassed at its sheer lack of originality, which he later confessed to the Pilkingtons he had offered as a throw away, off the cuff suggestion, and in a moment of flippancy. However, both Violet and Mrs Pilkington thought the name was perfect and anyway, 'didn't he know and appreciate that Bassenthwaite was the only lake to bear such a title?'

The first big mistake or assumption the professor made, was to believe that everyone would be happy and content with a quick registry office wedding in Keswick, followed by a small reception at *The Poachers Inn*. How wrong he was! The Pilkingtons, the vicar and probably the rest of the village had quite different thoughts.

"Doddy, you've already stated that you and Violet wish to remain here in Bassenthwaite and become a 'Cumbrian'. Well, surely you must go the whole hog and do it properly by getting married in our lovely church of St Bega's? You don't need to be reminded how close and involved we are, and I'm sure the Reverend Shepherd would be only too delighted to officiate at such a wonderful occasion. By the way, he's a great lover of poetry and has produced some creditable works of his own, so I'm told."

"That's what I want too," was all Violet said. It was a statement that implied no further debate was needed. The following day, a meeting was arranged with all interested parties present, namely Doddy and Violet, Eunice and Wilfred Pilkington and the Reverend Shepherd. Mrs Shepherd arrived later, having decided she needed to be part of the discussions and decision making. It was the reverend who had picked a suitable but neutral venue, the Dodd Wood, Old Sawmill Tearoom.

For some inexplicable reason, the reverend and the professor immediately hit it off. Horatio would not have been at all surprised, and probably would have stated that it was meant to be. The fact that the reverend had also been at Cambridge (Emmanuel College), before going on to the Nazarene Theological College in Manchester, in preparation for life in the Christian ministry must have helped. It was here that he also became a disciple (or at least a lover) of poetry! Hence, the new friendship was sealed when the reverend explained that Lord Alfred Tennyson stayed at Mirehouse (the grounds in which the church sits) in 1835 while he was writing his poem 'Morte D'Arthur' and St Bega's Church inspired the opening lines:

...to a chapel nigh the field,
A broken channel with a broken cross, They stood on a dark straight of barren land...

"I'll announce the first reading of the banns this coming Sunday, and I hope you and Violet will honour us with your presence, which is expected. As you probably already know, but I'll remind you anyway, the banns are required in law to be read on three Sundays in the three months before the wedding. They must be read in your parish church, as well as in the church where the ceremony is to take place. Am I therefore to assume that they are to be one of the same?" the reverend both stated and asked at the same time.

"They are," Doddy and Violet answered in unison.

"That's settled then, and I'm sure Eunice and Wilfred will show you the way, if not the scriptures."

Doddy liked the reverend, he had an honest directness about him that cut through any need to explain or apologise for past deeds. His wife, Octavia, was a chip off the same old block. The reverend had clearly married her for her warm-hearted but forthright personality and innate kindness, and not for her looks. She was a stout, some would say well-built lady, a plain-looking and plain-speaking woman but liked by all – what you saw is what you got. It was quickly becoming apparent to Doddy why his neighbours looked forward to their many church activities. Perhaps Violet could join the choral group, as she had a lovely singing voice, aided by a good set of lungs, no doubt, Doddy had thought to himself! In the meantime, the reverend and he could compare notes on their favourite poems and poets.

Doddy had soon come to realise that his decision to take early, an almost in haste premature retirement, was the best thing he could ever have done. Was the Oscar escapade the catalyst and beginning of it all? Horatio would surely have had an erudite answer to such a conundrum. The truth was not far wide of the mark.

In the meantime, Violet had asked Eunice for her help and guidance in doing up Lakeside Cottage. She had also been thoughtful enough to involve her mother, so as not to leave her feeling left out. Three women deciding on décor and dining room furniture is not the wisest of trios, but in the end, Violet was happy with what went in and what went out. In fairness, a clear out was long overdue. For years, it had been a holiday let; functional but not fashionable was how her mother succinctly described it.

Doddy had obtained Violet's divorce and the banns were being read, but a date had yet to be decided. It was finally made following a conversation between Sir Peter, who had agreed to be his best man. The situation regarding the likelihood of a trial date and predicted outcome had occupied most of the telephone conversation. The matter of the wedding was easily agreed, and they were to stay with the Pilkingtons, as they had insisted upon. The matter of where all the other invited guests would stay was up to them.

"They are all men and women of the world, Doddy, so please leave them to sort out their own logistics, as you used to instruct them to do not so very long ago." He therefore made this instruction clear when he sent out the long list of wedding invitations, not expecting so many to say, 'We'd love to come, just tell us when.' Sir Peter and Doddy took a huge gamble and picked a date in September! But before then, Sir Peter had best brief his clients.

Sir Peter Thornbury QC had been up at Cambridge the same time as Professor Dodderington. Sir Peter had gone on to become one of the country's most respected barristers, who had declined the repeated offer to become a high court circuit judge. He preferred the creature comforts of a happy family home life and regular trips to both France and Italy. The strictures and demands of a circuit judge were not to his liking. He also needed the cerebral cut and thrust demanded of the most complex and controversial cases, for which he had gained an enviable reputation. As a close colleague once shrewdly stated, 'Sir Peter has that rare ability to persuade and take people with him, rather than agen' 'im. It is a gift that few possess, and it is different from any other skill that can be taught. In his younger days he was a suave and handsome young beau, who reputedly could charm the knickers off a nun', it was reported, anecdotally − of course!

He was similar to Doddy, in that he was a large man with a stomach that indicated a love of good food and wine. Where he differed was in his dress and appearance. He still possessed a full head of hair, now silver in colour but well-groomed, which had been shaped and allowed to grow over the ears. He was of fair complexion with a smooth skin and piercing blue eyes. If not in a court of law, he would not have looked out of place as a film star. His suit was made in Saville Row and his shoes were handmade by Crofton's, his Hermes tie adorning a top-drawer shirt not known to the average man in the street. His overall appearance was of a man who transmitted success and a pride or possible vanity in how he presented himself. If his legal knowledge and skill was out of the same top, then Doddy had done well by both Oscar and Horatio, but only time would tell.

Before Sir Peter could hope to influence both the jury and the judge, he first had to gain the confidence and trust of his two young clients. His first success was to obtain approval to interview both of his clients together in the interview room, rather than have to repeat the laborious process twice over. This was considered acceptable by the prison authorities, as long as any interview could be overseen and monitored.

"Gentlemen, and I believe that is what you both are, notwithstanding your present predicament. Furthermore, it is my task to convince other people to be of a similar mind. I will, therefore, not waste your or my valuable time by going over the well-trodden ground of any regrets and self-recriminations. The deed has been done and it's my job to minimise or prevent either of you spending any unnecessary time in this and other suchlike institutions."

Both nodded, impressed by the confident but no-nonsense approach taken by the barrister who had generously been found, thanks to the efforts of their parents and good old Doddy.

"Now, gentlemen, again I need everything from the very beginning, and I mean everything. I require your complete honesty and recall, leave nothing out. What gave you the idea in the first place, and the exact article in the *Diamond Dealer's* magazine? How and why you chose Horatio and what's the third person's name?

"Raffer, you say, and that you can confirm you have no idea where he has gone, which doesn't help, of course. Where and how you purchased the car, clothes, make-up and any misgivings you might have had during the planning, which surely there must have been. Then you must go through every single step and what actions you took. All of this I need, in order to build up and present a picture for those that do not know you and might also take a subconscious resentment to intelligent, well-heeled students who are amongst the most fortunate few in society. These not unreasonable prejudices we need to overcome and explain your actions and subsequent remorse and guilty conscience for what it is, genuine and heartfelt. So much so, you have both been prepared to ruin any prospects of successful careers that would undoubtedly have been on offer. They may still be, but that's between us and the warder, who seems to have lost interest in our detailed conversations. I gave him 20 pounds to have a drink when he got off duty. I know it was a risk, but sometimes those that dare..."

It was almost an hour later, with the five-minute verbal warning bell having been shouted, when the last of their story had been told, and Sir Peter nodded his head in evident satisfaction.

"Thank you, men. You have given me more than enough to go away and work on. Your greatest asset is in your honesty and genuine regret. This comes through loud and clear and I am greatly heartened. It will now be my task to convince those that need convincing and to damage limit what you have done. There is much work still to be done but at least I have a good basis on which to work. If either of you remember anything else that you think has been missed, then give me a call." He gave them his card, shook hands and left. Both Oscar and Horatio were led away separately to think on what had taken place.

A long way from London in Madagascar, Raffer (now Rab) was settling into his new way of life. Not one to let the grass grow under his feet, he was now employed as a receptionist at the hotel in which he still resided. The only difference being his room was small, Spartan, but at least it was free. He soon learnt this island in the western part of the Indian Ocean had more attractions than first met the eye and was not unhappy with his choice of asylum.

His one big regret was not being able to share his whereabouts with any of his family. For the time, he had to make the best of his hasty retreat, having heard nothing in the media about any arrests or subsequent trial. For now, his best friend was his money belt.

Chapter 26

In the bowels of Woolwich Crown Court beneath Number One Courtroom, Sir Peter briefed his clients. Oscar and Horatio sat on a wooden bench in an otherwise empty and stark holding cell. Their knight in shining armour now appeared in a dark and immaculate double-breasted suit, wearing black robes. Oscar noticed the broad black braces which allowed the trousers to hang correctly onto highly polished hand-crafted shoes, the importance of presentation not lost on Oscar. The vision completed by the sight of a short wig and stiff white-wing collar, which had two white bands (strips of linen) hanging down – he was in uniform and ready for action.

"Well, gentlemen, the day of judgement is upon us. How do you feel, you both look all right?"

They had both opted to wear trousers with buttoned long-sleeve shirts – no cuff links and were sporting the King's College tie.

"Extremely nervous, and if the truth be known, a little frightened," Oscar volunteered. He was clearly conveying the same feelings of Horatio, who had nodded.

"Excellent. It endorses that what you have previously said and written was expressed with integrity and honesty. However, I require that you stand in the dock with shoulders pulled back and heads held up looking straight ahead, none of this bowed and soppy look, which would be quite unedifying and unbecoming and not what I want you to appear as. You need to convey an appearance of two young intelligent men – which you undoubtedly are – who committed a crime for which you now deeply regret and are fully prepared to accept the findings of those about to judge you. Tell the truth and fear no man, that's all I ask of you both and leave the rest to me.

"The judge is a Rufus Willmott QC, whom I've known for many years. He is highly respected by all at the Bar as a fair, if humourless old fart and not someone to play poker against or rub up the wrong way. It's rumoured he's not enjoying the best of health, an old man's problem, I understand, in the nether regions. Let us hope that any discomfiture works in our favour with a shorter rather than longer predicted trial. As it stands; and with your pleas of guilty, it is expected to be concluded within three or four full days of hearing. Then it will be a case of watch your fingers in the cell door – only joking." Neither Oscar nor Horatio thought Sir Peter at all funny.

"You will not be surprised to learn that your families are in attendance and occupying the front row of the public gallery, including the Fordhams. This I find a rather magnanimous gesture, especially as they still have not an inkling of where their son is. Professor Dodderington is also present, along with many others from King's. You two must have been good students or just popular good eggs. My learned advice is that you do not look at them throughout the trial. I have seen it happen on far too many occasions, which has only caused unnecessary distractions and distress all round. You will be better served by looking at either the jury or the judge, or the prosecuting counsel or my good self. You will also note that everyone stands when they speak and address the judge, who remains seated. The judge is always addressed as 'My Lord'. When he enters the courtroom, everyone will stand and bow as he takes his seat. In reality, they are not bowing or acknowledging him but the Royal Coat of Arms that you will see emblazoned on the wood-panelled backdrop behind him. In other words, it is an acknowledgement of the Crown."

"What do you think we'll get? We'd rather know, no matter how bad it's likely to be," Horatio enquired.

"I wondered how long it would take before one of you ventured to ask the obvious million-dollar question. The honest answer is – I don't know. But for what it's worth, I can give you my honest and most learned opinion of how it might and might not go.

"Firstly, the biggest thing in our favour is that you voluntarily handed yourselves in, admitted your crime to wit, you've pleaded guilty. You have already oiled the moving parts of law and order and enabled the wheels of justice to turn that much the easier. I can assure you, your retrospective action has made life much simpler and tidier for everyone, if not necessarily your own! Also, the fact that you were refused bail means that you have already accrued five months detainment at Her Majesty's pleasure by way of being incarcerated in Belmarsh High Security Prison, which I'm sure you found to be an enlightening if not enjoyable experience. This time 'served' will be taken into account when the judge weighs the sentencing considerations, together with the exemplary mitigation which I will be raising at the appropriate juncture.

"The real unknown and major worry that I have is the absence of your colleague, he really isn't helping your cause one jot. As you fully appreciate, his absence was the sole reason that your bail application was bluntly refused, no matter how unlikely you were to doing a runner. My concern is that it may cloud or influence both the jury's and judge's perspective, giving them justifiable reason to demonstrate that justice has to be done and not just seen to be done. Remember, your friend's name will also be read out and sentenced in his absence, with absence normally carrying a heftier tariff of sentence.

"My job will be to convince both the members of the jury and the judge that sufficient punishment has already been meted out. You have already spent time in prison, cheek by jowl amongst some of the most vicious and nastiest people you could ever wish to meet. You have shown genuine remorse and contrition in your voluntary actions, knowing and accepting that this would greatly damage any future career aspirations you may hold. I will implore that two highly intelligent young men, who had one moment of madness, should not be blighted or the rest of their lives ruined. Furthermore, it was a one-off and you are not habitual criminals, like those that repeatedly reoffend as surely as night follows day. Therefore, to punish you further would be spiteful, counter-productive and not true justice, although I may wish to couch these sentiments in a more subtle manner. After all, it is not for me to do the judge's job, only that he hopefully does our bidding. Judge Willmott has a reputation for fair play, which should be in our favour.

"I have one final point to make, Oscar, which is on a lighter note. Our mutual good friend, Doddy, who you have a lot to thank for, jokingly told me that it was his entire fault that you're in this pickle in the first place. He reckons you constantly and enviously eyed his montage of past pupils and decided that you wanted to be remembered for committing the perfect crime. The only flaw in his argument is that the perpetrators would never be caught, and neither would they hand themselves in or make themselves known! He was of course only jesting and is greatly distressed at your demise and fears for your aspirations to become a barrister. As you fully appreciate, the chance of you being accepted to the Bar with a criminal record, is on the wrong side of minimal if not entirely impossible. I'm sorry to share his concerns but I think you already knew this." Oscar nodded, the crassness of his actions hitting home.

"Anyway, it was jolly good of him to journey down from the Lake District with his wife-to-be! So, you clearly made an indelible and favourable impression on your tutor. See you both in court – shortly."

Before either of them could say a word or ask any further questions Sir Peter was gone, a uniformed guard kindly closing the door behind him. They were left to review all that he had said. Their conclusion was that the absence of Raffer could be the deciding factor, something they or Sir Peter had no control or influence over. Their thoughts were soon interrupted as the cell door opened.

"All rise!" the usher called out in a strident but clear voice. As the words echoed around Courtroom Number One of Woolwich Crown Court, everyone present did as directed by dutifully standing. Once the last discernible movement had ceased, the side door to the right of the elevated platform opened and Judge Rufus Willmott QC entered. Talk about making an appearance; he appeared resplendent is his white wig and full-length red and black robes. As expected, he looked the part as the court officials bowed as he slowly approached his chair.

What was not expected was the accompanying arrival of a red admiral butterfly, which had evidently fluttered and followed the judge in from the outside chambers, appearing to gate-crash the proceedings. There immediately followed an unseemly hubbub of whispering and pointing of fingers, which in turn caught both the ear and eye of the judge, who looked to see what the disrespectful noise in his courtroom was all about. The red admiral must have known that it had become the centre of attraction, as it carried out an aerial lap of honour around the full and large oak-panelled room. The clerk of the court and the usher made hopeless gestures of trying to shoo the butterfly out of the still open side door. They looked pleadingly towards the red and black robed figure, expecting the judge to become some instant lepidopterist. Whereupon the judge seemed to scan the entire courtroom, as if to confirm he had a full and attentive audience – he had. He then took his seat in a tall-backed and elaborately carved throne-like chair. Directly behind and above him a large and shining Royal Coat of Arms shield with the scroll *Dieu et mon droit* – God and my right, as if to remind everyone that this was indeed Her Majesty's Court, not that anyone was in any doubt. He clasped his hands, smiled benevolently and addressed the large assembly, with more than a few pairs of eyes busy alternating between bench and butterfly.

"Good morning, ladies and gentlemen. I have to tell you with all candour, this is the first time I've been upstaged on my arrival in court. But I'm sure you will all agree that we need to be patient and let this beautiful exhibit of nature's wonder have its few moments of fame, if only to remind us all that we only share this planet." Everyone in the courtroom, especially the officials, visibly relaxed at the judge's sanguine humour and wisdom. The butterfly briefly landed on the soon-to-be-used Bible. Was this a messenger and an omen sent from on high?

The judge's affable display was not lost or missed by Sir Peter (who missed very little), indicating he was in good spirits and of a favourable disposition, and not at all liverish due to any health discomfit, and this could augur well. It also eased the understandable tension being felt by both Oscar and Horatio standing in the dock. They had resolved to take Sir Peter's advice and not look in the direction of the public gallery. However, the distraction and flight path of the uninvited but popular red admiral made this impossible. There they glimpsed so many unexpected but familiar faces. On the front row of the long wooden form sat Mr and Mrs Ormsby-Waite, together with Mrs Featherstone. Next to them sat Mr and Mrs Charteris and son Tristram, Mr and Mrs Fordham with daughter Rosemary. The only family absentees being Horatio's former girlfriend Rebecca; both having agreed earlier to go their separate ways, rather than being pushed, thereby saving any undue embarrassment and ill-feelings. The only obvious person missing was Raffer, who by rights should have completed the in-dock trio.

Behind the families sat Doddy and his wife-to-be, Violet, and amazingly, the rest of Oscar's entire tutorial group. This included one American lady, heavy with child, Marie-Jo, with her husband and father-to-be. They had made the effort, having flown in from America, to be there for both the trial and the wedding. Next and most surprising of all sat Mrs B (who still made the best egg sandwiches in King's College), who had been Oscar's self-appointed surrogate mother, but now 'did' for the new occupier of his old room. Then most surprisingly of all, there was Malcolm Althorpe, the senior lecturer who had interviewed Oscar many moons ago. It was apparent that King's was a very special and caring college.

"Life must go on," Mrs B had said to the new incumbent, yet another undergraduate reading law. Next to her sat the new head of faculty. This was

Professor Dodderington's replacement, a Doctor Daniel Freeman, himself a past law student of Doddy's – well, who hadn't been? Beside him sat Doctor Michael Appleby, the head of Social Anthropology, obviously there to support his new designate member of staff; the exact date of his taking up the appointment was still to be confirmed! There, in addition to the usual cadre of reporters, almost lost on the back row sat a little white-haired old lady with no fingernails but with an indomitable spirit. In her handbag an open one-way El Al airline ticket to Tel Aviv! The appearance and surname of Doctor Freeman was not lost on Sir Peter, who, despite being a highly intelligent and accomplished advocate was also surprisingly superstitious and thought it another good omen and prepared to take anything on offer. Horatio, on the other hand, would have thought it just another silver thread on the tapestry of life, and merely a further indicator that all was set and preordained. Wasn't this just more proof, if proof were needed?

The red admiral must have soon realised the courtroom contained only nervous apprehension and not a crumb of nectar to be had; and miraculously found its way back out from whence it had flown, in its constant quest for food. With the door closed, barring any further flying visits, the judge interlaced his hands (it was habit which Sir Peter had picked up on) and spoke.

"Ladies and gentlemen, before we start, let me help you all by unravelling some of the myths surrounding a Crown Court trial. It will also prepare you for what to expect and more importantly, not what to expect. We lawyers are very good at assuming that everyone knows what happens at trial. Of course, many spend every day in the criminal courts so the whole process becomes second nature and they hardly stop to think, that for many people a courtroom is a strange and unfamiliar place. For many they may have based their knowledge on what they have seen in films or seen on television, which often bear little resemblance to reality and also are invariably based on trials in America, which are a little different to ours.

"In our courts, you will never hear a gavel pounding; you will never hear the shouting of 'objection' or judges responding with 'sustained' or 'overruled'. You will not hear counsel asking to 'approach the bench', nor will you see them walking up to the witnesses in the middle of cross-examination and shouting in their faces, and you will not hear witnesses take the oath and finish with the words, 'so help me God'. You will find we do things a little differently, and in a quiet, orderly and controlled manner. I therefore require and expect your indulgence and silence throughout, as any outbursts will not be tolerated. Also, to assist in any domestic arrangements, I expect the trial to be concluded before the week is out.

"I do, however, need to clarify why this case is being tried. A trial is normally required to determine whether or not the accused are guilty of a criminal offence. This usually means that trials only take place when a defendant pleads not guilty. If the defendants plead guilty, as in this instant, there is no legal need for a trial and the case will automatically go forward for sentencing. However, because of the unique circumstances involved, and to allow a fair and equitable hearing with the possibility of further charges being laid, a trial is deemed appropriate, if not entirely necessary in the eyes and the letter of the law. I trust this is not all too confusing and helps you a little to appreciate this complicated but justifiable ruling."

As the judge was speaking, Sir Peter looked across to the public gallery, searching out the old white-haired lady with no fingernails. She, on hearing the judge's caveat, and the likelihood of further charges, crossed her arms in a knowing way of satisfaction, with an old-fashioned smile spreading across her heavily wrinkled face, as she made eye contact with Sir Peter, and winked; it was a private communication that was understood by both.

The judge's fingers were once more interlaced (a sign that Sir Peter noticed indicated that the arbiter was ready to proceed). Judge Rufus Willmott QC then looked to the waiting and expectant officials, and with an economy of movement nodded his head once, almost indiscernibly.

The trial was about to begin.

Chapter 27

The clerk of the court announced, "The court is now in session." He then read out the charges.

"Mr Oscar Ormsby-Waite, Mr Horatio Charteris and Mr Rupert Fordham, who is absent, you are charged that on the 19th of April 2017, you carried out a kidnapping with the aim of extorting and obtaining diamonds, by means of blackmail. How do you plead?"

"Guilty," said Oscar in a clear voice.

"Guilty," repeated Horatio, also clearly heard by all. At this point, the judge interjected and addressed the silent courtroom.

"Ladies and gentlemen, as you will shortly learn, there should also have been a third person in the dock. He, however, has elected on a different course of action to those that stand here before you. Nevertheless, he will still be sentenced, be it in absentia, in order that justice can be seen to have been done." With that, he nodded to the bench of court officials that sat below him.

"Counsel for the prosecution will open," the clerk of the court announced in a clear and loud voice.

Sir Henry Tilehurst QC, unhurriedly stood up, turned to the judge and graciously bowed and nodded in one measured movement, before turning and facing the jury.

"My Lord, ladies and gentlemen of the jury, it is my duty and, with due governance, to set out the burden and standard of proof for this case. By that, I mean I will prove to you in specific terms that the offences were indeed committed by both of the accused you see here today, also by the absent third member. In the simplest of terms, I will tell you what they have done, by discharging the burden of proof and satisfying the standard of proof.

"You may have heard the phrase, 'beyond reasonable doubt'. Members of the jury be assured you will be in no doubt as to their guilt. The fact that they have already pleaded guilty makes this a straightforward case on which you can and should have no difficulty in reaching the right and unanimous verdict. That is all, My Lord."

Nothing to say at this early juncture, if it pleases M' Lord," Sir Peter replied. He too had stood and acknowledged the judge in a similar flamboyant fashion. The judge then took the unusual step of explaining the case background to the court, a procedure normally articulated by both prosecuting and defence counsels.

"Members of the jury, the two accused standing before you in the dock have pleaded guilty as charged, having submitted both oral and written statements describing their crimes, in great detail and with obvious candour. Therefore, I intend to adjourn this hearing until 2 pm this afternoon. In the meantime, you will all be given your own personal copy of the transcripts of their written statements. These you can read and familiarise yourself of the background facts. I'm afraid the rest of the courtroom attendees will have to make do with the emerging facts to be made public from those witnesses when called upon to testify." Again, there was a reassembling of the judge's fingers and a barely perceptible nod to the officials.

"Court is adjourned, to reconvene at 2 pm. All rise."

Judge Willmott stood and left via the same side door that the red admiral had also departed through earlier.

"All rise. Counsel for the prosecution."

Sir Henry Tilehurst QC, the prosecuting counsel on behalf of the Crown, stood up and in a confident and in what can only be termed as a casual almost friendly way, walked the short distance to face the jury. Every pair of eyes and heads now turned and followed his gait. This was his stage and one that he had performed on many times and was confident and assured without appearing to be arrogant or cocky. His aim was to gain the confidence of the jury, as if they were indeed on the same side and wanting the same result. Of course, none of this was implied, implicit or said, but the inference was there, but impossible to have explained or denied. It was a masterful skill that few could carry off or would dare to attempt.

"Members of the jury, this is one of those few cases where the decision and outcome is not in doubt or in dispute. I can state this with the utmost assurance as both of the accused have pleaded guilty as charged. Furthermore, you have now all had time to read your own personal copy of both written confessions. I think you will all agree that what they have said, confirms down to the smallest of details, the preciseness and meticulous planning that went into committing what was a serious and malicious crime. Therefore, do not be beguiled or taken in by the expressions of belated regret and remorse that the defence counsel will surely try to convey. Make no mistake, this was a well-planned and well-executed vicious attack on an elderly lady with serious health problems, and which could easily have had disastrous and long-term consequences. The fact that they gave themselves up, well, two of them, does not excuse or exonerate them from the extremely serious crime committed, as is reflected in the tariff of 'sentence considerations'. However, it would be improper for me to suggest the lengthy custodial sentences that the crime merits; I am obliged to leave that to others more senior."

At which point, the judge intervened, "Be careful, Sir Henry, you are in danger of knowingly making improper innuendoes. Members of the jury please ignore any references to lengths of custodial sentences made by counsel. It is not the prosecuting counsel's place to allude to terms of sentence or to guide you in any such thinking. Sir Henry, you have been warned, you are a person of many years standing at the Bar and you said what you said knowingly, and I will not tolerate such behaviour in my courtroom. Is that clearly understood?"

"Perfectly, M' Lord, and I apologise for any indiscretion, it won't happen again."

"I know it won't," retorted the judge, determined to have the final word.

Sir Henry continued, having been firmly rebuked. He didn't mind the admonishment as the suggestion to the jury could not be 'unheard'. "Members of the jury, let me say, and here I am back on safe ground, the two accused have committed a serious crime for which the law demands that they be punished in accordance with the statute and guidelines laid down. I would also make one further observation regarding the intended use of the money raised. They state that any monies realised would have been lodged with a reputable bank and allocated to named charities, with amounts issued on a monthly basis until the fund was exhausted. This is only their claim, and what's to say that they may well have changed their minds when the money was safely in their hands. One final point, the absent third member of the gang, thought differently and hoped the crime would go undetected, enabling them to carry on as if nothing had happened. That, members of the jury, is not the way in which normal law-abiding people think or react. To their credit, they concede they have done wrong and accept that they need to be punished accordingly. Therefore, I trust you will not disappoint them.

"Please, therefore, allow me as best I can to summarise what we now know. You have read the statements made by both of the accused, and I think you will all agree that they were extremely well-written. In all my years at the Bar, I have never read such comprehensive and perfect syntax submissions, perhaps the benefit and product of a university education where both attained first class degrees with honours. That, members of the jury, is where the honour ended, and the disgrace began.

"From the many pages of testament written, you will have formed more than just a passing impression, that the kidnapping of Mrs Birnbaum, albeit only temporarily, was a premediated and ruthless action. Indeed, the whole sequence of events was planned and carried out with meticulous attention to detail. It would, therefore, be fair to say, and by the authorities (the police) own admission, as we will hear shortly, they would have got away with it, as no meaningful clues were found. However, the thing they had not considered or taken into account was the matter of a subsequent guilty conscience, an ailment that most criminals do not suffer from."

To this last comment, there was a general titter-come-murmur from the public galley, which earned them an 'I'm-not-at-all-amused' look from the judge from over the top of his pince-nez glasses.

"Neither, I might add, had they taken into account the devastating effect the seriousness of their crime would have on not only those directly affected but the knock-on effect to others. Let us first take Mrs Birnbaum, whom I will call in due course, in order to hear at first hand the terrifying and harrowing account of what a helpless, frightened, Type 1 diabetic was forced to endure, whilst being deprived of her freedom of movement and access to her insulin. It would not be an exaggeration or overly dramatic to state that she could have died from what was a horrific ordeal. Furthermore, who is to say what the long-term effects might be? There could well be post-traumatic stress, flashbacks or even a nervous breakdown. Members of the jury, imagine the terror of people breaking into your home and then binding you to a chair and forcibly removing your wedding ring, and then forcing you to give them your husband's office telephone

196

numbers. All of which was to enable them to send a text saying that if he did not comply, he would not see his wife alive again!

"This was not some clever prank concocted by spoilt and self-opinionated university types who thought themselves above the law and intellectually superior by far. It was a heinous crime that they planned, thinking and knowing that they would get away with. And what's to say, having traded in the diamonds that they would then keep the money and not give it to charity as claimed. We only have their word for it.

"Then we have the act, the so-called honourable act, of giving themselves up, pleading a guilty conscience, and supposedly not hurting anybody. Perhaps they ought to ask Mr Birnbaum, who now lives on his own, his wife having left him for another earlier matrimonial problem. This was a problem that would not have come to light, had it not been for the kidnapping and blackmail. That is, to say nothing of Mr Birnbaum's ongoing enquiries with the police and his insurance company."

"Counsel is reminded that his latest remark is sub judice, and is currently under investigation, so please refrain from any further comments on this matter," the judge remarked again, looking over his pince-nez glasses.

"I'm grateful for My Lord's guidance and advice," Sir Henry replied (it didn't matter, the damage was done, as everyone had already heard and noted what had been said. There was no need to elaborate further, the message had been successfully transmitted and could not be expunged from the minds of those present, and as well the canny barrister knew).

"All of which leads us to the irrefutable and undeniable conclusion that they are indeed guilty of committing a serious crime, requiring of the appropriate stiff penalty. Wasn't the seriousness of what they had done, then realised by the absence of the third member accused? He knew that many years in prison awaited him, and was unable to countenance such a prospect, whereas the two now standing in the dock had a more cunning plan. Why not own up and fall on the sword, thereby accruing sympathy and maximum mitigation into the bargain. Any brief worth his salt would argue that the time already spent on remand was punishment enough.

"Members of the jury, I'm sure that my learned defence counsel colleague will try to persuade most in this courtroom," he was careful not to include everyone, "that exemplary mitigation would seem to indicate that they have been punished enough. I sincerely hope and trust this is not your own conclusion or reasoning. A serious crime has been committed and the guilty parties should now receive fair judgment and the full weight of what sentence is available. That, My Lord and members of the jury, is all I need and intend to say. I again apologise for any earlier indiscretion M' Lord."

The judge merely nodded, his poker face revealing nothing, silently he knew that Sir Henry had got his message across. Wasn't that what he would also have done in his shoes?

"I would now like to call Detective Inspector Beaumont, if only to confirm what we already know to be the facts," Sir Henry added.

It had been a masterly performance, conceded Sir Peter to himself, as he knew it would be. The Crown Prosecution Service could not argue with the thoroughness and repeated message again and again saying they were guilty and deserved to go to prison. The look on the faces of the jury was not the look that Sir Peter wanted to see. They would seem to have already decided on both of his clients' fate.

⌒·𝈀𝈀𝈀·∽

Having been duly called and sworn in, Detective Inspector Beaumont of the Metropolitan Police Crime Squad took the stand and explained the police involvement. This he did in a slow and laborious manner, constantly having to refer back to his notebook. He described how he had been placed in charge of the case, having been one of the two officers to collect the two accused from Cambridge. He had also arranged the forensic interrogation of the four crime scenes. He finally closed his notebook, by which time most in the courtroom had lost the will to live.

"You say four crime scenes, Inspector?" Sir Henry asked, knowing exactly what they were (but hardly scenes), which at least regained waning interest.

"Yes, sir, there was Mrs Birnbaum's house, the Citroen car, Mr Birnbaum's store premises and the drop point."

"And what was the outcome?" Sir Henry asked.

"No fingerprints were found due to the wearing of gloves and no clues to follow up on. The Citroen's two punctures we discovered had been deliberate, as explained earlier in my statement, but again no fingerprints. The waste bin on the lamppost was also checked but nothing found or expected. The only unexpected discovery was made in Mr Birnbaum's office regarding the diamonds, but I've been instructed not to elaborate as it's the subject of a further ongoing investigation." Sir Peter turned in his chair and again looked to the see the nail-less lady smiling and nodding her head in some secret and satisfying manner, with arms evenly more firmly crossed!

"Finally, Inspector, has there been any developments in apprehending the third gang member?" Sir Henry asked, with deliberate emphasis on the use of the word 'gang'.

"None whatsoever, sir, he has not been seen since he disappeared from King's College two days before the graduation," he again checked his notebook, "on the 19th of April. All airports, docks and ferry ports were notified but no reported sighting made. Both of the accused also stated they had no idea as to his whereabouts and neither did his family and other friends. It seems, if I may be permitted to suggest, that he may well have gone abroad without being detected, sir."

"Thank you for that useful suggestion, Inspector, that will be all," Sir Henry replied, without too much loaded sarcasm in his voice, whilst thinking the rank of inspector was probably one rank too high for Mr Beaumont.

It therefore came as no surprise when Sir Peter declined to cross-examine what had been a tortuously slow and pedestrian performance by the inspector, who was clearly relieved to leave the stand. For the jury, judge and counsels, it was merely a reiteration of what they had already been told or at least read. The only beneficiaries were those in the public gallery, who were given a running commentary of what had taken place from start to finish. So, in a funny sort of way, the inspector had done most in the courtroom a huge favour − albeit unwittingly.

"Ladies and gentlemen, I think we've heard quite enough for one day," the judge audibly sighed. "Court will reconvene at ten tomorrow morning. Members of the jury, may I again remind you not to discuss any part of this case outside of this building." The foreman of the jury (a secondary modern school headmaster) nodded, as if conveying the acknowledgement of all 12.

"All rise," again, the usher's dulcet tones were heard. Judge Willmott stood and slowly turned to face the public gallery, raising one long red-sleeved robe, as if acknowledging their silent good behaviour throughout the day. He didn't say that, in fact he didn't utter a word, but the action was received and construed as such, as he left the chamber, with no sight of any lingering butterfly.

Sir Peter quickly made his way out and downstairs, eager to have a word before Oscar and Horatio were whisked off back to Belmarsh for the night.

"How do you think it's going?" Oscar enquired, surprised but happy to see their advocate.

"As well as can be expected," Sir Peter answered. "You heard for yourselves what a performance Sir Henry put in. I know you both play tennis, so let me use a suitable analogy. He didn't miss a single point and I'm sure he left the jury with the impression that you two are the biggest pair of bastards ever to have walked the earth and deserve to get life! So, in tennis parlance, I would say it's thirty-love to them, with possibly two more aces yet to be served in the form of Mr and Mrs Birnbaum."

"Not good at all, then," surmised Horatio.

"Don't be so defeatist. I think this will go to five sets and remember there's no tie break, and I have yet to say my piece, and do not forget the importance of the mitigation, which could be a set advantage to us. See you tomorrow."

"Court is now in session," the clerk of the court called.

"Call Mr Birnbaum," said the usher, the beckoned witness appeared looking decidedly nervous.

Sir Henry began again in a seemingly seamless manner, as if there had been no recess or night of contemplation from when he had last addressed them.

"Members of the jury, you and the defence counsel have copies of your written statement. Therefore, we will spare you the obvious distress of having to repeat the entire terrifying experience in every horrifying detail." Sir Henry was clearly trying to build up the drama before Mrs Birnbaum took the stand. "Can you simply tell us what you remember most of the ordeal, and how you and your wife managed to cope in the face of such adversity?"

Mr Birnbaum was not in a good state and this was reflected in his edgy and sweaty appearance. He was in a quandary and not at all sure what he could say. A lot had happened since that eventful day, his life taking a definite turn, more a dive, for the worse. His wife had been outraged at discovering his engagement ring scam, and this she had used as a pretext for leaving him. Her short and dramatic departure had been totally unreasonable, in his opinion (whilst most thought he had been the unreasonable one). An opinion shared by a certain old lady in the public gallery named Ruby Cohen.

There was now the ongoing and worrying police investigation into the discrepancy between the number of diamonds he claimed to have handed over and the subsequent number recovered. Never in his wildest of avarice dreams did he expect the perpetrators to hand themselves in and return the diamonds intact and untouched! He was between a rock and a hard place. He was damned if he said anything and damned if he didn't! He knew he'd committed perjury, this despite having repeatedly being warned to be completely honest regarding what stock had been given, as both the police and insurers would need to be satisfied where hundreds of thousands of pounds are involved. His situation had not improved when the police found the incriminating diamond-filled envelope taped to the underside of his office desk. Perhaps it may have been better if he too had scarpered off to Madagascar!

His only plausible way ahead was to explain how he had acted as quickly as was humanly possible to prevent any harm or suffering befalling his wife. He'd done as demanded and had been the innocent victim for which he was now paying a hefty price. It was all sad but true, as Mr Birnbaum now stood in the dock a beaten man, where his irresistible greed and avarice had been his nemesis. He looked and sounded broken, despite the hollow words he uttered disingenuously and unconvincingly.

"I think we'll leave it there." It was the defence counsel's Sir Peter who eventually put the poor man out of his misery. "In view of the ongoing investigation by both the police and the insurers, we cannot delve further into the matter of the diamonds. Suffice to say, they were recovered in full and without damage." (Again, Sir Peter had conveyed sufficient information to the jury, with the only damage being inflicted upon the man now leaving the dock. One didn't need to be a rocket scientist, a detective or a diamond expert to know what had happened. As to how one damaged a diamond Sir Peter admitted he was at a loss to know.)

"We are all greatly obliged to your thoughtfulness and the need for sub judice," the judge added with heavy sarcasm, knowing damn well what Sir Peter had achieved without actually stepping outside of the chalked lines, whereby he could quite rightly have called the ball was out! Both Sir Henry and Sir Peter had played shots that had barely caught the edge of the court, but a puff of white dust kept them in play! Wasn't that why they were recognised as two of the two top seeded barristers?

"Call Mrs Birnbaum…"

The appearance and testimony that followed by the main witness was not at all what the prosecuting counsel had hoped to see and hear. To start with, her looks and demeanour were not that of a little terrified insulin-dependent diabetic old lady, as earlier and graphically portrayed by Sir Henry. Her recent and permanent departure from North London to the Bay of Haifa in Israel had been a rejuvenated fresh start in life, aided and abetted by the help and insistence of a loving daughter and understanding son-in-law. The situation would shortly be further enhanced with the soon to arrive friend, another elderly lady by the name of Mrs Cohen!

Mrs Birnbaum stood in the witness box, appearing confident and composed, whilst also looking to be fit and well. She wore a smart light blue two-piece suit, a plain white silk blouse set off by a light blue silk scarf, all of which complimented her recently acquired Mediterranean tan. The brown hands that rested on the wooden rail were still and steady, with not a ring or a diamond in sight. In a bizarre, illogical and confounding way, the intrusion had been the very making of her renaissance!

Her face displayed an enviable hue, not burnt but looking a picture of health. She was then asked, by the prosecuting counsel, to explain what had happened on that dreadful day, if it would not cause her too much distress or upset. Mrs Birnbaum had nodded and went on to recount what had happened in a clear voice and without elaboration… It was the refreshing honesty of her words, expressed in such a matter-of-fact way, that struck home and firmly implanted in everyone's mind.

"They were not rough or uncaring they were after all, women! I truly did believe they were French mademoiselles. Even when I was told later that they were in fact three university boys, I still found it hard to believe. In many respects, I have them to thank for leaving me the *Diamond Dealers* magazine, which was the catalyst or possible trigger for my move back to Israel and the start of a new life. Of course, it wasn't an enjoyable experience, and I was initially frightened, but to be honest, I never at any time felt threatened. I've since been told that they wish to see me and apologise and explain themselves – face to face. This I am more than willing to do, as it seems to be an honest and sincere gesture, if only to draw a line under the complete episode. I certainly don't want the intrusion (again the word intrusion) to ruin the rest of their lives. In an odd and fortuitous way their moment of madness has enabled me to begin a new chapter in what for many years has been a miserable existence. Had it not happened, I would still be living unhappily in Golders Green with nothing much to look forward to other than a few bagels and my weekly visit to the synagogue.

"I know this is not the damning testimony that the prosecuting counsel wanted or indeed expected to hear, but it's the truth, and isn't that what I swore to do when I placed my hand on the Bible?"

It was the judge who broke the silence, a silence that spoke volumes of admiration for a woman who was prepared to tell the whole truth in a way that captured the hearts of most present that day in Woolwich Number One Crown Court.

"Thank you, Mrs Birnbaum, for what was truly a breathtakingly honest account and assessment of what took place and delivered with enlightening candour. I suspect there will be no post-traumatic stress in your new home looking out onto the Mediterranean Sea," the judge replied. "I think we've all heard more than enough for one day. Court will reconvene at 10 am tomorrow."

"All rise."

Chapter 28

"All rise, counsel for the defence," the usher said.

Sir Peter got to his feet, coughed twice with exaggerated effect as he began his own performance; after all, he had two extraordinary acts to follow, that of Sir Henry and Mrs Birnbaum.

"My Lord, members of the jury, this has been a short but fascinating case on which you have been asked to adjudicate. As I hope you are all aware, we in Britain enjoy the finest judicial system in the world, which has served the nation well over its many years of enactment. Today, I have to confess, of being placed in the unique position of requesting, as I certainly cannot direct, that you consider the law to be an ass. This apologetic and confusing statement of course demands clarification."

It was the sort of dramatic statement he needed to make in order to grab everyone's attention. This he certainly did, as you could have heard a pin drop, or possibly hear the wings of any would-be passing butterfly. "Council for the prosecution has eloquently made the case against the two accused now standing before you in the dock. He has clearly articulated and described the course of events leading up to the crime and is to be congratulated on the number of times he repeatedly said they were guilty. This he achieved in a painstakingly detailed manner, from the very beginning when the letter of invitation was first sent by Mr Ormsby-Waite, through to their eventual surrender and confession. It has to be said that his task was made that much the easier by their pleading guilty to both charges, together with the most erudite and comprehensive statements that they made – both written and oral. Therefore, it appears to be a prima facie case, with nothing more needed to be said. It should now be a simple matter of due process with My Lord passing the appropriate custodial sentences.

"However, members of the jury, I crave your indulgence and attention for a while longer, whilst I give you other options and considerations for you to include in your ultimate deliberations. Before you now, stand two bright upstanding men who admit to having broken the law by committing a serious crime. Then, in the space of a relatively short period of time – no more than three months – they both came to realise the error of their ways. Theirs was a crime, some of you may reasonably consider, meticulously and cleverly planned and executed, by nothing more than spoilt, arrogant and self-opinionated intelligent young undergraduates from wealthy families. Therefore, shouldn't they be fully deserving of their comeuppance and the punishment commensurate and in line with what their crime merits?

"But do not throw away their cell door key yet, as I ask you to consider these other factors. Yes, they committed a crime, of that there is no dispute and to which they voluntarily surrendered themselves at the same as making full and honest confessions. We have also learnt during this trial, that it was a crime – in all probability – that they would have got away with. The police have been candid in admitting they had no clues or lines of enquiry that in anyway linked the two accused to the crime.

"However, what the two offenders hadn't taken into account or indeed planned for, was the innate but unpredictable gift we all possess called a conscience, and in their case a guilty one! So much so, they were prepared to sacrifice the prospects of successful careers in the desire to own up, if only for decencies sake and their own peace of mind, or possible forgiveness in some other form or another. This was a noble act and I do not use the word lightly, knowing they would irreparably damage themselves and hurt and shame their families.

"Their laudable decision to give themselves up, was made appreciably more complex by the refusal of the third member, who could not in any way countenance the plan of action they now proposed. His decision to flee the country, which we can only presume, did not help them, neither will it ultimately help him, as sentencing will undoubtedly be reflected in his decision not to surrender or confess to his part in the crime.

"A further point to be made is that they have already displayed genuine contrition by writing to Mrs Birnbaum, requesting that they be allowed to call on her, even at her new home in Israel if needs be, to express their personal deepest regret and remorse. The fact that they intended that any monies would be given to charities with no personal gain to themselves, maybe considered praiseworthy, although it is accepted that it was neither their diamonds nor money to make such a gift.

"Now, members of the jury, you have to decide whether the law is indeed an ass or should be upheld. A crime was committed, to which they have confessed and pleaded guilty. To this end, they have both spent the past five months on remand in Belmarsh High Security Prison awaiting trial. If you find them guilty as charged, then a substantial custodial sentence is likely. I would, however, ask you to consider the exemplary mitigation, this I will do as best I am able..."

The professor smiled to himself in the public gallery, knowing full well that Sir Peter was more than able to express himself clearly and concisely on any number of matters, and all done with never a hint or suggestion as to his preference for the cause or consideration stated in the explicit explanation.

Both sides of the case had now been presented, each in a persuasive and convincing manner. This was the silent conclusion made by Judge Willmott, who had his own persuasions and thoughts to make.

"That's quite enough for this morning. Court will reconvene at 2 pm."

"All rise."

Before leaving, the judge whispered a request in the clerk of the court's ear.

Ten minutes later, Sir Henry, Sir Peter, the clerk of the court and the foreman of the jury all sat in the judge's private chambers. This was a highly irregular meeting as everyone present knew, as they were offered either tea or coffee as a possible softener or precursor of what was yet to come.

"Gentlemen, I have never held such a tryst in all my years of serving as a High Court judge, as you might eventually wish to remind me so, or advise me that I am out of order. However, having now listened to all of the witnesses, including the wonderful Mrs Birnbaum, although the same cannot be said of her now estranged husband, I think we've all heard enough. I have, therefore taken this unique step of gathering you all here to listen to my strictly-off-the-record conclusions and proposal.

"Before I go any further, I need to remind you all, and indeed myself, of the judicial oath I took: 'I Rufus Willmott QC, swear by Almighty God that I will well and truly serve our Sovereign Lady Queen Elizabeth the Second in the office of High Court judge, and I will do right to all manner of people after the laws and usages of the realm, without fear or favour, affection or ill will'. I have, therefore, asked the clerk of the court to be present, to provide some measure of legality before he frogmarches me off to the tower if he deems that I am straying or suggesting something way outside of the remit."

"I have so pledged." Everyone smiled and sort of half-laughed, but anxious to know what this illegal and somewhat clandestine meeting was all about.

"Sir Henry, you have played a straight bat and presented the prosecution's case fairly and professionally down to the last crumb of minutiae. You cannot be faulted for your attention to detail, and also for your recommendation of custodial sentences. The fact of the matter is, that having pleaded guilty and there being no dispute as to what actually took place, it should be a simple case of sentencing. My dilemma and question are this: what good would it serve? They have already spent five months on remand in Belmarsh, and surely any further custodial sentence would be a futile exercise and a sheer waste of the taxpayers' money. I think we would all agree that these are not two common criminals, and highly unlikely ever again to step outside of the law. This leads directly to my proposition.

"It seems to me that should we follow the letter of the law, might the law itself be considered an ass? Or, as my oath requires, I do right by all manner of people, which I admit might be construed as cherry-picking and being somewhat selective. My question is, should we bend the rules to be commensurate and befitting the crime? Or do I abide by the rules as laid down in the sentencing considerations, which are invariably adhered to? Mrs Birnbaum has certainly demonstrated and displayed a forgiving and ambivalent attitude and questioning stance, and is she not leading by example? But as we all know, it's not as simple as that, it never is otherwise I wouldn't have invited you behind closed doors. Yes, they committed a crime, and yes, they pleaded guilty, and have already paid somewhat with their forced incarceration. The sticking point and problem are: the third member could not bring himself to take the same honourable route as his two colleagues. This fact cannot be ignored, and the law's due process must be done.

"As an aside, the unfortunate and wretched Mr Birnbaum, seems to have brought about his own ills, and is a long way from being out of the woods. As well we all know – be sure your sins will catch you out! What I am outrageously suggesting to you, foreman of the jury, is that you find the two accused not guilty."

There was an audible gasp of surprise from all those present; this was not what was expected. Everyone was expecting that leniency would be proposed, with minimum custodial sentences due to the extenuating and exemplary mitigation. But not a verdict of not guilty!

"I can see that has come as quite a surprise to you all, please let me elaborate and explain my thinking. Mrs Birnbaum is content to draw a line under the whole affair and paradoxically appears to be benefitting by it. The two are not criminals as we know, and this was clearly a moment of madness. If we were to find them guilty, it would forever taint them with a criminal record. Is that really what the law and society want? The Charteris lad has already been offered a teaching position back at King's, with a lifetime of respectable academia ahead of him, which can surely only benefit the hundreds of students to come. Ormsby-Waite obtained a first with honour in law, and has excellent prospects of becoming a barrister, this aspiration would immediately disappear."

"Perhaps he should have thought of that in the first place," Sir Henry spoke out.

"Is it that I'm in danger of being too judgemental and getting soft in my old age?" The poker face had disappeared, replaced by a warmer and open appearance. "I think that sufficient justice has already been done."

"I entirely agree," replied Sir Peter, greatly encouraged by what the judge had said.

"Within this chamber, I also agree," Sir Henry added. "However, forgive me if I do not share this opinion once back in court. I'm sure from our shared experiences we have come to expect the unexpected and the odd one or two who always fail to see or agree with the party line. I fear that what you are proposing may not come to fruition or indeed be acceptable, with the greatest of respect My Lord." Sir Henry knew Rufus Willmott well, but would never presume to use Christian names at such a gathering, despite being behind closed doors.

"I entirely agree, Sir Henry, but hindsight is a wonderful gift and gives us all 20-20 vision. Of course, they've done wrong, but should it blight or ruin life's prospects of two highly intelligent young men? Surely, if Mrs Birnbaum can find it in her heart to forgive them, perhaps the law should be equally as magnanimous.

"However, your point Sir Henry is well made and taken. Therefore, if the foreman cannot persuade the entire jury to arrive at a unanimous not guilty, then the law must play its part and a verdict of guilty returned. That is my dilemma and proposal, which you are under no obligation or pressure to acquiesce. At the end of the day, it is for the jury to come to its own decision, and I hope this suggestion has not put anyone feeling in an invidious or awkward position. You must do what you consider is right, it is merely an option which you may wish to float," the judge ended, interlacing his fingers once more.

The foreman of the jury looked around, as if wishing to obtain some tacit approval to speak. Everyone looked in his direction, as this was clearly expected.

"I can see where you're coming from, My Lord, and I think that what you are suggesting is pragmatic and eminently sensible. However, my own gut feeling having been with the other 11 for the past two days is that most would go along with what you have proposed, but not all. There are one or two – no names, that would pick a fight in an empty room, if you get my meaning. So, I'm not at all hopeful."

"That's fair enough, if it's not to be then it's not to be, but at least I'd like to think that I've honoured my oath in full and given it my best shot, even if slightly and legally askew," the judge concluded.

"Sir Henry, you were absolutely right to point out the likely googlies or leg breaks, but at least you are now aware of which end of the crease I'm bowling from." The judge was an ardent cricket fan (not tennis) and knew full well of Tristram Charteris, and his meteoric rise in becoming the captain of Kent County Cricket Club, of which he was also a board member like Sir Peter.

"Let's hope we win the toss and get a good declaration from the jury," Sir Peter added, if only to continue the cricketing analogy, underscoring his love of the game, which he considered far superior to the somewhat genteel and convenient game of tennis. There was clearly no point in either Sir Henry or Sir Peter adding anything further, the judge and the foreman had said it all. The clerk of the court left with the foreman of the jury, a mightily relieved man that he didn't have to escort his lordship off to the Tower of London!

"All rise," the usher called out, as everyone stood. By now, the courtroom rituals had become familiar, with the usher's directive not really necessary or indeed required, but protocol demanded. The judge entered, stood and looked to all four corners, as if to indicate and imply that now was the moment of reckoning. He then took his seat and interlaced his fingers. His eloquent summing up began, at the end of what had been a short four-day trial.

"Members of the jury, when I read the case brief, I thought it straightforward, done and dusted, as simple as 'ABC', or falling off a log – this has proved not to be so. For the letter *A*, we have heard of ambition, ability, audacity and anguish. For *B*, there has been boldness, blackmail, benevolence and Belmarsh, and for *C*, culpability, contrition, compassion and now conviction.

"It is, therefore, my onerous duty to present to you the facts of this case without bias, fear or favour, and not to wear my heart on my sleeve, which I must admit I have been tempted to do, as my learned colleagues now know. Members of the jury, this should have been an easy and straightforward task for you all, in reaching the verdict of guilty on all counts, inasmuch that two of the three accused had given themselves up and admitted to their crimes. I will take this strong and valid mitigation into consideration when passing sentence. We can all be wise after the event, all I'm suggesting is that you think outside of the legal box, if only as an option.

"You may consider, on balance, contradicting the logic and letter of the law by returning a verdict of not guilty. However, for you to do this requires a unanimous decision by all 12 of you. If, however, all 12 cannot agree, with one or any number of dissenters, then a verdict of guilty is mandatory. Whatever decision you arrive at, I am obliged to accept. In short, what I am asking or suggesting is outside that of normal protocols and accepted lawful procedures, but for the reasons I have endeavoured to convey in good faith, I trust you can now understand, if not in agreement with.

"Court will now adjourn until 10 am tomorrow, when I hope you will have reached your verdict."

"All rise."

"All rise."

"Members of the jury, have you reached your verdict?" the judge asked, as he looked across the courtroom at the 12 faces that had become familiar to him over the past three days. It was Thursday. The trial had only lasted three and a half days, probably due to the pleas of guilty and the small number of witnesses. This would enable the judge to go and watch Kent play Surrey at the Oval for the next two days, not that this was his aim in what had been a foreshortened trial.

"We have, My Lord – guilty."

"Thank you, Foreman, both to you and the rest of the jury for your attentiveness and due diligence throughout this trial. You have discharged your duties in a totally satisfactory manner. Normally, I would defer sentencing, but not in this case. I have already decided on what sentences to pass, whichever way the verdict went. This I will now do, rather than cause unnecessary anxiety and frustration with an unseemly and inconsiderate delay.

"Mr Fordham is sentenced to one year's imprisonment."

"Mr Ormsby-Waite and Mr Charteris, you are sentenced to 125 days imprisonment, this being the exact amount of time you have already served in Belmarsh Prison whilst on remand. In addition, you will both complete 200 hours of community payback work, to be accomplished within the next two calendar months in and around the North London district of Golders Green. You are now free to leave."

"All rise."

Everyone in the courtroom stood, obediently silent as the judge turned to leave the courtroom. This time it was broken, as was the protocol of remaining so until the door had closed, although the judge must have heard the excited whispering that had already begun. The judge smiled to himself, he was content that he had made the right decision and there would not be any appeal demanding an increase in the sentences' severity or length. There was no prize for guessing what the topic of conversation was!

The first person to greet both Oscar and Horatio outside of the courtroom was not Sir Peter, or their parents, but Mrs Birnbaum and Mrs Cohen. The two old ladies were evidently nimbler on their feet and quicker of mind than many of the younger ones, of which there were many.

"I understand you both wished to see me?" Mrs Birnbaum greeted them with a warm smile on her face. The next ten minutes was spent with sincere regrets and profuse apologises being made and gracefully accepted. All the time, the parents and Sir Peter stood politely by, happy at what was taking place. Eventually, two charming and gracious ladies left, they had a plane to catch!

It was then Doddy's turn, with Violet dutifully and tactfully keeping well away from all the commotion. The professor was easily recognised, wearing the same green corduroy suit, with yellow silk handkerchief that hung precariously from his top pocket and on the verge of committing Hari-Kari by jumping ship. The shoes still hadn't seen a lick of polish and the shirt looked none too smart, but the smile and warmth was genuine enough, the handshake firm. It was not difficult to see who the barrister and the absent-minded academic were. These were the private thoughts of the nearby Mr O-W!

"Oscar, you blithering idiot," that was Professor Dodderington's greeting to his last star pupil. "There was I worrying about you burning the midnight oil with all that unnecessary swotting, when all the time you were planning some brilliant diamond heist! Well, from what I can gather, you both got off as lightly as was humanly possible, but you've buggered your barrister hopes. I suppose you know that?"

"Thanks for reminding me, DD, but it's good to see you anyway. I think I'll take up your UNICEF suggestion; it will get me abroad and at the same time I'll still be using my legal knowhow. We're both eternally grateful for your prompt action in sorting out Sir Peter for us. He's been an absolute star, as you've seen and heard for yourself, and I understand he has still another duty to perform?"

"Yes, rather, he's going to be my best man, this coming Saturday, to which you are chief usher! We took a huge gamble on the date, but it all turned out well in the end. Now you better come and meet my wife-to-be. I've told her so much about you." Oscar wasn't sure of how much Doddy had told her, or had she learnt enough already? Violet was duly introduced as his bride-to-be by a proud and beaming Doddy.

Later in the comfort of a hotel lounge, there sat a large gathering of extremely happy people. In addition to the families and Sir Peter, there was Doddy and Violet, together with Oscar's entire tutorial group, one of which in imminent danger of giving birth, plus of course, two convicted free men. After the initial excitement had elapsed, Sir Peter explained what efforts the judge had tried to make on their behalf. It transpired that only one member of the jury was adamant that a guilty verdict was returned – there's always one!

Oscar and Horatio consoled the Fordhams. It was clear they were putting on a brave face, still feeling the hurt of their son's disappearance and now the spectre of prison, which did little to alleviate their loss and despair. They both promised they would keep in touch. It was only then the Fordhams confessed they'd known for years of his bisexual orientation and more worryingly of his bipolar condition. They had wisely decided not to say anything, what good would it have done? They loved him for what and who he was, and there was no arguing with their logic. After all, he'd got to Cambridge, which was no small feat; so perhaps they were right after all.

Eventually Oscar and Horatio went their separate ways to dine with their families. Mr Ormsby-Waite had forgiven Oscar, and all was well. Time is a great healer and be thankful for what you've got, not what you wish for.

Epilogue

If one tells the truth, one is sure, sooner or later, to be found out.

Mark Twain

Should you (heaven forbid), be of a mind that you've read enough or have suffered sufficient then stop now with no harm done? All that can be reasonably hoped is that you enjoyed the yarn and still of an inquisitive nature, whilst retaining some glimmer of dormant if irresistible idle curiosity. If so, then all is now thoughtfully explained, revealing what became of our main cast of players.

The beginning of the story told of an African farmer, who dreamt of striking it rich. He was not unique. There was another man, let's call him Al Hafed, who lived on the banks of the River Indus, who had a nice farm with orchards and gardens, excess cash, a beautiful wife and children. He was wealthy and contented. Then an old priest visited him and one night related how the world was made, including the foundation of all rocks, the earth, the precious crystals and stones. He told the farmer that if he had a few diamonds, he could have not just one farm but many. The farmer listened. Suddenly, he wasn't that happy with what he had thus far acquired in life.

He sold up and went travelling in search of diamonds across Persia, Palestine and into Europe. A few years later, what money he had was gone, and he was left wandering around in rags. When a large wave came in from the sea, he was happily swept under it! For the man who had bought the farmer's land, it was quite a different story. One day, walking his animals in the stream that ran through the property, he noticed a glint in the watery sands. It was a diamond. In fact, it was one of the richest diamond finds in history: the mines of Golconda would yield not just one but many acres of diamonds.

(Golconda is a district of Hyderabad in India. The region is known for the mines that have produced some of the world's most famous gems, including the Koh-I- Noor, the Hope and Nassak Diamonds.)

Perhaps a third such farmer is a man called Mr Isaac Birnbaum, who now ekes out a lonely and sad existence in a one-bedroom flat in Brent near to Golders Green in London, having lost the most valuable things in his life − his family. Sadly, his deep-rooted meanness and greed has left him without a friend in the world, as he counts what little money he has remaining, instead of counting the blessings of what he once had, but without ever fully appreciating or deserving of them. The moral is surely: be grateful for what you have and be careful for what you wish for.

The wild, hair-brained and irresponsible scheme carried out by three undergraduates to execute their own diamond heist had serious and lasting implications on a number of people. To some, it was detrimental, but not to all, as in some cases it proved to be a definite bonus!

They do say that every cloud has a silver lining, and that when the lion feeds, someone else suffers. This proved to be the case with both sayings. Well, at least the first adage had justifiable credibility, according to at least two fringe participants, in what could be termed a modern-day Shakespearean tragedy, or should that be a love story?

For the Birnbaum family, it was far from being a love story. For Mr Birnbaum, the pleasure of getting his precious diamonds back was short lived. His avarice and deplorable treatment of his immediate family cost him his marriage with future visits to the courts to explain his far from truthful statement. Most important of all was the fact that his wife had finally decided that enough was enough. For many years − more than she wished to remember − Mrs

Birnbaum had suffered in silence at the hands of a husband – who was in reality married to money. Greed has an uncanny knack of leaving a nasty taste in the mouth with pernicious habits manifesting themselves in every day-to-day life, with alas, unforeseen consequential side-effects.

One such side-effect was the ongoing enquiry by both the police and the insurance company into the claim made by Mr Birnbaum. At the time, it had been a confident and outrageously exaggerated claim, no doubt made with the sure and certain knowledge that the diamonds would never be found. Now, there existed the somewhat amazing but embarrassing situation, whereby the diamonds had been returned – intact and voluntarily!

Mrs Birnbaum had not been happy for many years; she never should have married him in the first place; her wise old mother had unsuccessfully counselled. But, having made her bed, she was determined to lay on it. However, her husband's meanness and his constant desire to make and have more money clouded and overshadowed any marital happiness that there was. It was learning of the diabolical trick he had played on his own daughter and not the intrusion that was the final straw. She went with never a hint and without his knowing, she had left, not saying a word, save that of a brief note, informing him that her solicitor would be in touch to set in train divorce proceedings on the irrefutable grounds of his long-term unreasonable behaviour. This he ably illustrated by retaliating and informing her that she would not get a penny piece and he would fight her in every court in the land. He naively and incorrectly assumed she had no money and that she would be forced to return, cap in hand begging forgiveness, how wrong he was. What Mr Birnbaum had not known was that Aalijah Birnbaum was a wealthy woman in her own right. Her grandparents had bestowed on her an appreciable largesse, which had remained a secret – in case of a rainy day. Now was such an inclement time to put up the umbrella of self-sufficiency and financial independence.

The ensuing and protracted court appearances cost him a small fortune, but such was his blind pig-headed nature he didn't know when to call it a day. This despite being advised so by the wealthy lawyers, who continued to demand their hefty fees. In addition, he then decided (unwisely) to defend himself in court against the charges brought against him by the insurance company. Again, he should have put his hands up and come clean, but he couldn't it was not within his adversarial nature. The predictable outcome was that he was forced to continue to fork out for two courts cases, which eventually exhausted all of his financial reserves and more. In the end, he had to sell both his house and his company; he'd lost everything. He now lives alone in a small one-bedroom flat with not a friend in the world. His acres of diamonds were now no more than a dump of despair, with the prospect of becoming a prison cell.

Conversely, where life was now doom and gloom for Mr Birnbaum, for Mrs Birnbaum it was now sweetness and light. The silver lined clouds proved to be so. In a perverse and ironic sort of way, the intrusion and learning of her daughter's ring were the absolute making of her. It provided the impetus she required (and justification) to leave her husband, which had been encouraged to do, and for a long time by her good friend and neighbour, Ruby Cohen. The final endorsement and plea coming from her daughter, asking that her mother join them back in Israel. This she had done and with surprising alacrity and speed. Then, after living with her daughter for a short spell of two months, she had found a well-appointed first-floor two-bedroomed flat some ten miles further along the coast. Aalijah then made a similar suggestion and plea that Ruby come and join her. Needless to say, Mrs Cohen needed no second bidding. They now live happily together with a lovely group of neighbours-come-friends. Near enough to her daughter, but not too near, to give everyone the space they needed.

Not far away, there lived an extremely rich Jewish jeweller and his family. It was rumoured, but never proven, that he had made an absolute killing out of the Antwerp Diamond heist, but no one knows how (that is except of course a certain Leonardo Notarbartolo, who would love to have known where he now resided).

Whilst Mrs Birnbaum flourished, Mr Birnbaum never did see the error of his ways. Even now in his one-roomed flat, he still seeks a way of trying to make a fortune. There are two further sayings: *There is no fool like and old fool*, and *Fools never prosper*.

For the families of the three misguided graduates, it was a scarring chapter in their lives, now needing time to heal the deep and hurtful wounds. There is another saying: *Time is a great healer*, and so this proved to be the case except not for the Fordhams. Sadly, they never did see or hear from their son Raffer, remaining an ever-open sore.

For the three main players, in a production that should never have been staged, the curtain calls produced interesting results. The audience (you the reader) will hopefully surmise that the human spirit to survive and make the best of a self-imposed bad deal is truly remarkable. As one anthropologist was later heard to say, 'it's almost as if it was preordained and meant to happen'. None of it would have happened, if a certain student had not immersed himself in reading *The Diamond Dealers* magazine and of the Antwerp and Hatton Garden robberies. The gang that carried out the latter still languish in one of HM prisons, whereas a certain Leonardo Notarbartolo had recently been released. He no longer resides in Turin, but has moved across the border into a beautiful part of southern Switzerland in the Italian-speaking canton of Ticino bordering Italy and handy for the town of Lugano – the best of both worlds!

Having been released from the Belgium prison, he had returned home to his family, and to put the finishing touches to a plan he had had plenty of time to arrange. The removal vans arrived and the Notarbartolo family moved into a small hotel for two nights. They then drove through the Alps to their new home. On the way, in one remote stretch, of which there were many, Notarbartolo left the car to disappear off road, ensuring he was unseen. This he did on five separate occasions, but all within the distance of about one mile. It would seem that the Italian Alps did indeed contain acres of diamonds!

Before finally turning to the three main players in our drama, we need to spare a thought and mention the role played by Oscar's mentor, who had found them their courtroom saviour – Sir Peter. It is of course the main supporting part played by Professor Dodderington.

After Doddy's initial disappointment on learning of his star pupil's erring, he had rallied and done all that he could to help, and more. Privately, he had been bitterly disappointed by Oscar's action, and illogically blamed himself, which of course this was not the case. Over the past three hardworking years He'd spent many hours with Oscar, in his room and walking along the riverbank and thought he knew him well. He decided that in future he would only have complete trust and have faith in poets and musicians who had already departed this mortal coil – better the devil you know!

In addition to the Oscar and Co affair, the professor had also decided to retire to the Lake District, where he had experienced the unexpected emotional highs of falling in love and a subsequent matrimonial union. This was certainly not envisaged or a hitherto planned retirement regime for this die-hard, slightly eccentric bachelor, whose two main loves in life had been Wagner and poetry, and probably in that order.

It was the most strangest of matrimonial unions but it worked. Upon reaching his 60th birthday, Doddy had paid a flying and unexpected visit back to the Lake District and confronted the Pilkingtons with a proposition, which they agreed to whilst being tickled pink with what the professor had proposed.

Having received the Pilkington's approval, Doddy made his way to the lower end of the village of Bassenthwaite and called upon a certain Violet Thackery. He smilingly asked if she would like a drink in the nearby *The Poacher Inn,* to which she was already well acquainted. There over a pint of best bitter and a gin and tonic he took her small, pudgy and calloused-hand and asked if she would do him the extraordinary privilege of consenting to be his lawful wife! He did so, knowing full well that the other occupants were listening and looking on with avid expectancy.

"Doddy, you bloody old fool. Do you mean it?"

"Of course I mean it. Why should I pay to have you come in and clean the cottage which I am shortly to be the new owner, when you can share it as my wife?"

"Of course I'll marry you, my adorable hunk," Violet replied, as she wrapped herself around him, knocking his almost full pint of ale all over the floor! There was a thunderous round of applause, with the landlord bringing him a full and replenished glass.

"Congratulations Professor and you too Violet. This one is on the house." Having finished off their drinks, the happy couple disappeared to go and tell Violet's mother. The response was one of unexpected delight.

"'Bout time 'yon made an 'onest w'man out of 'yon. Best you stay the night," Violet's mother said, winking to Doddy, which meant more than a thousand words ever could have. It was true they made the oddest of couples. Doddy was big, bulbous and awkward. Violet was small and even more bulbous. He was highly intelligent and well-educated; she dim and barely literate. He loved Wagner and classical music and poetry; she adored *Coronation Street* and girly magazines. And so, the saying proved true: *Like poles repel, whilst unlike poles attract.*

They were married on the Saturday, only two days after the completion of the trial. Sir Peter had returned the compliment of being best man and Oscar the chief usher, ably assisted by Horatio. The timing and the wedding in Bassenthwaite could not have been more perfect. Oscar had spent one night with his parents in their new chocolate box home before travelling north. There, he was free (literally) to help Doddy and Violet in making the last-minute arrangements. The decision to invite and involve Horatio had been Violets kind afterthought.

The wedding was a grand affair and Bassenthwaite had never seen anything like it. St Bega's church was full to overflowing; the spare remaining rows of pews filled by members of both the upper and lower parts of the village. Morning dress was the order of the day for the bridegroom and best man and also for Oscar and Horatio. It was the first time that Oscar had seen his dear mentor in anything other than a green corduroy suit. Violet wore a voluminous and necessarily loose-fitting cream outfit, which did little to disguise the fact that she was a small but extremely large lady. Sir Peter had amusingly (but unkindly) remarked that she resembled a mobile marquee, but happy with her choice of guy! She was given away by the inn's landlord, who'd hosted and paid for Violet's small hen party the previous night.

The reception was held in the grounds of the nearby Old Sawmill tea rooms with over a hundred other guests in attendance. The wide eclectic range of outfits was something to behold, but as Eunice Pilkington sagely commented, "Well, this is Bassenthwaite and not Buckingham Palace."

The reception, whilst thoroughly enjoyed by all, was not, however, without incident.

Marie-Jo's waters broke, and it was clear that baby was on its way. Without further ado, Violet and Eunice took charge and cars drove them back to Lakeside Cottage. What should have been the newlywed's home and honeymoon suite became the venue for the safe arrival of 'Lester Maybank Hartington Jnr' to make an appearance into the world. It was Doddy who remarked that young Lester probably didn't realise that Bassenthwaite was the only... The freshly married couple generously turned their Lakeside Cottage over to the Hartington trio to spend the first two nights of their married life in the spare room of *The Poacher Inn*. From that day onwards, the hitherto invisible lines, which had denoted the upper and lower parts of the village were expunged forever, not that many had ever known of any such demarcations.

It was a good marriage, with Doddy and Violet continuing to live happily together next door to their good friends and neighbours the Pilkingtons. They have not, as yet, been persuaded to become regular visitors to church, but do accompany them on the daily walk around the lake. Doddy still enjoys his music, poetry and mountaineering with his undiminished love of both K1 and K2!

Horatio Charteris was unquestionably the most gifted of the three and would undoubtedly have succeeded in any pursuit or career he chose. Even from the beginning, when first approached by Oscar, if you recall, he had had reservations about the wisdom of the 'adventure', and had said, 'against my own better judgement'. He did, however, not blame or try to make excuses. Instead, he took it all in his stride − 'just one silver thread on the tapestry of life' − as he would eloquently explain to his fellow inmates. Needless to say, they neither understood his flowery language, nor for a single minute accepted his philosophical pragmatism of justifiable imprisonment. Horatio saw it more in simplistic terms, merely as a hiccup or a sneeze, and not influenza or terminal in anyway, but rather using the five months on remand to his advantage and good effect, with plenty to do.

Despite his small, slight and slender build, women found him both irresistible and desirable. This magnetic attraction may have had something to do with his bolt of blonde wavy hair, piercingly blue eyes and the complexion of fine porcelain. But more likely due to his innate understanding of what made them tick. Throughout his time at King's, he had had a host of relationships, but always conducted with care and reticence. There was never any boasting or bragging of bedroom conquests, with no one ever demeaned or debased, which was duly appreciated by all.

Horatio understood women and what satisfied the female form. He had the knack, ability, flair, talent – whatever appropriate label you wish to append, of knowing how to reach and excite the erogenous zones. This, coupled with the ease and charm of making them feel as if they were the most special of all, made him a formidable Don Juan. This in stark contrast to most colleagues, who never knew such places existed and even if they did, they knew not how to get there! The ultimate skill was in not appearing patronising or false in any way, but in a manner that derived pleasure and contentment to both participants.

Horatio's other pastime – apart from women – was his love of hiking or mini mountaineering, as he preferred to call it. By this, he meant enjoyable days spent with a friend walking or clambering at height over the occasional rough and rugged terrain. Not, he would hasten to add, the difficult and dangerous domain of altitude climbing, which required base camps and oxygen. That was for the really committed or insane! His climbs were demanding enough, but sufficient to get the adrenalin flowing and the heart beating.

Apart from this love of climbing over mountains and onto the top of numerous women, his real true love was in the subject matter of anthropology. Whilst in Belmarsh, Oscar had asked him, 'what is anthropology, anyway?' Horatio had remembered what the Anthropologist Ruth Benedict (1887-1948) had so accurately and succinctly stated: 'The purpose of anthropology is to make the world safe for human difference'. This short answer was far too accurate and brief for his cellmate who never enquired further!

Yet, in a strange way, the questioner had in an unwitting way prompted and provoked Horatio's into his next course of action. With both clarity and boldness, he wrote to Professor Robert Kingsnorth, the vice chancellor of King's College, setting out his stall. In essence, he explained that now as a postgraduate, he felt a calling, if there is such a thing, to a life in academia helping other undergraduates and graduates tackle this most humanistic of all the scientific degree courses that any university could possibly offer. Before this, he had candidly explained his present position and demise, with no attempt to obfuscate or excuse himself.

The vice chancellor was impressed with both the eloquence and honesty of the unexpected letter and duly consulted. He was to learn that Horatio Charteris had been an outstanding graduate, head and shoulders above his peers, who had displayed incredible perception into such an all-encompassing and complex subject, especially for one so young as a 23-year-old. The overwhelming consensus was that he would be an enormous asset to the teaching staff, notwithstanding his present predicament.

The letter that Horatio received two weeks later was more than he could ever have hoped for.

Dear Charteris,

Thank you for your letter and your honesty with its refreshing candour. It takes courage and strength to admit one's failings, and in this case, your guilt and it does you great credit. Having consulted widely, you will be pleased to learn that you were held in high esteem and in many cases – admired.

We therefore propose the following course of action for you to consider. Depending upon the outcome of your trial, and hopefully your release, you take up your intended travelling sabbatical (which can only enhance subject knowledge and background), prior to serious consideration given to you joining us here on the staff, for what should prove to be a full and immensely rewarding career in academia.

We look forward to hearing from you in due course. I'm also a keen hiker, so perhaps we could mix business with pleasure?

Yours… 14th October 2017 King's College

A full year later, Rupert Archibald Fordham was still in Madagascar, his chosen country of refuge having fled the country, albeit living under an assumed name. Had it been a brave or a cowardly decision to go the way he had? It was something that he'd wrestled with on a number of occasions during the following days and months. He decided on reflection that it had been sensible but spineless, and that was something he had to live with.

He had learnt, via some circuitous route, the outcome of his friends' trial and of his own sentencing to one year in prison. He knew then that he would never be returning to England and that was final. In some respects, he privately owned and regretted not staying and seeing it through with them, but it was too late now and there was no point whatsoever in saying, if only or I wish. He was where he was at – so best be making the best of it. This he had done, and three months had elapsed since his King's college lover, Damian, had joined him. How this was contrived and achieved remains a secret between the two of them, but they seem very happy together.

Life for them living in the capital of Madagascar – Antananarivo, had proved busy and successful. They had been incredibly lucky, being in the right place at the right time, when a property became available in the downtown district, in the heart of capital, on the *Avenue de L'Independence*, on the main shopping artery. Here, nearly every corner seemed to bustle with activity. Motorcycles whizzed down the avenue, slicing through a sea of bodies and cars. Stalls sold fruit, flowers, bamboo, cell phones and even live animals on the side of the thoroughfare. Locals gathered in the green spaces to share the day's gossip and host impromptu music sessions.

The Madagascan capital is one of the liveliest in all Africa, and Rupert and Damian's restaurant was situated in its very centre, absolutely ideal and where they owned and lived in the flat above. Here, in this hectic mile of eclectic boutiques and shops, was the perfect location for a small but successful restaurant, which catered for all types and genders! Their success was largely due to their ability to speak French. The island's official language being Malagasy, but French was widely spoken but not English. Rupert and Damian's schoolboy French had paid dividends and they were soon speaking like natives!

In the little spare time they had, they amused themselves as members of the local drama society and this satisfied Rupert's underlying thespian aspirations and desire to act in one way or another. They were both outward going young men and were well liked and popular and soon accepted as a 'couple'.

His only deep and lasting regret was that he could not bring himself to contact either his parents or Oscar and Horatio. He was afraid that if he did, one thing could possibly lead to another, and he'd end up back in prison. Both he and Damian had decided that better the devil...even though he knew how much it still hurt him and indeed his parents. There is a saying, *You make your bed...*

Life for Oscar never turned out as he had planned when he had first arrived at Cambridge. His aspiration to become a barrister never materialised, which may well have been the case, had he not picked up and became engrossed in reading the *Diamond Dealers* magazine. After the trial and the wedding, Oscar returned home to Kidderminster (near to Malvern), a home or house he had never visited. Here, he was welcomed by his mother and his father, the building of bridges between father and son had begun. This due in no small way by the pragmatic insistence of his mother, who rightly stated that life is too short, and we could lose him forever like the Fordhams had. Is that what you his father want? It was also true that Feathers played a tactful and healing mediatory role.

Both parents were reluctantly understanding and supportive of his decision to work abroad. He'd already written and been offered a legal position in UNICEF, based in Dar es Salaam in Tanzania. He confessed that it was not his preferred choice, but beggars could not be choosers with his recent pedigree! He would be responsible for a number of countries on the African continent, where his legal knowledge could be invaluable. It was a two-year assignment, which suited all.

The job and the place were better than he thought and life in Dar es Salaam was not bad at all, especially after meeting a fellow Dutch UNICEF worker by the name of Lotte De Vries. If it was not love at first sight, it was certainly lust, and within three months, Lotte had moved in with Oscar and they are still together three years on, as partners which seems to be the modern way. The agreement reached between them was that, knowing of his 125 days criminal record, that if she fell pregnant, they would get married. One bastard in the family was enough! The following year, Oscar and Lotte invited Horatio and Rebecca (now back together again and engaged to be married) out to Dar es Salaam, as a pre-marriage treat. The invitation was taken up on the understanding if they could possibly include a flying trip over to Madagascar, only some 1,600 kilometres away, and the capital a mere eight kilometres from the airport. This they did and all went well, with Lotte and Oscar first showing them their own Tanzanian sights.

The highlight was still to come, as Horatio now a seasoned academic in Anthropology at King's, understood what a fascinating place Madagascar was with so many animals unique only to the island. On arrival, the four of them booked into the Hotel and Spa *Palissandre*, one of the capital's favourites. It was Oscar's treat, having recently been promoted to head of the African legal department for UNICEF. They decided to investigate downtown and dine out amongst the locals and soak up the atmosphere. Imagine then their surprise and shock when they walked into a crowded and noisy restaurant and straight into the arms of Raffer!

"Actually, it's now Rab – Rupert Aulde-Been!"

The End